The Baron of Bad Behavior

by

Elf Ahearn

Scandals by the Ton

Cover Art by *The Wild Rose Press, Inc.*

The Wild Rose Press, Inc.
PO Box 708
Adams Basin, NY 14410-0708
Visit us at www.thewildrosepress.com

Publishing History
First Edition, 2025
Trade Paperback ISBN 978-1-5092-6203-8
Digital ISBN 978-1-5092-6204-5

Scandals by the Ton
Published in the United States of America

Dedication

To Jano Fairservis, a creative being who somehow kept her madly creative family functioning.

Chapter 1

Like a felt blanket, the night draped thick and airless over Brettingham Hall. Open windows and doors in the ballroom strained to catch the tiniest breeze, and each zephyr was as welcome as an unmarried prince. Weighted by a petticoat that clung to her legs and hampered by stockings that chafed wet against wet, Lady Nefertiti Albright—Snap to anyone who didn't want a punch in the sneezer—slogged about the ballroom with the rest of the dancers. Though it was mid-May, some fluke in the weather had them all dripping and red-faced—the lot of them growing drunker as they cooled their throats with champagne. The lemonade disappeared hours ago.

As Snap brushed a sticky curl from her forehead, she saw her sisters melting on the sidelines. Eleanor—better known as Ellie—and Margaret—who everyone called Peggity—listed grimly beside a long row of mamas ringing the room. No longer possessing the energy to monitor their daughters' and sons' partners, the mothers waged war with gravity by leaning on the armrests of their gilded chairs as they fanned their faces. On the balcony, the musicians paused to wipe sweat from their eyes, leaving chunks of the melody to be carried by instruments holding the harmony. Everything seemed smeared by the heat. It was as if the ballroom were sliding slowly into a boiling cauldron.

The scent of cooked food hit Snap like a death blow. "Not a hot meal?"

"Please no," groaned a man sporting a glistening face and sodden cravat.

"The scandal sheets must report this bonfire a success, even if it means we cavort till dawn," Snap whispered to the swain in the tailcoat as they completed a twirl.

She returned to the line to await her next partner. Weaving a little, a soldier in crimson wool strewn with military buttons and gold braid, stepped out from the row of men. His face was green and blotched in red and white patches. With a glazed look, as if he vaguely understood where he was, he stumbled toward her. She lifted her hand for the turn. He lifted his, then his knees buckled and he dropped to the floor, brushing her gloved hand as he fell.

Quickly kneeling beside him, Snap fought with the gold jacket buttons, struggling to untie the soldier's sweat-soaked neckcloth. She'd managed to unfasten two buttons when someone wrenched her to her feet.

The steely voice of their hostess, Lady Pemneux, cut the molten air. "Leave him. He'll be back and dancing in a trice." The woman fixed her hawk-like eyes first on the fallen soldier, and then on Snap. "Disgraceful," she hissed.

Two footmen parted the crowd and dragged the poor fellow away.

The music swelled, and the dancers forced their reluctant bodies back into line, all eyes fixed on Pemneux's back as she stalked away. Snap, however, was too stunned to move.

"Pray she doesn't remember you, or you'll never

see the inside of Almack's," said Jane Rackyer-Williams, her eyes flashing malice. "Rather improper, undoing his buttons."

"If I'd known you would be so offended, I would have left him to die," Snap said, mustering her sincerest look.

Jane abruptly turned her back.

Silly hen. If my reputation's tarnished for rescuing a man from stifling outerwear, then great heavens, wait till they learn the rest of it.

Snap wiped her brow and was about to rejoin the ranks, when, like a Biblical flash, she recognized her situation: with no dance partner, the only proper thing was to leave the floor. Sometimes Society's rules were perfect!

Quickly she headed for the terrace in hopes of cooler air, but a wall of humanity blocked the French doors. Seeking another avenue of egress, she noted all the exits from the second story ballroom. The game and smoking rooms were out of the question for a young lady, the dining room only connected back to the ballroom, and the ladies' retiring room was full of...ladies. There was the grand entrance... A quick glance ruled that out too. Lady Pemneux stood guard two steps up. Her mouth spoke to a cluster of guests, but her gaze roved the floor. Then across the room, Snap saw a deliciously unguarded window partially hidden by a potted palm.

Adopting a casual attitude, she slipped past the wilting matrons and stupefied gentlemen. Four windows down from her goal stood her sisters, waving their fans in front of faces shining with dew. They smiled at her approach, but when she halted at the palm,

Peggity, the eldest, gave Ellie an alarmed nudge. Tapping it lightly with a toe, Snap moved the plant a few inches out onto the floor, then gathering her skirt in one hand, slithered behind its sheltering leaves. Peggity's eyes flew wide. Ellie's fan ceased fluttering.

Keeping an eye on Lady Pemneux and moving slowly so as not to be noticed, Snap edged her bottom onto the window sill. Peggity frantically mouthed "Nooooo" and shifted toward her, but Ellie snagged Peggity's arm.

Like a hound sensing an intruder, Lady Pemneux's head came up and her gaze traveled the faces of her subjects one by one. Hiding behind a palm was bad, and sitting on a windowsill was enough to leave a girl's future in tatters. Just as those judgmental headlamps were about to penetrate the palm's foliage, Ellie sneezed at full volume. All eyes cranked toward the perpetrator, and without a second to spare, Snap snagged a handful of ivy on the outside wall and swung out into the night.

****

As she clambered down the ivy, it felt as if the humidity were thick enough to keep her aloft should the vine give way. Crickets and tree frogs hummed in the heavy atmosphere, and the pungent scent of ivy filled her nostrils.

On the ground, she peeled off gloves, dance slippers, and finally, stockings. Every inch of skin freed from its layer of clothing made her giddy with the thrill of escape, but the grass between her toes was only a degree or two cooler than that wretched dance floor. *Pish to propriety, they're all mad to stay in that oven.*

A blurry sliver of moon made it just possible to

catch the outlines of walls and trees, but little else—a plus, considering her state of undress.

Somewhere on ol' Pemneux's estate there'll be a fountain.

She bundled her slippers and gloves together, then wound the stockings around them and stuffed the lot deep into a boxwood hedge. Keeping to the deepest dark on the lawn, she commenced exploration.

Around the corner of the house, she spied either a hedge or a stone wall that likely fenced the garden. As she drew closer, she found it to be a low hedge with the delightful sound of splashing water in the near distance. Gathering her skirts, she jumped it, and to the relief of her bare feet, landed on grass.

The night seemed darker in the garden. Even vague outlines disappeared. She let her toes feel for safe passage. Confident, she'd found the path and lured by the music of spilling water, Snap picked up speed until her foot hit something hard. She stumbled, caught herself on a slick mossy surface, slipped, pitched forward and splashed to a landing on her knees in a pool about a foot deep. A mad scramble kept her from a thorough soaking—anyone less agile would have gone in completely, but only half her gown got wet.

But oh, how wonderful that icy water felt! Holding her sodden skirt high with one hand, she submerged her arms to the elbow, then cupped a puddle and let the divine cold slosh over her face.

From the far end of what she now recognized as a reflecting pool, came the sound of water pouring into water. Looping her skirt over her arm so high her thighs were thoroughly exposed, Snap waded toward the sound. The silhouette of a statue of Venus came briefly into view via the flash of a small fire. A moment later, the glowing tip of a cheroot flared in the darkness. She froze, scarcely daring to breathe.

A long minute passed. The cheroot brightened as the stranger, a man no doubt because no woman would dare smoke at a Pemneux gathering, took another puff.

"White's a god-awful color to hide in," came a masculine voice. "Next time wear black or brown—something suitable for a hedgehog, perhaps."

Snap dropped her gown, feeling it splash against the waterline. *He saw my knees... He saw my thighs!*

"Have you been watching me?" she demanded.

"It's a dark night—there's nothing else to look at."

"Well, it's not gentlemanly."

"Did I claim to be a gentleman?"

She swallowed. "If you're not, then what are you doing at Lady Pemneux's ball?"

"I wasn't invited."

She shifted uneasily. He didn't sound like a tradesman or servant—his accent was refined.

"But you're lurking about her garden?"

"The fact is, I'm a desperate pirate, here to steal money and jewels from the *ton*." His tone was bemused, flirty.

"So, is your band of brigands hiding behind that statue?" she said, beginning to enjoy the conversation.

"No need for 'em."

The cheroot flared, and she strained to see his face, but the night was too dark and the light too brief. She waded closer. "If you're going to raid the ball single-handed, I'd avoid the hostess; she kills with a glance."

He chuckled—a delectable sound, savory and rich as butter.

"Ahhh, so it's fear of her glance that's got you unchaperoned and standing in a pool in the dark with a pirate. A pirate, mind you, who should scare you more than any regular fellow out for a smoke."

"Considering I'm not the least bit afraid, I'll assume you're like me—just a person escaping a stuffy room."

"Then you'd be wrong."

These words carried an irresistible undertone of danger.

"Pish," she said, sauntering closer. "You sound as terrifying as a vicar giving his first sermon."

He chuckled, soft and low. "Saucy as toffee pudding."

When the cheroot glowed again, she slogged closer, but caught only a shadow that might be a mustache. "If you must know, Sir Pirate," she said, moving ever nearer, "I'm here because it's beastly hot in that ballroom. When you make your attack, consider stealing a lady's fan first."

Having got almost got to Venus's water spouts, all Snap needed for a prime view of him was another pull on the cheroot, when a strange bird call came from the direction of the house. It sounded vaguely like a crow, except crows roost at night.

"Duty caws," he said.

The glowing tip of the cheroot floated toward chez Pemneux and disappeared with the crunch of footsteps on a gravel path.

Would he really truly steal? Churning after him through the wet, not caring if her gown were soaked and spoiled, Snap hit the pool's rocky edge with a shin. Painful, but not enough to slow her pace, she left the water in one graceful leap and sprinted across the lawn.

As she gained on the tiny glow of fire at the tip of his cheroot, she realized her quarry was headed for the house's grand entrance. The well-lit drive stopped her in her tracks.

Three men stood at the door beneath the roof of the portico, a massive construction consisting of eight pairs of Ionic-capped columns. Two of the men puffed pipes; the third, a square-built gentleman with a fuzz of hair and a large pot belly, brandished a cheroot. Snap's heart plummeted. How could a pirate be... be so portly?

Then a figure moved silently between two of the columns. Instead of joining the smokers, the man, who had to be her pirate, braced his back on one column and pressed a bare foot against another. Quietly, stealthily, so that the smokers were unaware of his presence, he edged up between the columns, applying so much pressure with his feet and back that he was able to ease himself all the way to the capital. Terrified he'd plummet to his death in the transition to the roof, she stifled a gasp with both hands covering her mouth.

He didn't hesitate. Reaching past the portico's elaborate molding, he gripped the roof. Snap watched in awe as he swung a leg onto the housetop, leveraged first one elbow, then the next onto the slate shingles, and summited the structure.

He stood, brushed himself off, emptied tailcoat and shoes from under his shirt, put them on, and elegantly stepped through the open window.

Chapter 2

Lady Pemneux freed her melting guests at 2 a.m. By that time everyone in Snap's family was either too drunk or too exhausted from the heat to utter a syllable during the coach ride home.

All night Snap lay awake contemplating her pirate. He must have stealthily stripped them of their jewels and money during a distraction. Otherwise a great clamor would have ensued.

Lud, the man was a clever climber! Never had she imagined two pillars could be used to access a roof. What else might he know? Would he teach her? Did he have a mustache?

At 9 a.m. she sprang out of bed and dashed to the dining room where the footmen were laying out the breakfast buffet. Whitey came through the servants' door carrying a basket of rolls. His eyes were glazed and puffy, as if he was barely awake, and he bumped into one of the dining chairs.

Snap tweaked his sleeve. "What are they saying downstairs about the Pemneux ball?"

He looked at her bleary-eyed. "Hotter 'an blazes, and the upstairs staff is to-the-nines trying to get the stink out o' the formal wear."

"Yes, but did anyone say there was an unusual event?"

After wearily putting the basket down, Whitey

leaned against the side-table. "Don't you wish we was back in Exeter? There's no heat like in London; it must be fearsome come high summer—none of us's slept a wink since it come on."

"Whitey, did anything noteworthy happen last night?"

"The serving class must be too fagged to get the word out." The footman slumped toward the door. "I'll tell ya if I hear something."

Whitey's verdict, Snap realized, was that she'd have to wait for a family member to come to breakfast before she could learn of her pirate's deeds.

She was sipping orange juice when her brother-in-law, Crewe Burnett, the Duke of Hanesford, entered the dining room. He was unshaven, his neck cloth was missing, and he looked rumpled, but since that was his natural state and he no longer drank, she thought nothing of it. Before he married Peggity and replaced his brother as duke, Crewe was a well-respected pugilist, and he had the musculature and flattened nose to prove it. There was nothing pretty about him; he was all shoulders and brawn; but Snap adored the man. Of all her brothers-in-law, Crewe was the only one who truly shared her rebellious streak.

"Morning," she said brightly.

"Morning."

When he'd made his breakfast selections and settled at the table, Snap, as casually as possible, said, "Were you in the game room last night?"

"Aye."

"Did you win at cards?"

"Aye."

Crewe was never very talkative in the morning:

"Did you see anything interesting—for instance, out or in the window?"

His brow furrowed. "The night was pretty dark for viewing, lass."

Just as she was about to launch another volley, Peggity wandered into the dining room, where she gave Crewe a peck on the cheek.

"It's cooler today," she told him. "Maybe we can take a nap later."

His head popped up, and he looked at Peggity with a gleam in his eye. She responded with a flirty shrug that Snap pretended not to see.

As her sister scooped eggs at the sideboard, Snap said softly to Crewe, "You were about to say something about the window to the card room—the unusual activity…?"

"I was?" He gave his elbow a thoughtful scratch. "You must be talkin' about me friend Ga—"

At that moment, Hugh walked in, followed by Snap's sister Ellie.

With a subtle cut of his hand, Crewe urgently signaled an end to their discussion.

A clue. If this Ga-fellow can't be mentioned in front of Hugh, that mysterious climber has to be a man of ill-repute. I met a real pirate!

"Is everyone finding what they want for breakfast?" Ellie, playing hostess, asked while absently looking about the room.

"I was talking to Crewe about the game room last night," announced Snap.

Peggity gave her husband a pat on the shoulder. "You did quite well, didn't you, my love?"

"I done all right."

"I did all right," she said, gently correcting him.

Snap turned her attention to Hugh, the Earl of Davenport and Ellie's husband. Of the spouses, he was the handsomest. A dusky curl flopped between eyes the color of jet, and even a scar that slashed across his right cheek, failed to mar his good looks.

"How was your luck last night?" she asked. "Did you fill your pockets with ill-gotten gain?"

Hugh laughed and tousled her hair as if she was still a child.

"You can't do that anymore," she scolded, giving his hand a little slap. "I'm almost eighteen."

"My apologies, milady." Hugh bowed. "Does your interest in my winnings stem from a need for ready cash?"

Snap's mother gave her a generous amount of pin money, but more was always welcome. "You know how close-fisted Papa can be…"

With an indulgent wink, Hugh reached in his pocket, but came out empty handed. "Huh? I must have left my money in my dress jacket."

"I'll look!" she cried. Before anyone could object, she flew out the door, down the hall, and up the stairs, taking two at a time.

In Hugh and Ellie's room, the house's stunningly appointed master suite, she went straight to the mirrored dressing room across from their satin-curtained canopy bed. The jacket was the first item she found. Digging in one pocket, she came up empty-handed. Her excitement grew. The next pocket offered a long expanse of nothingness until, at the bottom, she found a lump of folded paper. It was a large bundle of bills, as much as a hundred pounds.

Disappointment came like an unwelcome cloud across the sun. So he wasn't a thieving pirate... She drifted out to the hall.

"Sweeting, are you going down to breakfast?" said Claire, accompanied by her husband, Viscount Flavian Monroe.

Snap sighed heavily as she waited for them to catch up.

"How are you feeling this morning?" said Flavian in his deep baritone. "The party didn't wear you out, did it?"

Claire, who knew everything about medicinal herbs and curatives, took Snap's hand and patted it. "Nothing shy of braving a blizzard in a spring coat could keep our Snap in bed."

"Humm..." she responded.

Pivoting her, Claire looked carefully into her face. "You seem a bit down. What's the matter?"

On the verge of saying castor oil wouldn't help, Snap noticed something extraordinary. "Lawks, Claire, your pearl earbobs are missing!"

Feeling one ear and then the other, her sister's eyes flared with panic. "Oh dear!"

****

"Papa, I'm going to run off with a pirate," said Snap shortly after breakfast.

Her father paused in his headlong rush down the hall. Pushing his glasses up the bridge of his nose, he caught her square in the eye. "Have you seen that scrap of papyrus about Thutmose III?"

Snap narrowed her gaze. "My fiancé has a terrible smoking habit, and a reputation as a jewel thief."

"Well, it was right on the table in the library and it

seems to have gone missing." A black cat mewed at her father's feet, wrapping its tail about his leg. "Could I have left it in the Roman invasion pile?" he asked the feline.

Before either the cat or Snap could respond, Lord Albright hurried off the way he had come, with the black kitty in hot pursuit.

"And he's murdered people by the score," Snap called after the retreating figure. When her father failed to respond, she sighed. "I should have said he steals Roman antiquities…"

With nothing to do, she went to the window, then angled behind the curtain to see if anything interesting were happening in Mayfair. It was possible a runaway horse would gallop by, or maybe a fight would break out. But only a man with a monocle swinging from his neck sauntered by.

London was a dreadful disappointment. They'd arrived from Exeter six days ago to prepare for her come out, and the single exciting thing that had happened was meeting her pirate. With a zing of pleasure, she recalled the stranger's buttery voice and the scent of his tobacco wafting across the reflecting pool. He'd said he wasn't invited to Lady Pemneux's ball…but he'd also claimed to be a burglar, yet not a ha'penny'd disappeared that night. Claire found her earbobs on the dresser. Why then, had he taken to the darkest part of the garden for a smoke…? A gentleman would smoke in the game room, or just outside the house. So, he's got to be at least a little bit criminal.

The next question was how to find him. Truly, it wasn't ladylike to approach every man with a cheroot to his lips. Besides, that horrible lady's maid, Malloy, who Ellie insisted she use, would forbid it. The woman kept such close watch, Snap had barely managed to sneak unaccompanied into Hyde Park, let alone tear through London's streets looking for smokers.

There was only one solution—naturally, it wasn't proper... She really oughtn't to do it... However, this was a serious matter in need of immediate attention. Snap bolted down the narrow kitchen stairs at the back of the house. If she was to find the most notorious fellow in England, the best place, nay the only place to start was with the servants.

The scent of baking bread and the cackle of good company leaked from the kitchen, yet the moment she pushed open the door, the gang at the table went silent.

"Oh, don't mind her," said Whitey, one of the footmen who had accompanied Snap's family from their Exeter estate, "she's more us than them."

Snap flashed a smile.

"It's not done." Malloy glowered.

"Oh pish," Snap replied, taking a seat. "Tell me all the dreadful things happening in London."

When the table remained quiet, Whitey took the initiative. "There's scandalous doings over there," he said, jerking his chin at the house next door. "The lady wants her portrait done, and the master don't like the artist she chose."

"Why?" asked Snap. "Does he paint in his shirtsleeves?"

"He do a lot worse than that," said a red-faced scullery maid, her eyes fierce with indignation. "He poses 'em in their skivvies!"

Snap's jaw dropped. "And ladies do that?"

"They does it for him," the maid replied, raising

her brows suggestively. "He's wicked handsome, that's why."

"Enough," Malloy barked. "My lady, your come out is only a few weeks away and—"

"Do you think he could be spied on through a window?" Snap blurted, wondering if her pirate knew the artist. Disreputable people befriended disreputable people.

Mrs. Dibble, the cook, swung a wooden spoon in the air. "No artist be coming within a mile of the neighbors, not with the shouting I heard last night."

All heads turned for further details. "Here I was checking on the leg o' lamb because I weren't certain I'd brushed it with the herbs yet, and it got to sit like that for hours or the flavors don't—"

"Yes, but what were you saying about the fight?" Snap pressed. As a member of the family rather than a servant, it was her privilege to interrupt.

Mrs. Dibble folded her arms and primly replied, "They were just tiffing, is all."

"Oh, Mrs. Dibble, I've upset you," Snap said, leaping from the bench and taking the cook's arm. "Please tell us. I promise to hold my tongue."

"You shouldn't be in the kitchen anyway," the cook complained. "Young ladies ought to be curling their hair and puttin' on dresses, not jawing with the below stairs help."

Malloy nodded vigorously.

Stepping back but still holding Mrs. Dibble's arm, Snap applied her most innocent expression. "You're so right, and I am being horrible, but it would be awful to be sent away without knowing even a little of what happened last night." She lowered her gaze and slid out her lower lip in an abject pout.

Mrs. Dibble's arm, which had been tight to her side, relaxed. "Well, his lordship's screaming, 'This painter, Julian van Eck, is the worst kind of gambler and rogue.' Said just touching him was enough to defile a woman, and if she go near him, he'll put her in Bedlam and leave her there."

"Oh, that artist got a fearsome reputation with the ladies," the scullery maid added. "One look, and all them grandies want to lift their skirts and give 'em an heir."

Snap covered her mouth and giggled. "He can't be as good looking as all that."

"There's not a swell in the world could do that to me," said a voice from the far end of the kitchen. Stationed next to a sack of potatoes stood a girl Snap hadn't seen before. Scarcely paying attention to her work, she sliced a potato so deftly and with such speed, it looked as if the knife was an extension of her hand.

"And who are you?" asked Snap.

The girl laid down the blade, wiped her hands on her apron, and crossed to the table. Offering a bumpy curtsy, she replied, "I'm Lizzie Widcomb."

Something about her seemed different from the rest of the staff. A light in her eyes, an almost masculine spring in her step. As Snap gazed at the slight, sinewy miss, she recognized in Lizzie the one thing she needed most in London.

A fellow adventurer.

Chapter 3

The problem with Malloy was two-fold: not only was she a high stickler, she also played lady's maid to Snap's mother-in-law, the Dowager Lady Aurelia Davenport, which meant every tiny transgression was reported.

Though Lizzie was not exactly a lady's maid, she was a maid, thereby fulfilling half the requirement of an escort for a young lady of fortune and position. Therefore, Snap felt only a little guilty when she told her mother and Ellie she was going for a stroll in Hyde Park, and yes, she would be accompanied.

Now, as they stood on the cobbled street at Julian van Eck's address, Snap took a mental survey. On the top floor of a three-story limestone building, was a bank of north-facing windows. It simply had to be his studio.

The building next door, a squat little red brick, was only a narrow alley away from van Eck's exterior wall. Her palms dampened with excitement.

"So what's next?" Lizzie said, breaking Snap's concentration.

Pointing to the red brick, she answered, "First, we find a way in there and make our way to the roof. Then we leap across the alley and onto the terrace outside Mr. van Eck's studio. We can spy on him from there. If we're lucky, he'll be seducing someone."

The maid's jaw dropped in horror. "Why don't we

just walk through the front door, like everyone else?"

"A young lady of my standing can't do that," Snap said, shocked by Lizzie's ignorance. "The neighbor's husband was yelling his head off because Mr. van Eck is far too scandalous for a lady of society to be seen with."

"Then I ought to be bustling you off this street right now," said Lizzie, planting fists firmly on her hips.

Snap chuckled. "You should, but you won't because it's far more interesting to spy on a notorious artist than to peel potatoes." As predicted, the maid's eyes traveled back to van Eck's atelier and her mouth puckered like a fish—excellent signs of relenting.

"Humph," said Lizzie. "And how do you propose jumping that spread in all that fabric?"

Snap swished her skirts. "I stuff it into the waistband of my petticoat."

"So your legs are sticking out for all the world to see?"

"Oh pish. No one in this neighborhood will look up. See them? Working folk, every last one of 'em. They've got far too much on their minds to star gaze."

Glowering, Lizzie cast a distrusting glance about the street.

"Go ahead and knock, I'll be right behind you."

But the maid didn't move an inch. "I ain't exposing my undercarriage just to see a bang-up swell."

"You have a lot to learn about being a servant, Lizzie Widcomb," Snap said impatiently. "When I tell you to do something, you're supposed to hop to it."

"Well, you can tie that idea to a hitching post." Lizzie gave Snap a cool look. "A young miss looking for trouble ain't ordering me to put my neck in a noose." Without so much as a backward glance, Lizzie began walking away.

"Now you hold on," demanded Snap, but the maid paid her no heed. It was obvious from her stiff back and squared shoulders that the girl was not about to obey.

Should Snap be caught scandalously alone on the streets of London, the society chatter would ruin her come out party. She darted after Lizzie, and catching her arm, ended her retreat. "Fine!"

"Fine!" Lizzie barked back.

"Go up to the door and give it a knock." Snap gestured toward the brick house. "Don't worry, you're with an aristocrat."

Lizzie rolled her eyes, but tromped across the street and slowly dragged her carcass inch by inch up the stairs to the front stoop. Snap followed, but remained on the sidewalk and adjusted her skirts to look as ladylike and grand as possible.

The knocker clinked, and a half minute passed. Lizzie swiveled around, ready to give up.

"Give it another," Snap said, raising her chin to look even more commanding.

With a downward twitch of her lips, Lizzie applied the knocker once more, and this time a woman shouted, "Hold your horses!" Uneven footsteps followed.

The missus who opened the door sported one shoulder that was so significantly higher than the other, she appeared to be standing on a hill. "What's this about?" she snarled.

"My lady wishes to speak with you." Lizzie stepped aside.

The moment the woman saw Snap, her eyes went

wide. "How may I help you?" she breathed, nearly falling to her knees in supplication.

One could always depend on the English class system to get one's way.

Snap flashed a tolerant smile. "My papa," she said, pressing the vowels past her teeth in an explosive *pahpah*, "is interested in purchasing a building in this neighborhood. However, he's curious about the view. He's asked me to look about, and I believe the best way is to see its configuration from the rooftops, wouldn't you agree?"

Struck dumb, the woman nodded.

"So you won't mind if we take a gander from yours, will you?" Without an invitation, Snap ascended the stoop and swept past Lizzie and the befuddled owner. As she climbed a narrow staircase toward the second floor, she shot over her shoulder, "There's no need to accompany us, and we'll be a bit of time up there. I know you won't mind."

The woman moved her mouth but emitted no sound. When Snap looked back, she was peering at them, her crooked frame like the living embodiment of a question mark.

On the third-floor landing were two doors to a pair of bedrooms, Snap guessed. At the end of the hall, though, was a square cut in the ceiling with a hatch door.

"That's our destination," she whispered to Lizzie.

They took two steps toward the hatch when the door to one of the bedrooms opened and a hairy man in his underdrawers burst into the hall. In a flash, he ducked back in the bedroom and slammed the door.

"Mrs. Miller," he bellowed, "ya coulda said we got

guests!"

The crooked lady clumped up the stairs, shouting, "They come in sudden-like, Mr. Miller, and I didn't have the chance to warn nuthin'.."

"My mistress," Lizzie said, clearing her throat, "is lookin' to look… at something for her da, and we need to get on the roof."

Mrs. Miller's brows furrowed with puzzlement. "Whatcha lookin for?"

"A view," Snap replied brightly. "You live in an interesting neighborhood where artists abound and—"

"We got no bounders here," called Mr. Miller through the bedroom door.

"She ain't saying 'bounders,' Mr. Miller," his wife admonished. "She's saying artists—plenty of 'em."

Snap moved under the square. "There must be something in the view that attracted them, don't you think?"

"It were the low rents," the missus mumbled.

"Perhaps. Have you a ladder, madam?"

Mrs. Miller opened a closet, and after fighting back a pile of unbalanced trunks topped by piles of faded cloth, she wrested a ladder from the mess.

With a broad smile, Snap took the ladder and propped it beneath the hatch. "We shall go unassisted," she announced. "I need time and concentration to absorb all that my father the earl will need."

Reluctantly Mrs. Miller drifted toward the stairs. Snap watched, keeping a formidable smile fixed on her face until the woman faded down to the first floor.

Satisfied, Snap stripped off her spencer jacket and bonnet, then tossed them to Lizzie. "Hold my reticule."

"So I'm a pack mule, eh?" Lizzie mumbled, taking

the things all the same.

Snap hitched her voluminous skirts over one arm and climbed the ladder. A moment later, Lizzie hurled jacket, bonnet, and reticule up, then shot through the hatch at lightning speed. Before Snap said a word, the girl hoisted the ladder and dragged it, bumping and banging, across the roof.

"This'll suit better 'an a hop."

"Lud, you'll wake the dead with that racket," Snap growled. She lifted an end of the heavy wooden apparatus and resumed walking. "You see, it's all about subtlety. One simply can't disrupt the populace and expect to gain one's goal. For instance, Mr. Miller is far more likely to come up and check if we make noise. Then, poof, there goes our chance to peek at Mr. van Eck."

"Humph," grunted Lizzie.

"Adventure is a refined art."

The maid halted at the edge of the roof. The gap between buildings was twice what it appeared to be from the street. She lowered the ladder across to Julian van Eck's terrace. It barely reached, leaving only about three inches on each side.

"Well, it's going to get less refined now," she said grimly, pointing at the alley below.

It was piled with wheel spokes and broken barrel staves that pointed up, deadly as swords.

Lizzie stuck a fist above her hip. Her brows were raised in a "Do you really want to risk this?"

"There are always obstacles to overcome," she explained to the maid. "This is nothing. I once had to stowaway on a fishing boat in Exeter. They'd never have found me in the hold if the mackerel weren't running that day."

"Why'd you hide on a boat?"

Snap gave an impatient huff. "Like we don't have more important things to discuss, but, if you must know, Rory O'Shannessey was said to be dabbling with Mrs. Gillis, and I had to follow him to find out if it was true."

"And was it?"

"Yes, Lizzie, that's the beauty of it!"

Lizzie turned away and emitted a low "Humph." "Well," she added after a moment, "you go first. I'll hold the ladder."

Snap studied the distance to the ground and the pointy edges of the detritus below. After a deep breath, she said, "Right then."

Lifting her skirts high, she tucked as much fabric as possible into the waistband of her petticoat, creating an enormous puff. Her legs were exposed well above the knee, but one had to forgo decency at times like these. If Julian van Eck were half as handsome as the rumors said, however, some naked knee was worth it.

Snap lowered herself onto the ladder and her bottom, by necessity, stuck into the air. Lizzie uttered an explosive snort.

"Hush!" commanded Snap.

Cautiously she crawled forward, gripping the ladder's rungs. Yet, when she felt her boot leave the edge of the Miller's roof, the image of her huge rump waddling back and forth, brought on a fit of the giggles. The fragile ladder shook.

"Keep crawling!"

"Do I look silly?" The ladder rocked as Snap's hysteria grew.

"Aye, but get on now or you'll fall."

Snap clambered forward. "Have you seen the hippo at the zoo?"

"No."

"That's what I must look like."

Merriment caused Snap's arms to tremble. She stopped midway and tried not to think of her backside, which only made her laugh harder, and then she heard a crack. Panic replaced mirth. "What was that?"

The rungs were fine. Another crack rent the air.

"Devil take it, the glue's breaking. She's gonna split!"

Snap froze, clinging to the two sides of the ladder, but she could feel them wiggle loosely. "Do something!" she whispered.

"Don't breathe."

A subtle change in stability meant Lizzie had let go of the ladder. "What in God's teeth are you doing?"

"Hush!"

Behind her, the maid moved quickly, though Snap was too afraid to turn her head to see.

Then the stability returned. "I tied her off with my stockings. Careful now, or she'll come apart at the end."

Terrified, Snap inched forward until at last she reached van Eck's terrace. The last few rungs were so loose they shifted beneath her knees, and if she hadn't held the rails tight, they would have clattered to the alley below.

"Now, that was exciting," she said with a gleeful shudder.

"Right then," said Lizzie. "Tie 'er off with your stockings on that end."

"Have you gone mad? This thing's as safe as a viper's nest," Snap declared.

"That's so, but you can't be seen unchaperoned."

"It's not my intention to be seen."

"But what if he looks out the window?"

Resigned to Lizzie's logic, Snap replied with an exasperated huff, but unloaded her skirts from her petticoat, unlaced her half boots, and pulled off her stockings.

"Weave 'em in-and-out, in-and-out, like I done, and tie 'em up real tight."

Once Snap had completed Lizzie's directions, Lizzie, with the majority of her dress secured in her petticoat, picked up a knife, bit down, and started across the rickety bridge. Though she resembled a pair of swaying pillows neither of them laughed. Safely across, she slipped the blade into the waistband of her apron and unpacked her dress.

Snap raised a brow. "A knife?" she whispered.

"Aye. You should see me gut a deer."

"I can only imagine." Turning toward the studio, Snap mouthed, "And now, on to victory!"

Chapter 4

Crawling on hands and knees across the terrace, the girls peered around a corner, and then, ever so cautiously, through a panel of large-paned windows. But blocking their view of Julian van Eck's studio was a chaise upholstered in red velvet on a frame of gold leaf that sported panthers at the headrest. Snap had never seen anything so wicked. Her blood raced. By lying flat, however, she saw the legs of two easels, an elegant chair, and a large utilitarian table. Spatters of paint carpeted the floor and canvases leaned against the walls—all of them were of naked ladies. Snap's jaw dropped. She grabbed Lizzie's hand,

"Look!" she gasped.

Pushing in front of her, Lizzie gasped too. "They ain't got nothing on!"

"Not even ear bobs."

"I never seen nothing so scandalous."

"Me neither," Snap said, a thrill zigging down her spine.

Just then a door opened in the studio and several dogs scampered across the floor. The boots of two men followed. One pair was finely cut but worn at the sole, and the other appeared a cheap imitation of expensive hessians.

Snap pressed close to the glass. "Which one is Julian van Eck?"

The first man to come into view had a bald patch ringed by pale hair gathered in a beribboned braid at the back. A slight paunch curved over the waistband of his trousers. His only attractive feature, from Snap's view, was a pair of blue eyes mounted over well-rounded jowls. She shifted her position for a better view of the second man, when Lizzie pulled her back.

But it was too late. A black-spotted beast with a shaggy coat cocked an ear and trotted toward the window. With a quick dive, the dog went under the chaise and barked like a mad thing. Two additional canines stuffed in next to the first, yowling and snarling to wake the dead.

The girls scrambled back and Lizzie raced for the ladder. At that moment a man burst onto the terrace. He was the most extraordinarily handsome being Snap had ever seen. The power of him, the intensity of his green-flecked eyes and the cascade of dark Byronesque curls that curled across his brow, would have been enough to overwhelm her, but the muscles that bulged through the fabric of his jacket threw her mind into a state of shock. Thoughts of the pirate vanished. She took a few steps back just to distance herself from this man's astounding masculinity, when he lunged forward and grabbed her arm.

"You'll go over the brink," he said, pulling her to his chest.

Snap found herself captivated by the straight lines of his cheek bones, the dashing black mustache, and his hazel eyes, warm with merriment. Scarcely knowing she was about to speak, she yelped, "I want you to paint my portrait!"

****

Usually they came hooded and cloaked, and they took the stairs, unlike these stocking-less roof crawlers. But the girl in the aristocratic, though rumpled, dress looked at him with such wide open admiration he found it embarrassing.

"Did you hear that?" he called into the studio. "She wants me to paint her portrait."

"I thought we were on our way to the pub."

"In a moment." He led her into the studio, noting she frantically signaled her maid to come as she stepped over the threshold.

"Huh," said his friend, looking up, "she is a fine subject." Straightening some brushes on the table he added, "Let's see what we've got. Take your clothes off then."

The girl's eyes went wide and red shot to her cheeks. Her maid covered her mouth in shock, but the pair caught each other's eye, and finally the aristocrat said, "Where is the dressing room?"

Picking a fingernail with studied disinterest, he pointed. "Behind that screen."

She swayed a little, but went resolutely, catching her lady's maid by the arm and yanking her behind the barrier. Then the dogs packed in with them.

The chit couldn't be old enough to have her papa's permission for a portrait, but her obvious daring amused him—that, and her pert figure which revealed itself despite all that cloth. He was quite expert on what lay beneath folds of fabric. Chuckling, he strode to the table and moved a few brushes. A sea shanty drifted through his mind, but he couldn't recall the lyrics.

"Feel like laying odds?" said his friend.

"And how're you going to pay when you just said I

took your last quid?"

"The girl's coming out in shoes, shift and shawl."

"I say no shoes, no shawl." This one had light in her eyes.

Behind the screen the girls urgently whispered. And then there was silence; the kind of silence that spelled a decision. A minute later, out came the aristocrat, barefoot, shawl-less, but still in her shift.

Elbowing his friend in the ribs, he said, "I'm on a winning streak. So how much more do you owe?"

Her chin went up. "Winning streak?'

"That's right. We laid a bet on you, and I won."

A look, dark with challenge, narrowed her features. "Bet that I'd do what?"

His collar went tight, so he gave it a tug and shifted his weight. "It's all right. A young damsel isn't expected to—"

"To what?"

Her cerulean blues darkened even more, and her head went high as a defiant horse's.

"To... ahem..."

"To imitate Lady Godiva." His friend chuckled.

Her pupils dropped to slits, and an instant later she tugged her shift far above her knees and kept lifting, offering a view of the two most comely legs he'd ever witnessed.

"Keep your bleedin' eyes to yourself!" shouted the maid, yanking down the shift and turning on him with a knife in one hand and the studio shawl in the other.

But it was too late, with a roar of blood, his manhood leaped to attention and the ropes that bound his heart ripped in two and flailed in the air. Just the thought of her perfect ankles, her pink, round knees, and, Heaven help him, the curve of her alabaster thighs left him fighting for breath.

Realization struck with a jolt—the girl was practically fresh from the nursery. "God's teeth." Ignoring the glinting blade, he sprang to the vixen's side, grabbed her arm, dragged her to the screen, and as the maid tried to throw the shawl over the chit's translucent shift, he shouted, "Put some bloody clothes on! Where's your father? He should chain you to a wall until you're old enough to know better. Don't you ever, ever gallivant around unmarried men again!"

The dogs launched into a frenzy of barking, then turned on one another in small skirmishes. He paced the floor in a fury as the maid snarled and growled, clearly forcing the girl back into her dress. Overcome with rage, he slammed out onto the terrace and dragged the ladder across from the neighboring building. The girls' stockings were tied to the damn thing! After wrenching them free, the ladder disintegrated in his hands; rungs clattering into the alley, leaving him holding only the braces.

"Great bloody hell!"

The hounds circled, banging his legs with their tails in an ecstasy of excitement.

A giggle came from behind. He dropped the boards, and whipped about in time to catch the chit tittering.

"What in God's name are you laughing at?" he bellowed. "Do you know how easily you could have been killed?" He took her slender wrist with a grasp that could have wrapped around a second time, and hauled her to the edge. "Look down there. What do you see?"

She laughed so hard she held her stomach. He dragged her back from the edge and was on the verge of administering a spanking, when she quit her cackle and melted into eyelash-batting remorse.

Gazing with breathtakingly blue eyes, she said so sweetly a wild boar would cease its charge, "Now don't be so upset. We tied off the ladder, so it was perfectly safe. We're very clever that way, you know."

Every inch of her radiated contrition, and his anger pooled like syrup. "Be that as it may…" he said, gruffly. "Well, go and put your stockings on."

When she turned to obey, he noticed the back of her dress. Half the laces and buttons were in the wrong holes, and bunches of cloth puckered along the seam. "Now, what's going on with this?"

The maid threw her hands in the air. "And what am I supposed to do with that many fixings? They none of 'em wants to lie flat."

"Lizzie is new at her job."

"How new?" he demanded.

"Today," the girl named Lizzie shot back.

He rolled his eyes. "Well, throw the shawl over her back, Lizzie, and let's get you two in a hack."

Little Miss Blue Eyes appeared shocked. "I can't be seen in that shawl. Do you know how many scandalous pictures you've painted in which it's appeared? Everyone in London would recognize it!" Then an innocently seductive yet mischievous look brightened her eyes. "No, you must button me." She backed toward him.

"Me?" He put his arms in the air so as not to touch her, but she sidled closer. So close, the perfume of her rose-water-cleansed skin circled his brain and made it lose all reason. There was no question he knew how to fasten a woman's gown. How to unfasten them too... But if he touched her... Sweat dampened his forehead. Slipping around her, he called in the door to the studio. "Come on out and help with these buttons, eh?"

A sly smile bisected his friend's face. "Seems to me you can do the job just fine."

If he argued, he'd look like a frightened fool, and he was a frightened fool, though he wasn't about to admit it to anyone here—dogs included. *She's just like every other silly chit, so button her and be done with it.* But the moment his fingertips touched silk, the heat of her poured into his body like an upended pitcher. His cock leaped to attention, and he jerked back in shock.

"Go ahead," the blue-eyed vixen said, proffering her shoulders.

"Damned indecent," he growled. "You don't understand the half of what you're doing. Now, face the wall."

She turned, tossing an impertinent peek over her shoulder. He clenched his fists.

The ties and buttons fell away revealing a sliver of her back halved by the delicate hills of her spine. More blood drained to his nether region, causing blurred vision and a buzzing sound in his ears. One last tie and the mess could be corrected. But when undone, that tie exposed not just spine, but the swale at her waist, foreshadowing her bottom. He vehemently denied himself the pleasure of looking more closely at that delicious upward slide. However, no matter where he rested his gaze, her skin shone pale as the inside of a clam shell. And then, what got to him most, what wrenched his heart from its cave, was a single brown mole on the edge of her shoulder blade. A dot on that perfect landscape of skin, as innocent as a lamb in a field. Breath hissed through his teeth and he barely caught a moan before it sneaked past his larynx.

Something had to be done before he lifted her into his arms and took her on the chaise in front of everybody. Staggering away, he caught the handle of the studio door and was about to escape the roof when Lizzie's voice stopped him. "She's half undressed, where're ya going?"

"Close her up, but start at the bottom. Work slowly." He had the door open.

"But you're supposed to," said his tormentor.

"I'll get you a hack to take you home."

He allowed himself a quick glance in her direction. The point was to assure her that she held no power over him, but the glance was a mistake.

With those clear blue eyes burrowing into his soul and arousing his every male instinct, she said, her glistening, rosy lips dimpled in disappointment, "Are you sure I can't persuade you to paint my portrait?"

Chapter 5

"This is your home?" van Eck asked as they dismounted from the hack.

"Not mine, really. It belongs to the Earl of Davenpor—"

"Hugh Davenport. I know the man." A troubled, slightly frightened look darkened his features. He ran fingers through his hair several times as if he were pondering whether to stay or go.

Determined to keep him by her side until he agreed to paint her, Snap reached for the doorknob. He stepped past and clanked the lion's head knocker three times. Loudly.

"We can just go in," Snap said. "I live here."

"Nevertheless, we shall wait for the butler."

He had the most dashingly masculine voice. It caused ripples of excitement. Plus, he stood straight and tall beside her—like a royal guard. *If I die trying, I'll convince him to paint my portrait.*

About a quarter minute passed, and van Eck reached to give the knocker another clang, when Truss, the Davenport's butler, opened the door.

"I would like to speak with this young lady's father."

Ever so subtly Truss passed Snap one of those "now you're in for it" looks. She raised her brows and shot back a "you'll see" expression.

Truss turned on his heel and disappeared around the bend to the library. Oh, how she despised those glances—especially because they were so ludicrously wrong. Her parents wouldn't blink hearing about today's adventure.

"My papa will ask if you know anything about the Roman conquest of the Britons and leave it at that."

"Then I shall have to persuade him of the importance of keeping his daughter well chaperoned until she's mummified in a suitable marriage." His eyes flashed in Lizzie's direction.

The maid's jaw dropped. "Me only startin' this morning, I'll not take the blame for this one's doings. There's no stopping 'er once she sets her mind. You'll find that out soon enough."

Snap noted a pleasantly alarmed look in his eyes.

As they entered the salon, she deliberately waited for him to sit on the couch and then tucked in beside him as close as propriety would allow.

"Move to that end," he demanded.

Ripples again. How she adored that stern brow. Obediently, she scooted over.

The scuffing sound of her father's slippers approached. To demonstrate her complete lack of concern, she dangled a hand over the end of the couch and hummed a ditty.

Lord Albright arrived in the doorway and absentmindedly surveyed the contents of the room. "You wished to see me?" Then his glance landed on van Eck, and he poked his glasses up on his nose. His spine straightened, and she'd swear his hackles rose like on the back of a dog.

"Captain Gareth Hart," her father spat, "what are

you doing with my daughter?"

"Lord Albright." Gareth got to his feet and Snap followed.

"No, no, he's Julian van Eck, Papa."

"Leave this house, Captain. You are never to step foot in here again, and I will not tolerate your presence near my child."

"My lord, your daughter crawled across a rooftop to visit that notorious—"

"Enough!" Her father drew himself to his full height and appeared about to attack. "Remove yourself at once."

"Of course, my lord. Only try to keep your daughter—"

"How dare you! How dare you!"

Her papa trembled with rage. In fact, she'd never seen him in such a puff. It was very dramatic and exciting.

"I do sincerely beg your pardon."

Truss made a show of opening the door extra wide, and once Gareth had slipped out, the butler closed it firmly behind.

Captain Gareth Hart. How did she not recognize him?

After burning down their horse barn and trying to steal their mares for his horrible uncle, Baron Wadsworth, Captain Hart lay with a back injury for a month in the front parlor, too disabled to rise. Papa refused to speak to him.

But she, at only nine years old, nursed him back to health with hardly any help from her sister Claire, the healer of the family, or the servants, or anybody. And he'd told her the most marvelous tales of his escapades captaining his father's cargo ships, and of his heroic deeds during the war, and of his exploits in London's gaming halls, and of his wild seductions of the doyens of society. Hidden under that mustache lurked the face of a man who'd inhabited her every dream of love, adventure, marriage, and... and...other things...

"Go in the parlor and sit down," commanded her father. "Sophia," he called to Snap's mother, "Please convene the girls."

A chorus of concerned voices answered from upstairs. "What is it, Papa?" "How can I help you, dear?" etcetera.

"Come, I say!" He stormed halfway up the stairs, and Snap, wishing to follow his command, yet consumed by a desire to catch another glimpse of Captain Hart, sped into the parlor and pressed close to the window. Three dogs with their heads out the window of a hack, passed by with Captain Hart sitting by them straight and grim, one hand resting on the pug's back. Lud, was there ever a more attractive man?

Ellie caught up to her. "Is that Captain Hart? Oh Snap, you mustn't. He still works for his uncle!"

But Snap ignored her sister's protestations.

"Are you even listening?" Ellie barked, giving Snap's elbow a shake. "Papa wants to speak to you."

"I insist you sit, Snap," her father boomed.

Peggity stormed across the dining room and took Snap's arm. "You take the other side," she commanded.

Instead, Ellie guarded the rear as they marched Snap into the dining room.

Ugh, the lecturing would be endless.

Peggity and Ellie would certainly have words for her. Mama and Claire, though they could be counted on not to scold, would say gentle things, which was often worse. But Papa in full steam? Rare. Snap considered pretending a need for the privy and escaping to her room via the dumbwaiter.

"Now listen to me, young lady," Lord Albright bellowed. "Sophia, tell her!"

"Tell her what, dear?" said Mama.

Everyone except Mama glared at her until she sat—the family aligned on the far side of the table, with the exception of sweet, dear Claire, taking her usual position next to the accused—a sympathetic pillow cushioning a bed of nails.

"Baron Wadsworth is an enemy and a threat," Papa said, forcefully rubbing his glasses against his vest, his pale blue eyes bright with outrage. "That man, that wretched Captain Hart, whom you just admitted into your sister's home, is the baron's nephew and chief henchman. Have your forgotten that the baron is determined to lay his clutches on your mother's pearl necklace?"

"He's terribly dangerous," Ellie said, leaning across the table, as if her words could burn more effectively the closer she got.

Snap shrugged her shoulders. "I didn't know. I mistook him for the artist Julian van Eck. But even if I did know, don't you remember how Captain Hart forced himself from bed, though his back pained him so terribly he could scarcely walk, and then sacrificed himself to his uncle so the wretch would cease blackmailing us? That was heroic!"

"He hasn't left his uncle's employ ever since," Peggity said, her voice hard with rancor. "He collects gambling debts. Threatening poor, bankrupt people for their last farthings to keep Wadsworth in luxury and himself from an honest day's work."

"Did you hear that?" Lord Albright exclaimed. "Listen to your sisters."

"Not once, Papa, did you speak to Captain Hart while he was in our care. If you had, you'd know of his extraordinary feats of bravery against Napoleon. He probably saved thousands of lives."

"How old do you think he was eight years ago?" Peggity said, eyebrows high and head tilted in that way people do with an answer that's not at all what you want to hear.

Afraid to hazard a guess, Snap grumbled, "Pish."

"Seventeen," her sister said, triumph ringing in her voice. "At sixteen a man can buy a commission to become a lieutenant. It takes three years of service before he can purchase a higher rank, which means he couldn't have been a captain."

"They promoted him because of his deeds of valor."

"Poppycock!" Brandishing his glasses, her father added, "That rogue took advantage of your naïveté and filled your head with fairy tales."

"On top of that," cried Ellie, "the man's a charlatan! He seduces widows for their money."

Doubt crept into Snap's mind. During his recovery, the dowager often visited. Claire said they had a "special friendship," which at the time, Snap thought that meant they played together... Obviously, that wasn't correct... And had he made up stories about the war? If nothing he said was true... Well, wasn't it wonderful he liked entertaining an unkempt, untamed little girl, largely forgotten by her preoccupied parents?

He'd been so warm and kind—and best of all, so happy to see her and have her near.

"Sweeting," said her mother, reaching across the table to take Snap's hand, "Regrettably, you were given a great deal of free rein growing up; your father and I are at fault for that. But in London, dear, you must adopt the restraint of a young lady of position and fortune. An individual such as Captain Hart could only enhance your feral inclinations, leaving you unattractive to gentlemen of the *ton*. And we do so want you to marry well."

"In other words," Peggity said fiercely, "if you so much as lay eyes on that man again, we shall send you back to Exeter and your come out ball will be cancelled!"

Snap gripped the arms of her chair and cast her most baleful expression on the assembly. "I shall be eighteen in six weeks, and I will not be treated like a child! Besides," she added, deciding to give them what they wished to hear rather than let them turn her against the man she'd loved practically forever, "you're all making a fuss about nothing. I haven't the least interest in Captain Hart. All I wanted was my portrait painted."

The room fell silent.

Then Claire touched her arm. "That's true, I'm sure," she began gently, "but unfortunately you have that look in your eye, my darling Snap."

"Yes," Peggity cried, "you've got that look in your eye."

Looking apologetic, Mama nodded in agreement, while her father gripped the edge of the table, his knuckles turning the milky color of a fish belly. "Snap," he said sternly, "you are not to associate with that unfortunate man. Do I make myself clear?"

The next word of her father's scold was in mid-formation, when Lord Hugh Davenport, Ellie's husband, ambled in. "Who're we talking about?"

"Captain Gareth Hart," Ellie proclaimed as if she were reading notice of the plague.

"Dear God, never say that name in front of Mother," Hugh said, eyes wide with alarm. "She's still speaks fondly of the man."

"I doubt that sincerely," Lord Albright said, vigorously polishing his glasses on his sleeve. He cut Snap a grave squint: "That reprobate's name shall never again be spoken in this house nor shall it pass through your lips."

Snap dipped her head in submission. "Yes, Papa," she whispered, secretly crossing her fingers. "I promise."

Chapter 6

"Oh Lizzie, I've never seen Papa so angry," Snap said in the privacy of her bedroom. "And all because of Captain Har—the man whose name shall not be spoken." She threw herself backward onto the bed and grinned in delight. "I absolutely must see him again."

"Are you touched in the nob? They'd hang you before they'd let you near him. A man livin' off widows and breakin' fingers to collect a few shillings. That ain't a fellow deserves more than the gallows."

Snap sat up. "Were you eavesdropping?"

"Servants don't need to listen at doors to know what's doin'."

"Just because my sisters said it, doesn't mean it's true." She flopped back on the pillows.

"You said yourself he burned down a barn and tried to steal your horses. If that ain't a hanging offence, I don't know what is."

"If you say it in that negative fashion, it seems like he behaved badly. But we had the nicest time together, and his uncle, the very worst of characters who has a twitch and everything, forced him to do it."

Lizzie shook her finger. "A man don't burn down another man's barn if he ain't a slick one himself."

"Oh pish." Snap added another pillow behind her head. "I took care of Captain Hart as he recuperated, and he wasn't 'slick' at all. Me, at only nine years old, spooned him willow bark tea and told Claire when he needed laudanum for the pain and put cool compresses on his forehead when the fever got him. And when he was well enough, he told the most enchanting stories. Did you know that during the war, they had to use a hole instead of a chamber pot, and whole bunches of them did their business at the same time. With no privacy."

"Ugh," said Lizzie.

Snap stuffed another pillow behind as she warmed to her subject, and then patted the bed for Lizzie to sit.

"One time three horses escaped and they were very important because they pulled a cannon. He volunteered to go after them even though the French were everywhere just looking to slice an Englishman to bits. Very quietly, he sneaked through the woods, following the horses' tracks, and then he spied them. The French had all three in a pasture with their own horses; maybe twenty of them, probably more. Well, one of those three escapees was a mare named Bettykins who was as bossy as they come. Get her, and all the rest would follow."

Lizzie untied her boots, kicked them off and sat Indian style on the coverlet. "What did he do?"

As Snap worked the laces of her own boots, she said, "It was broad daylight, mind you, and even though he could be seen, Captain Hart knew the French soldiers would never expect an attack. He climbed into a tree that overlapped with another tree, and that overlapped with a third tree with a big limb hanging over the pasture fence. He waited hidden in the leaves until lunch when he knew the men would be distracted by their rations and groggy with food, then like a stealthy, stealthy cat, he jumped from one tree to the next. Then he inched out onto that limb over the paddock.

"He throws a little grain on the ground, and a horse notices it. Then the others get wind and in no time bossy ol' Bettykins is right under him. He drops down next to her, slips the lead on her halter, and sinks to his hands and knees. With the rope in his teeth, he crawled to the gate. And it was all so slow and natural, those soldiers didn't know what was happening until that gate swung open. Then he sprang onto Bettykins, kicks her into a gallop and brings the whole herd flying back to the British garrison."

Lizzie clapped. "Lawks, he's either a clever liar or a clever horse thief."

Snap shot bolt upright. "Why couldn't he do deeds of great valor so they made him a captain? That's not impossible."

Lizzie took a deep breath and leaned against the bedpost as if she were about to explain something to a dull child. "Folks with money buy a commission. They don't need to do nothing brave, so stealing horses—"

Snap jumped from the bed, grabbed the girl's ankles, and commenced dragging her off the coverlet. "Unsay it!" she demanded. "Unsay it this instant!"

Lizzie clung stubbornly to the bedpost and pedaled furiously to free herself. "I'll not! I'll not!" After jerking her legs from Snap's grip, she scrambled to the far side of the bed. "What are ya so upset about? Every word I hear about him, he's makin' off with another nag. What else am I supposed to think?"

"You don't know him as I do," Snap said, stomping her foot. "He's a gallant gentleman, and as I live and breathe, Lizzie Widcomb, I'll prove it to you and everyone else!"

A humphing sound whistled through Lizzie's teeth, but she didn't utter another word.

Chapter 7

A roast chicken was the sole occupant of Gareth's plate as he sat at the dining table in his Albany House apartments.

"Wasn't that the most interesting encounter today?" he inquired of the three dogs ringing his chair.

The trio, Rascal, Mimi, and Springer, fixed hungry eyes on him, their concentration exclusively on the chicken.

"I did a terrible thing to her family years ago," he murmured. "The worst I've done in a life of rottenness." He winced at the memory.

"It was long before you were puppies, perhaps before your mama and papa were puppies."

He took a bite of roast chicken. Mimi, a short-haired Pekinese, whimpered.

How did he bring himself to empty the Albright barn and fill each stall with the carcass of a dead horse from the knacker's yard? The stench and weight came back to him, along with the clouded look of the beast's lifeless eyes...then the fire.

The shame was even worse. Dealing with their kindness, the Albrights keeping his sick bed in the parlor so he wouldn't be alone, dosing him with laudanum to dull the ache, and little Snap, pouring her sweet tales of adventure into his broken heart.

Abruptly, he put his fork down. By God, she'd

grown into a fine young woman.

Mimi put a delicate paw on Gareth's leg, her soulful eyes a calling card for chicken. As he removed the contents of his fork and fed it to the peke, his mother's troubled expression drifted to mind. In a quavering voice, she said Uncle Wadsworth, her own brother, threatened her and Gareth's sister Laura. Gareth must steal the Fitzcarry pearls, or they would pay the price... And she did pay for his failure... Paid heavily.

Memories to tear a man in two.

He wiped his mouth with a napkin. No sense dwelling on the past.

He pulled off a few strands of meat and tossed them. The pack scrambled, wolfed, and reassembled.

Things needed doing tonight: collect ten quid from Lincoln Richards, perhaps visit Lopey and ask for more pocket money... Or take one of the baron's uglier jobs for the extra quid in commission.

Strung between brass candlesticks on the table hung three slightly tattered lace-rimmed handkerchiefs. He fingered a corner to see if the cloth had dried.

The familiar twinge of pain burned in his back, but...

"Snap..." He chuckled softly, and the dogs wagged their tails. "She's not little anymore..."

Heat like brandy flooded his senses. Legs long and trim at the ankles, that Albright blond hair, pale as corn silk. Springer licked his hand.

"I'm a rogue for thinking about her, but God's blood, a man can't easily get rid of an image like that."

Springer offered her paw.

Devil take it, you're practically engaged to Lopey.

Stick with the widows—they're safe, and lucrative.

A commanding knock sent the dogs leaping and barking at the door. Gareth waded through the scrum and admitted Crewe Burnett, a former boxer and the recently titled Duke of Hanesford. He'd married Peggity Albright, Snap's oldest sister, in fact. Nothing happened, Gareth reminded himself in a panic. You didn't touch a hair on her head.

"Tell this lot to keep their voices down!" Crewe roared as he dropped to his knees to greet the excited pack.

"Hanesford, what's brought you to my humble abode?" Gareth said, trying not to sound alarmed.

They might be friends, but dallying with his wife's sister… A sound beating wouldn't be out of order.

"The Albany ain't humble, laddie, so keep up the good work with your widow."

Crewe left off the dogs and kicked a chair out from under the table. Sitting backwards with his arms on the top rung, he said, "I'm gettin' up a round of fisticuffs." Absentmindedly he removed a drumstick from Gareth's dinner. "I'm depending on you to keep the betting on the up-and-up."

So that was the reason for the call. Relieved, Gareth said, "When's the bout?"

"Whenever the magistrates ain't lurking."

"They wouldn't arrest a duke."

Crewe grinned. "They might cause a stir and alert the wife."

"She sees those black rings around your eyes, and she'll catch on quick enough."

"Here's to the other fellow wearin' 'em." Crewe lifted the drumstick in a toast.

Rascal gave a short, impatient bark. Crewe tossed him a bit of chicken skin, which the creature caught in midair.

A single knock sent the hounds baying again, but without waiting for an invitation, in burst Gunner Swift. Through the din, he politely yelled, "It's us."

Following silently and sedately, came Ambrose, Marquess of Harrowgate.

In one quick motion, Gareth snatched the drying handkerchiefs from their string, stuffed them in his pocket, and hoped Ambrose hadn't seen. "Lud, let a fellow answer the bloody door."

Paying no heed, Gunner took a chair at the table, while Ambrose sauntered to a green velvet chaise trimmed with fraying gold fringe. He pursed his lips in disdain upon noticing a tear in the upholstery.

If Ambrose goes nose up to my furnishings, why in hell does he always chum along? "Doctor Swift, at your service," Gunner said, planting a beatific smile on the fighter. "Which part of your body do you wish to injure this time?"

"Not me; it's Beam Murphy what'll need the stitches." Turning to Gareth, Crewe added, "And do I get your permission to beat the stuffing out of your foremost bully boy?"

Gareth shrugged. "The first blow's on me, mate. What'd he do now?"

"Broke my footman's arm for a five guinea debt, the bastard. And how about you, ol' Radcliffe?" Crewe twisted in his chair. "What's your opinion of a duke takin' on the dumbest muscle in England?"

Ambrose glared. "It's unseemly."

Crewe and Gareth roared with laughter, while

Gunner shook his head and hid a smile.

The foursome told others they'd met at Cambridge, which was a bald-faced lie. It was attending Crewe's fights that brought them together: the boxer, the collector, the doctor, and his shadow.

"Hey, I've a bit of news," said Gareth. "Today an old acquaintance appeared on the rooftop of Julian van Eck's stud—" He halted in horror. What was he doing? If Crewe heard his sister-in-law crawled over roofs to meet Julian van Eck, he'd... Gad, seeing Snap had him fuddled.

Ambrose gazed out the window. "By 'old' acquaintance, I assume you mean a former conquest, Captain Hart," He added. "A highty-tighty with a fortune and enough wrinkles to map the Amazon, no doubt."

"Radcliffe, you could turn a tea party into a brawl," Gareth replied.

Ambrose's mouth curled in disgust, but his sharp gaze left the window.

Prying loose a wing, Crewe leaned closer and gestured with the appendage. "Are you going to reveal the lass's name and attributes or shall we start runnin' down the list?"

Gunner chuckled. "She must be a fine specimen; you're looking feverish, ol' man."

"Buxom?" asked Crewe, his brows rising.

"I'll not dishonor her with a crude description," Gareth said, suddenly overcome with emotion, "but war made me forget that something as, as...happy and spirited as...this woman...existed."

Ambrose offered an embarrassed cough, and Crewe scratched his elbow.

"Do you think he's going to burst into song?" asked Gunner.

Irritated, Gareth threw a chunk of meat to the dogs. "Don't be daft. She was just another woman—and anyway, I'll be anchoring permanently with Lady Whitlocke soon."

A sharp, cynical, "Ha," came from Ambrose.

"Widows are welcoming, lucrative, and the fastest way into Society," Gareth snarled. "Are you going to deny it?"

Gunner and Crewe passed a look, but the Duke of Radcliffe cleared his throat. "Society has no use for an outsider."

"I won't be an outsider when I'm married to Lopey—she's a doyen of Almack's."

"My dear lad," Ambrose said, radiating gentility, "you are a pretty folly meant to dote on Lady Whitlocke in front of her friends, little more."

Gareth shot to his feet. "Retract that statement, Radcliffe, or I'll sew your poxy eyes shut!"

Before Gareth could move, Gunner caught his shoulder and Crewe blocked the path to Ambrose.

"I've a patient. We should go," Gunner said, crossing to Ambrose and moving the duke's legs off the chaise. "Come, accompany me."

After rising languidly, Ambrose ambled toward the door. "He'll learn soon enough."

"You want my footprint on your whore pipe?" Gareth shouted as the duke sauntered by.

Crewe held him back until the door swung shut.

"What do you want with the *ton* anyway?" Crewe asked, pulling Gareth's dinner plate closer. "Bunch of feckin' peawits, as far as I'm concerned."

"You were born into the aristocracy, so you haven't faced the cuts I have."

"Aye, it's noble blood in my veins; enough to get me through their doors and send me out the back near vomiting from the falseness of 'em. You're missing nothing, chappie."

Gareth slapped the table and paced the length of the room. "You and Ambrose have titles, and Gunner has a profession, but me—my looks are my fortune, and they won't last." He turned to Crewe, jaw aching with emotion. "Marrying money is the only way, and Lopey Whitlocke's willing. I've got to get out of my uncle's grip before he slashes my face so badly a bleedin' whore wouldn't have me."

"He'd not do that."

"That mawworm cut a baby in its mother's arms for a three-shilling debt. There's no eviler man on Earth than my uncle, the esteemed Baron Wadsworth."

"But it's been on to eight years you've done his bidding. If he was going to do it, don't you think he would've by now?"

Gareth slumped on the edge of the chaise and tried to regulate his breathing. The dogs gathered in sympathy.

"It's coming to a head. He's going to find my sister Laura and her child. They'll never be safe without the protection of money and position."

Crewe folded his arms on the table. "So you're content with the widow Whitlocke, eh?"

"Of course. Naturally." He cleared his throat. "Very content. Yes…"

"Sounds like this woman you seen today's a bit more interesting."

"She's not!" Gareth said, nearly shouting.

Crewe laughed, yanked the other wing off the chicken, and shook his head. "You've got yourself a dilemma, laddie."

Chapter 8

Something was afoot. Through closed doors came the unmistakable music of secrets being whispered. Whatever this secret was, it was big; most of the servants had disappeared, which meant something was too exciting to miss.

Just as she passed the door to Crewe's bedchamber, his valet, Johnny, burst into the hall, wild with hurry. "Pardon, milady," he said, dipping his head then turning tail and racing away.

The man was entirely too startled for innocence. Keeping her distance so he wouldn't suspect, Snap followed. Down the stairs he flew, then out the back. Through a window, she spied him running toward the barn. Clearly, her brother-in-law was up to something he didn't want Peggity to know about.

Certain there were too few servants about to catch her, Snap used their tight little passageway through the house to slip into her room. There, she threw on a bonnet, snagged her reticule and a shawl, then stealthy as a cat, sneaked back down the passage and out the first floor window—the one with the hedge against it. She made two tiny taps and a scraping noise on the kitchen window; it was their signal for Lizzie to join her.

About to step from the bushes, Snap drew back. Blackfire—saddled and ready. Crewe approached the horse. Strides, purposeful. Fists, clenching and unclenching.

Now she knew…

****

Standing tiptoe on a crate at the back of Daffy's tavern/fight club, Snap craned to see through a soot and smoke-stained window.

"They'll come out and say where the fight's to be," Lizzie said, standing on another crate beside her. "Then we got to step quick to keep up."

"Is that Beam Murphy?" asked Snap.

Lizzie wiped a peep hole in the coal dust. "It's himself."

"Lud, he's big as a Stonehenge rock."

Crewe came into view, approaching Beam who sat at one of the tavern's long tables. The duke said something, and suddenly a roar shook the window panes. Beam bolted to his feet, knocking over the bench. His neighbors sprawled. Tankards of gin jumped and sloshed as the fighter's massive fist hit the table.

Crewe stepped back, and Gareth appeared. The breath caught in Snap's throat.

"He's a king amongst men," she whispered, putting a palm to her heart.

"A lily in a thorn bush," said Lizzie.

The man she loved should not be called a *lily*, but before Snap could demand a correction, Gareth said something to Beam. The monolith shoved the table at Crewe, who roared incoherently and ripped his own jacket off.

Daffy's erupted. Gin-soaked men slammed into each other, cursed, dragged tables to the corners, and bumped into the paintings of pugilists lining the walls, which clattered to the floor.

Beam, with fingers thick as cucumbers, worked the ties at his shirt collar.

"Where's your knife?" said Snap, gripping her companion's shoulder.

In a flash, Lizzie produced the blade.

"Break the glass; we've got to hear what's happening."

Without a second's hesitation, Lizzie stabbed through the window; the tinkling of glass drowned by the thunder of excited men. A scent of tobacco and gin rolled through the gap. Appearing unbothered by Beam's frenzy, Crewe tossed jacket, vest, collar, and shirt to someone just out of sight.

Never having seen a man's naked chest before, Snap gawked at her brother-in-law's pectorals, the cords of muscle across his stomach, the curling hair bee-lining toward the waistband of his trousers. God's teeth! Did Gareth look like that too? She fervently hoped so.

"That's Grub Street news, Beam. Your wife's not playing the blanket hornpipe with ol' Neddly," Gareth told the mountainous beast. "Get a grip, man. We'll hold the fight at—"

But Beam, eyes red as coals, would have none of it. Giving up on untying his shirt, he ripped the linen off and flung it to the floor. Whereas Crewe's body's was cut and defined, Beam, from brain to breeches, seemed to be one vast muscle.

"Lizzie, that man's going to kill the duke!"

The opponents raised their fists.

Snap clutched the sill and gasped in terror as the first punch landed.

****

Beam didn't wait for Crewe to settle into a stance. He lunged, and swung hard, nicking the duke's jaw.

"Eh, eh, eh!" shouted the crowd. "Fight fair! Fight fair!"

Worry tightened Gareth's gut as Beam, crazed and gin-swollen, hunkered low, driving Crewe against a table. *Beam's a prime piece of stupid, but he knows how to cheat in a fight.*

A killer right fist swung for Crewe's head, but the duke twisted away and the blow winged past his ear. No longer hemmed in by the table, Crewe pummeled Beam's ribs, the *thwack, thwack, thwack*, cutting the tavern's smoke-laden air, until a vicious left ended the series with an explosive breath from Beam.

Pain angered the bull, making him even more careless. He kicked for Crewe's knee, a tactic Gareth had seen him use on runaway debtors. Fortunately, his boot only partially connected as the duke leaped out of range, but the crowd roared at the move, some in outrage, others in blood lust.

Crewe's face pinched in agony, and a flash of fear rose in his eyes. Fisticuffs were one thing, but this was a St. Giles brawl.

"Keep it out of the gutter, Murphy!" Gareth shouted.

At the next swing, Crewe dodged right, throwing off Beam's balance and he crashed into a portrait of Gentleman John Jackson. The picture withstood the impact, but rocked on its nail.

An onlooker blocked Gareth's view, so he only heard a bone-breaking thump. Then another and another. Dread crammed his throat. Shoving the onlooker aside, he saw Crewe had the brute flailing to ward off punches. Then, with a southpaw slam to the ear, Beam twisted, teetered, slid down the wall, and fell. The floorboards shuddered.

A pair of urchins at the window jerked out of sight as Gareth went to the fallen fighter.

"Peawit," he growled. "You're bloody cup-shot. How many bumpers of gin did you swill before you heaved into Daffy's?"

Beam glared back.

Spiney, a grizzled old boxer with a flattened nose and rat eyes prodded Beam with the toe of a worn out shoe. "Get your arse up; your thirty seconds is done. And this round, use your feckin' hands!"

Sullen as a storm cloud, Beam got to his knees, and batted away Gareth's offer of assistance.

Gad, there's more genius in a box of hair. Rolling his eyes, Gareth left the man to figure out how to stand by himself. Of all the thugs in England, his uncle had paired him with Beam Murphy—a lummox of the first stare. Collecting debts with Beam was like carrying a club too heavy to lift.

"Round two," rasped old Spiney.

Crewe danced toward his foe, his knee heavily wrapped in gauze by Gunner. "Get em' up, Murphy, or tell your wife to bunk at ol' Neddly's tonight."

A twitch ran through Beam's body, and he scrambled to his full height. Huge, menacing, he towered over the duke and everyone else in Daffy's. Then Gareth caught a grin on Beam he'd seen before. That grin meant trouble. That grin meant Beam Murphy was about to do something deadly.

"Step back!" Gareth shouted, but almost before the

words left his lips, blood splashed across his face.

Too stunned to move, Crewe still held up his fists as blood from a gash to his knuckles poured down his left arm.

And then Gareth saw it—a little flash between Beam's clutched fingers. The poxy devil held a piece of glass!

Beam slashed again, but Crewe blocked the blow with his arm. That left Beam free to grab the duke's hair with his left and yank him forward to ram the glass through the jugular. As his giant mitt pulled back for the kill, Gareth took the bench the lummox broke and jabbed it into Beam's side. Pain and surprise battled across the beast's dull features, and he let go of the glass shard.

Crewe staggered toward the crowd, and Gunner came forward with a ready bandage.

All eyes were on the duke, when Gareth turned on his partner. "You're the prize fool of London," Gareth said, shoving Beam onto a bench. "Daffy's will ban you for life."

Beam said nothing, just pawed at his side with fat fingers, searching through the blood for splinters.

"Drunk to madness, and picking up glass to even the odds. If there were any justice, I'd use your guts for garters."

Glowering, Beam only grunted in response. The grunt, while hostile, contained a tiny note of apology.

Everything about this brute irritated Gareth, but he couldn't help feeling a bit sorry for him. All the fool knew how to do was fight, and believing his wife was cuckolding him, Beam's manhood was a stake.

Sighing in exasperation, Gareth said, "We've got

work in the morning. Seven Dials, my man."

The big head nodded as his fingers paused in their search for more wood fragments.

A few patrons approached, looking for their payouts. Bad enough that Beam had shamed himself in front of the entire Fancy, the blasted fellow didn't need to hear them brag of the money they'd scored betting against him. Gareth waived the men off.

"Have you the blunt for a hack?" he asked.

Beam's head lowered a fraction. "The baron ain't paid for the last job."

"Holy hell." Picking up the fighter's tattered shirt, and his jacket and vest, Gareth added a pound note to the pile and shoved it under his nose. "Take this, and get your arse home. But know this, leather-head, your wife went to ol' Neddly's for salt pork."

The vast ridge of Beam's brow wrinkled, and he gazed at Gareth with puzzlement.

"You're wondering how I know? I gave her the coin to buy you meat because today's your bloody birthday."

****

As the girls hid in the alley behind Daffy's waiting for Gareth, the duke, and the household servants to leave, Snap whispered, "Did you see the captain, Lizzie? I told you he's a heroic man."

"I seen him collect money, like your sister said."

Snap folded her arms and treated Lizzie to her most disapproving glare. "So you failed to watch him save my brother-in-law's life? And you didn't catch him being kind to that big bloke?"

Without looking the least cowed, Lizzie glared back. "You mean that bloke what tried to kill your brother-in-law?"

"Oh pish," Snap grumbled. "Clearly he's a friend of Crewe's, in fact, of all the gentry at Daffy's. And our footmen and stable hands seemed to know him too."

The swish of a broom and the tinkling of glass leaked through the broken window. Nervously Lizzie fingered the handle of her knife, which was sheathed at the waistline of her apron. "Ya think one of them shards I made is what cut up the duke?"

Snap listened to the glass skittering across the floorboards trying tell if the pieces near the window were large enough to be the one used in the fight. It was useless. Every stroke of the broom sounded the same.

"I don't think so… That big fighter was quite far from us…"

"He weren't though, that's the truth of it." The maid scratched her head, skewing her white cap to the side. "You ain't gonna say anything?"

"Of course not," cried Snap loudly. She clapped a hand over her mouth and taking Lizzie by the arm, led her quickly down the alley. "Anyway," she continued *soto voce*, "I'm almost one-hundred percent positive that glass came from a picture."

"How?"

"Because I know these things."

Chapter 9

For three days, Snap, with Lizzie as escort, scoured Hyde Park for signs of Gareth and his canine entourage. They had towed around Scout, the dowager's spaniel, as cover, but this morning, footsore and exhausted, the dog refused to leave his bed.

Yet body and soul, Snap thrummed with the need to see the captain again. He glowed in her mind like the Holy Grail so that every thought began and ended with him. The way he saved her from falling into the alley at Julian van Eck's studio, how he saved the duke by whacking that leviathan, then giving the beast a pound for a hack home... The memories pulsed through her heart.

But ever since the fight, that horrible silver-eyed Malloy surveilled Snap and Lizzie to the point where leaving the house without a solid excuse was impossible. The situation became desperate until this morning when Ellie suggested a shopping trip.

As they dressed for the outing, however, the nanny tending Ellie's son Sebastian injured her ankle hunting a pigweasel. This imaginary creature was Sebastian's arch enemy. Poor Nanny had to relinquish charge of the boy to Lizzie.

Now, ensconced in a coach on its way to the Burlington Arcade, Snap scrutinized the landscape for signs of Gareth. Then Ellie interrupted her thoughts.

"Ackerman's has a charming picture of a white gown trimmed in white with white embroidered flowers," she said. "So pretty and refined."

"If the gown is to be white, I want it to be terribly low cut," Snap said brightly, knowing it would send her sister into a fret.

Lizzie lifted a brow and gave her a "What are you up to now?" sort of glance, but Snap's sister straightened and took on an authoritative air. "Don't try my patience, Miss Nefertiti Albright."

" 'Don't try my patience, Miss Nefertiti Albright,' " Snap mimicked. "Lud Ellie, Mama would never use such a silly tone, and I expect better from a woman who rides astride."

The rosy-cheeked toddler gazed questioningly at his mother, then sucked loudly on the handle of his silver rattle.

"Sebastian," Snap said, addressing the babe, "if your mama ever uses that high and mighty inflection with you, bite her on the nipple."

Ellie gasped. "You insist on being outrageous!"

"Only because you pretend to be outraged."

"I am outraged."

"No, you're not. You think that just because you're a mother now, you should become dull. It's ridiculous."

"There's no reason my child—"

"Sebastian, do you know what stories you'll love most when you grow up?" Snap said. "The one about how your mama dressed as a jockey and won the St. Leger on her mighty steed, Manifesto, and how Auntie Claire faced down a murderous madwoman, and how Auntie Peggity made a duke out of a boxer. But best of all, there will be the exciting tale of Aunt Snap's revealing bodice!'"

The little boy pulled the rattle from his mouth and waved it, a drooly grin stretching his chubby cheeks.

"Yes, it's thrilling," cried Snap, just before the rattle bonked her on the nose. "Ah, so you're planning to become a swordsman, little one," she added. "That's a perfect profession for a daring Albright."

"*En garde*." With an index finger, Snap parried the toddler's rattle.

"Well, I'll be...," Lizzie said softly, interrupting the swordfight.

Snap followed Lizzie's gaze. "I'll be, what?" And then she saw them—three dogs sitting outside a hat maker's shop. One was a droop-eared spaniel, another a peke, and the third, a furry black and white thing of indeterminate origin that was lifting its leg on a hitching post. Snap barely stifled an exclamation.

Fortunately, Ellie was too busy cooing at her son to notice. Folding her hands neatly in her lap, Snap said, without a hint of excitement, "Perhaps we should stop here. There look to be some interesting shops."

Ellie poked her nose out the window, and just as her forehead wrinkled into a "not here" declaration, Lizzie blurted, "Besides, I got to use the privy."

"Thank you," mouthed Snap to Lizzie, as Ellie tapped the roof to signal the driver.

"But I do," Lizzie mouthed back.

As the ladies disembarked, Ellie handed out her son to Snap.

"Oh, what sticky fingers," Snap said, bringing the toddler to a horse trough and dunking his digits in the water.

"No!" cried Ellie, but it was too late.

Squawking with pleasure, Sebastian splashed until his sleeves were soaked, and, as Snap predicted, until his bottom was warm with urine.

"Oops, he's wet," she said, putting him down.

Ellie's eyes blazed. "Of course he is. That's what cold, splashing water does to babies."

With eyes wide, Snap replied, "I had no idea. But perhaps you'd better change him at the King's Swan Inn."

Lizzie took the little boy's hand. "I'm headed that way right quick."

For a moment, Ellie looked undecided.

"She's not as gentle as some," said Snap, jerking her chin at the retreating figures, "but I'm sure she can handle those big diaper pins. They're not much different from knives, are they?"

"Where will you be?" Ellie said sternly, walking backwards as she crossed the road after her son.

"There's a milliner's just there with some lovely bonnets in the window."

"Right then." Ellie eyed the spot. "We'll get the baby cleaned up and meet you there."

Forcing her lips into an expressionless smile, Snap waited for her sister to turn around before sauntering, ever so casually, toward the milliner's and the three waiting dogs at its entrance. The canines wagged their tails at her approach and circled her knees.

"Is he in there?" she asked the peke, who answered with a lick to Snap's palm.

Upon entering, she expected to see Captain Hart among the men's hats, but he appeared to be studying bonnets. Tiptoeing to his side, she blurted, "Will that be a gift to a paramour?"

He jolted in surprise, then seeing her, furrowed his brow, though not before a flame of want lit his gaze. "I thought I'd seen the last of you."

"When?" asked Snap.

"What do you mean, 'when'? When I dropped you off in Mayfair and was told by your father never to darken his door again."

"Ah, well, it might as easily have been when you hobbled from our home so many years ago to sacrifice yourself to that dreadful uncle of yours—for the safety of my family." Before he could object, she snatched up a hat. "Do you remember how you were so bent over with pain you could barely walk? We thought you would die if you left my care." She put the bonnet on and posed for him. "Do you like it?"

He turned away as if afraid of seeing how becoming she was in the *chapeau.*

"Clearly I wasn't on death's door, because I'm fine now."

Jouncing a curl of ribbons, she said, "Too many gew gaws?"

"Take that dreadful thing off, you shouldn't even be in this store."

Puckering her lip in her prettiest petulant frown, she removed the head covering and patted her pale locks. "I've as much right to shop here as you."

He moved quickly away. "Yes, but I got here first, and your father objects to my presence."

"Oh pish." She turned her back on him and tried on another bonnet. "He's simply forgotten how marvelous you are."

Gareth folded his arms. "I'm not marvelous in the least."

"You're lovely then."

She got close enough to lean past him and reach for another hat. He smelled divinely of frankincense and wet dog.

"Men are not lovely," he said, blocking her reach. "I'm especially not lovely, and it's time to leave." Then using his body as a barricade, he herded her toward the door.

He'd have her out soon if she didn't think quickly. The knob bumped her rump and the bell above the entrance tinkled at the disturbance. "You were lovely to a lonely little girl," she said, keeping her back pressed to the knob so he couldn't turn it.

"Lonely? You? I seem to recall at least a dozen urchins standing in the parlor, watching you put cold compresses on my forehead, and begging you to come out and play."

He attempted to gain the knob, but she refused to budge. "But I was lonely," Snap said. "You were the only adult who talked to me; who wanted to hear about my adventures with the fishermen, and my rat, Napoleon."

That made him laugh. For a fraction of a second, he looked delighted.

"Remember, I let you feed him a lima bean," Snap continued, "but he wouldn't eat it. He hated them as much as you and I do."

He smiled, but then his brows angled to seriousness. "He was a funny rat, but you'll be eating nothing but lima beans if your father catches you with me. Now, let's get you going."

He lifted her under the elbows, plunking her down out of the way. Before he could nab the knob, however, she dashed out of reach.

"I have to put this darling chapeau back on the shelf."

With fists planted on hips, he let out an exasperated breath. "Sly vixen." Shaking his head in disapproval, he strode after her.

At the hat's shelf, she scampered further across the store, so he stalked purposely after her. The hunt was on!

"Lady Albright," he said, barely managing to keep his voice stern, "for your own good, please leave."

Scooting around the far side of a display, she shook her head, "I won't until you buy your paramour this, this—" She galloped to the next display as he made a grab for her arm. "This magnificent piece of finery."

From its place of honor on a hat block, she lifted a pale blue bonnet with a high conical crown trimmed in rosettes and pink ribbon. Wrapped like a squirrel's tail around that crown was the most luxurious blue ostrich plume she'd ever laid eyes on. That feather would be noticeable above the thickest crowd.

"Put that back," Gareth demanded, "or your father will show you the hot side of Hades."

Deep beneath the glowering eyes and furrowed forehead, he was hiding a secret joy in the game. She could tell.

Glaring fiercely at him, every fiber tingling with excitement, Snap said, "I will not, nor will I leave until you've purchased this hat. She will love you forever."

"I don't need her, or anyone else to love me forever, but I do need you to depart before your papa loads his pistol." He took another swipe at her arm, but she dodged left, nearly toppling a mannequin.

Safely out of reach, she said, "I shan't," and lifted her chin for emphasis.

He shook a finger at her. "This is not ladylike behavior."

Snap flashed him her most brilliant smile. "I know."

A startled guffaw sneaked out before he could suppress it, and she knew she had won.

"So, you'll be gone if I buy that bonnet for my 'paramour'?

She nodded.

With a great show of impatience, he motioned for the headgear and went to the shopkeeper. "How much?"

Snap crept to his side—head bowed—the picture of feminine subjugation.

The cashier bit his lip. "Five pounds, sir."

"Five pounds!" Gareth cried. "Are you serious, man? I could buy enough silk for two frocks and a pair of gloves for that kind of money."

"Aye, sir, it's our very best."

Gareth turned on Snap, who sprinted behind a shelf of top hats. Leaning over the arrangement, she exclaimed, "Not one step if you fail to buy that hat!"

His lips twitched toward a smile before he got control and frowned. Back he stormed to the cashier, who already had a round box waiting. Showering oaths, and bestowing unconvincing looks of exasperation at her, Gareth fished coins from his wallet and dug deep in several pockets before five pounds lay heaped on the counter. He shoved the currency toward the shopkeeper, but just as he was about to lift the box, Snap whizzed by, snatching the parcel as she flew out the door.

Safely across the street she turned back and waved. "I'm your paramour, Captain Hart, and I can't wait for you to see me in your present!"

"You thieving kinchin cove!" Gareth blustered. Then, as a laugh crinkled the corners of his eyes, he jerked his head toward the dogs. "And where were you while she was robbing me blind?"

Chapter 10

Gareth sat on a sofa in Lopey's Rococo-infested saloon, a ledger spread in front of him, overwhelming a small table whose legs barely accommodated his knees. Quill in hand, he paused before tackling a fresh row of numbers.

"Why Captain Hart," a feminine voice said, "I do believe you're grinning."

Lady Penelope, the Earl of Whitlocke's widow, gazed at him admiringly through an ornate gold lorgnette. "I don't believe I've ever seen you grin."

"No?" he replied.

"You don't grin, yet it suits you."

"Then I shall greet you with at least one smile per day, Lopey," said Gareth, displaying his row of perfect pearly whites.

She chuckled. "Oh, you smile all the time, Captain, but it's an obligatory smile. What I just observed was a happy grin, and I'm afraid, dear one, that you are rarely happy these days."

"Being in your company makes me happy," he said, and that was true.

Lopey was the latest in a long line of affairs with widows who included the Dowager Lady Davenport, but Lopey was different: pear-shaped, prone to wearing turbans and spouting eccentric philosophies, such as the influence of ghosts on politics or the moon on carriage horses, he couldn't help but adore her. Or, to be more accurate, he adored the hope she instilled. Unlike past lovers who knew exactly what to do with their husband's money the moment those unfortunate gentlemen were sent to the worms, Lopey was adrift. She'd truly loved ol' Whitlocke. In her despair at losing him, she had made the mistake of entrusting her fortune to her oldest son, Finnegan, an untalented poet with no interest in numbers.

The lad never checked invoices or communicated with the stewards of the Whitlocke estates, and as a result, he paid extravagant prices for the simplest things: three pounds for a rake, seven shillings for a fistful of radishes, and a sovereign for an ox's nose ring. Otherwise honest stewards, merchants, and tenants seized their opportunity, and Lopey had no clue what was happening until one day Finn complained at dinner that bread cost twenty shillings a loaf.

"Bread is but sixpence and not a farthing more," Gareth had exclaimed.

Everyone at the table looked at him in shock. That was when he knew—despite a deep desire to live a life of leisure—he had to take over the care of her estates.

Now, instead of having to perform the beast with two backs for a new suit of clothes, Lopey bestowed on him the responsibilities of the lord of the manor— a position that, unfortunately, did not come with the freedom to use her money. She'd established him at the Albany, London's most fashionable bachelor housing, but only on rare occasions did she remember to reward his work and attentions with coin. No matter. When they were married, all that would change.

"Look at these numbers, my darling," he said,

shifting the ledger so she could read it. "You're in for an exceptionally comfortable winter, and doubly so if the harvest does well."

She studied the page, her knuckles going white around the lorgnette's handle. Tracing a finger down a row, she said, "There are a lot of figures, aren't there?" With a frown, she pushed the account book back. "I suppose you'll be trotting out of my life soon."

Gareth was taken aback. "That's not my plan. Why would you say such a thing, Lopey?"

"This morning there was a fat toad on the garden doorstep, and he looked quite lost."

Gareth moved the table and ledger aside. He crossed his leg and gave Penelope his full attention. "So I'm a toad, eh?"

Pensively, she licked her lips. "Well, there are no more slugs eating the herbs, so what's that poor toad going to eat next? It's in his nature to hop to the neighbor's garden. Now that my accounts are in order, you'll grow bored."

"Not at all. I'll grow indolent as the rest of the aristocracy—a state I've been seeking for a long, long time, my love."

Lopey shook her head mournfully. "By next month you'll be itchy, the following you'll have found some new interest, and the month after that, you'll be gone."

"Never. You are my sole occupation, Lopey."

An unwanted vision of Snap in the hat shop, mischief sparking like a Roman candle, shot heat to his groin…and panic to his brain. In the next instant, her image was usurped by his sister Laura's pale cheeks and trembling hands. Gad, he had to act quickly or everything would be ruined.

"In fact, I'd like to make my commitment to you official."

She laughed, then propped the lorgnette on her nose, and her eyes, magnified to the circumference of the lenses, stared into his. The sensation was unnerving, yet Gareth was getting used to Lopey's ways.

"You say that as if you mean it."

He reached for her hand. "I do mean it," he told her seriously. "You've made me a stronger, better man, and in return, I am forever yours."

She waved him away as if batting a fly. "A hot-blooded male such as yourself saddled with an aging bovine like me? Nonsense."

He moved to a footstool at her feet, and ran a thumb across the back of her hand. The skin wrinkled like chop on a lake, and he hated himself for noticing.

"I prefer mature women," he said, as the recollection of Snap's alabaster skin replaced the sight of Penelope's loosened flesh.

Hurling the image from his mind, he focused on Lady Whitlocke's not unpleasing face. Never again would Uncle Wadsworth blackmail him into carrying out his filthy orders. Never again would Laura… sweet Laura, and baby Clementine have to hide from his evil… if Lopey married him.

Ardently, he pressed her fingers to his lips. "Women like you understand the world. You offer a man peace and tranquility." Snap's brilliant smile flamed in his thoughts. "And a woman who's been married doesn't engage in silly, provocative behavior."

Lopey patted his hand. "My, my, such a fervent speech. I imagine, though, with your good looks you've had a number of mademoiselles misbehaving for your attention."

"Indeed," said Gareth, beaming his most charming smile.

Her keen gaze met his. Shaking her head in wonder, she slumped into the silk cushions and waved vaguely at the sideboard. "Weren't you going to fetch us a drink?"

"Not until you say yes, my love."

She wrinkled her forehead, then rose and went to the window. He held his breath and prayed a mosquito wouldn't whine, that leaves wouldn't rattle, that a cloud wouldn't temper the sun's rays; she could interpret anything as a bad omen. Blessedly, the sky remained its usual, pristine gray, and apparently the rest of nature held its peace.

"I will," she said, giggling and hiding her face like a schoolgirl.

Gareth hopped to his feet, planted a kiss on her plump cheek, and led her back to the chaise. "I'm exceedingly happy. Truly, my love. And now I'll fetch a drink to toast our blessed union."

By the time he turned around with her ratafia, however, Lopey was thrumming her fingers on her chin, a shadow of worry darkening her features. "But you were grinning before you asked me." She sat up straight and pointed. "You're in love."

He froze with his brandy in midair. One telling move was all the lady needed.

"No, I am not," he said slowly. "Except with you."

She bit the side of her index finger.

"I bumped into an old friend today, is all. We had marvelous times together back in the bad old days," he added a wicked wink.

Lopey sank back, the furrow smoothing on her brow. "Oh, what a disappointment," she said, with a flick of the wrist. "I thought it was something more exciting. Fellow sailor, I suppose?" She took a sip of ratafia.

"High seas, yes," said Gareth. "Fellow sailor, no."

"He sounds intriguing."

"Just someone who's undergone a remarkable transformation."

"Heathen to gentleman, eh?"

"Something like that."

He ought to discuss wedding dates, honeymoons, dresses and ceremonies, but it felt as if his insides trembled. Pulling the tiny table and ledger to his knees again, he tried to concentrate on the ink scratches covering the page. The number five, however, reminded him of Snap swinging the hatbox; the three of her small, firm breasts, and the eight, worst of all, brought back thoughts of her figure, scarcely hidden by the sheath she wore at van Eck's. He punched his thigh. *By God, the girl's off limits.*

One row of figures later, however, another grin sneaked onto his face.

Chapter 11

Snap lay on her bed as sunshine poured through the window in a brilliant rectangle that marched across the parquet, up the coverlet and across her skirt. She glared at it, then slammed her book shut. Reading was impossible on a day like today, and no one, not Ellie, not the dowager Lady Davenport, not Malloy, nor anyone else should expect her to lie here doing nothing. The trouble was, they did expect her to do nothing, or at least nothing that would jeopardize her reputation, which amounted to nothing because even glimpsing Gareth Hart was apparently a crime in this city…

It had been four whole days since she'd whisked that bonnet from his grasp, yet she hadn't figured a single way to discover where he lived, since the servants refused to give even a hint. Restless as a baby strapped in a pram, she pounded her bare heels into the coverlet until its embroidered satin surface lumped into foothills. It was childish, she knew, but times like these called for childishness. Outside a mockingbird had the nerve to park itself on a nearby branch and sing.

"*Toohee*, yourself," said Snap grumpily.

Excruciating day after excruciating day, she'd been wracking her brains for a way to get Captain Hart to see her in the bonnet. Every time she lowered it over her curls she looked prettier: its blue rim highlighted her eyes, its pink ribbon brought out the blush in her cheeks, and its perfect shape accented her oval face. One glimpse of her in that magical *chapeau* would guarantee a proposal. But how to find him? Just lumbering around in a coach all day on the off chance of seeing him wouldn't do. Snap picked at a loose thread jutting from a white lily embroidered on the coverlet.

"What to do, what to do, what to do," she mumbled.

The mockingbird gave a full throated *toohee* and flapped into the azure sky. Its flight distracted her, and then she heard, faintly at first, the meow of a cat. One meow, two meows, and then a chorus of who knew how many meows accompanied by the excited woofing of Sport.

Snap leaped off the bed, dashed to her mother's room across the hall, and leaned her full torso out the window. Around the corner came the cat's meat man with his wheelbarrow of scraps considered unfit for human consumption. At his heels were dozens of yowling felines. Even the slinky strays boldly approached his cart. In every house at least one dog had its nose pressed to the window, paws working the glass and adding their voices to the cacophony.

Of all the peddlers in London, the cat's meat man was the most likely to know Captain Hart's address!

Without bothering to put her slippers on, Snap bolted from the bedroom and slid down the banister. Truss, the butler, was striding toward the front entrance to open it for her, but Snap beat him to it. She twisted the knob and raced onto the sidewalk before the cat's meat man was halfway down the block. Kitties scattered as she bounded up to him.

"Sir, excuse me, do you provide meat to dogs as well?"

The man tried to answer, but his words were drowned by an insistent choir of meows. The noise was deafening. Quickly he cubed some meat and threw it to the crowd. The voices died as the cats pounced.

"Eh?"

"Dogs?" Snap shouted, as the chorale began immediately. "Have you meat for them too?"

"Aye, milady," he said, tilting his head in puzzlement. "Do you want to buy?"

"Oh no," she assured him, "Cook will do that, but there's a trio of dogs I've seen recently that I thought were simply adorable. I wondered if you know where I can find them?"

"Perhaps, milady" the man said, frowning. "What'd they look like?"

"One's a brown spaniel. Then there's a white pug-nosed creature, and the largest of them is a fluffy black and white."

His frown deepened and his eyes narrowed. "I know 'em."

"Could you give me the address? I'm ever so interested in finding out if that shaggy black and white has any pups."

"If ya look close at 'em, milady, you'll see the beast is male."

In tandem, a tuxedo and a calico leaped onto his cart, leaving him just enough room to slice as the rest of the gathering swirled about his feet. He cubed and tossed, and the feline phalanx split and quieted.

"What about the Pekingese?" said Snap, offering a sweet smile. "She seems like a dear little thing."

"Aye, the peke's a nice 'un, but the man what owns them dogs ain't the sort a young lady should be consortin' with."

"Why ever not?"

He wagged his head noncommittally, but Snap got the impression he didn't think it was proper to discuss such things with a member of Society.

Placing a hand to her heart, Snap widened her eyes to achieve an appalled expression. "My goodness. Well, thank you, sir, for your expertise."

Back inside, she stomped up the stairs. "Oh lud!" *Now, what shall I do?*

But she hadn't ascended more than four steps before an alternate plan to find Gareth popped into her brain.

Forget cat's meat vendors, all she needed was a costume...

Chapter 12

Gareth studied his cards as he sat playing piquet with Lopey. He let her win another trick. She adored winning, and frequently cheated. He'd found a cache of face cards stuck in a seam under the table. It was never assured that she'd pay him back. Sometimes the butler passed him a purse as he left the house. Today?

A hankering to be out in the sunshine crawled into his toes, crept to his knees, and thrummed in his thighs. The hankering grew until it was impossible to concentrate a moment longer on keeping score. Though he could put it off serving his uncle's needs till evening, he decided to use him as an excuse.

"My darling?"

She peered through a gold lorgnette.

"I've got to be on to my next, far less pleasant, employment, and you'll bankrupt me if we keep playing."

"Poor captain," she replied, pursing her lips in sympathy. "That dreadful baron has you doing his bidding today?"

"I'm afraid so." He laid the cards down, kissed her forehead, wove through an obstacle course of gold leaf and inlay, and finally escaped out the front door.

A hack brought him to the edge of St. Giles, where the carriage halted. "Not a step further, Clara," he heard the driver tell his horse.

Gareth tossed the man a shilling and took the few strides necessary to bring him into the chaos of the rookery. The wail of babies blended with the shouting of men and women, throaty and raucous in their gin-soaked state, the stink of sweat and piss steaming from their bodies as the sun beat upon the cobbled street.

He found a pebble and launched it at a window. "Ay oh!" he called, then leaning a shoulder against the rough limestone of a pawn shop across the street, commenced waiting. A shanty came to mind, that he sang softly to himself.

"Soon we'll be warping her out through the locks,

Way, ay, roll an' go! Where the pretty young gals all come down in their flocks,

Timme rollickin' randy dandy O!"

The verse reminded him of Snap. His blood heated in a rush, so he had to force his mind to other things. He ceased humming.

A gang of hardened lads rounded the corner, arms across each other's shoulders, singing a totally different tune. "I wish I was a diamond ring, on my Lulu's hand," they caroled at the top of their lungs, "and every time she scratched her butt, I'd see the Promised Land." They burst into discordant cackles.

A stout one used his hat as a cudgel on the smallest of them. "What're you tittering at? You ain't never seen the Promised Land, and I spec' you won't in a lifetime."

Gareth recognized the little one as Quick Rope. Only about nine, the lad was auditioning for a spot with the gang, so he gave as good as he got, whacking the stout one with a felt ruin he had had perched on his head.

"I will sooner'n you, fatty!"

"Feckin' call me Fatty!" roared the bigger boy, making a grab.

But Quick Rope dodged fast, and seeing Gareth, made straight for him. "Eh, Cap'n," he cried. "Is ya makin' a visit? Who's the lucky pigeon today?"

The others held back, their sly, feral eyes watching.

"I'm seeking Tommy Taylor. Is he about?"

Quick Rope gauged his mates' mood. "I ain't seen no one," he said, jerking a grubby chin at Gareth.

"Well, if you find Mr. Taylor in a pub or the like, you boys will let me know, eh?"

They laughed dangerously. "What'll ya give if I find him?" crowed Kid Bowman, the leader, mockery gleaming in his dark eyes.

"A shilling," Gareth replied coolly.

"How much ya got on ya?" another asked.

Studying the tips of his white gloves, Gareth replied, "Enough."

"He been collectin' all morning," the stout one said. "I'm bettin' he's got blunt comin' out the arse by now."

The air went taut as a bow string. Greed, hunger, envy fired in the ring of faces.

"Eh Quick Rope," said Kid Bowman, licking his lips, "tell your rich friend we'll find Tommy so they can both get their crowns kicked in together. A double hanging, eh fellas?"

Cackling, harsh and menacing, followed.

Gareth snorted, and slowly tugged off his gloves. "Don't get too ahead of yourself, youngling."

"Call me 'youngling,' you bloody, feckin'—" But Kid Bowman didn't wait to finish his sentence. He lunged at Gareth and the other boys lunged with him.

Deft as a leopard, Gareth leaped onto a push cart, caught the iron bar of a gas lamp hanging over the pawn shop door, swung on it until he got his legs high enough to hook around the iron bar from which the shop's three ball sign was suspended, and then clambered onto a thick stone window sill above it.

He'd just gotten comfortable, dangling his legs over the edge, the boys shouting and leaping below, when Beam Murphy lumbered out of the tenement across the street.

Like a great, dull ox, Beam ignored the shouts of the pack and looked for Gareth both ways down the street, swiveling his enormous frame as if his neck were too muscle-bound to turn his head. Gareth rolled his eyes. It would be kinder to call out, but these jobs for his uncle always turned ugly with Beam around. Tommy Taylor was three weeks in arrears. No doubt he'd already downed his pay at a gin house, but having his thumb broken wouldn't help.

Gareth reasoned he could tell his uncle he'd waited for ol' Beam, but the idiot was still quaffing his hair when Gareth had to high-tail it from a thieving band of brats. The lie would have just enough truth in it to be believed.

Using the sign pole to help him stand, Gareth found a handhold in the crumbling mortar above the window sill and a foothold on a decorative scroll, and another handhold on the sill of the third story window, etc., etc. until he gained the roof. From there, he leaped the gaps between buildings until he reached the end of the street—far enough away that Beam wouldn't spot him.

You're a lucky man today, Tommy Taylor.

****

"Truss, send Widcomb to my room," called Snap as she flew up the stairs.

Her headlong rush was halted midstride when Lady Davenport's breasts stopped her shortly before the woman emerged from her apartments. "I thought that unseemly pounding of feet might be you," she said.

"Oh dear," Snap replied, layering the sweetness on thick as jam. "I'm afraid you've caught me again. When will I ever learn?"

"Which is why I'd like to speak with you."

"Of course, my lady," replied Snap, "But please allow me a moment to meet you in half dress instead of this frumpy ol' thing." She flapped the fabric of her simple gown, fit only for the house or mad dashes after cat's meat men. But as Snap attempted to skirt the dowager, her passage was blocked by the lady's famously large bosom.

"If I let you escape, you may not know before your come out ball what a woman of grace and beauty does with her person," Lady Davenport said, reaching for Snap's arm with the intensity of one who has something of tremendous importance to impart.

That peaked Snap's curiosity.

"It is critical," the woman said, her eyes somber in her lined face, "to learn the art of moving with refinement."

"Do you mean walk a certain way?" asked Snap. "Because I can pick that up quick as a wink. Right now though, I've got the most awful—"

"We glide." Lady Davenport gripped Snap's arm and led her a few paces down the hall. "Smooth strides."

"Smooth strides," Snap repeated, imitating her.

Together they flowed over the floorboards, the dowager digging her trim nails into Snap's flesh. Despite the pinch, it was nearly impossible to keep a straight face; Lady Davenport looked like a masthead on a windless day.

As they reached the far end of the hall and turned, Snap asked, "Do you remember Captain Hart?" She hoped she didn't sound too interested in the answer.

Halting mid-stride, Lady Davenport clasped her hands under her chin. "That enchanting young man?"

"So you liked him. Did you find him dashing and heroic?"

"I adored him. Perhaps even loved him." The dowager sighed. "We were planning to escape his uncle by sailing to New York, but that unfortunate incident with the horse stealing and the barn fire... Those were foolish times."

"But you came often when he was at our house. I remember you tried to dose him with willow bark and laudanum, but he only wanted me to do it."

"He was quite fond of you."

The elderly woman's gaze shifted as if she saw her affair with Gareth play out on the wall. Then her shoulders slumped slightly: a breach of posture Snap never expected to see from her in-law. The impropriety lasted only a few seconds before the dowager straightened and gave Snap a piercing look.

"Why the sudden interest in Captain Hart?"

"I saw him...at a hat shop."

"Ahhh, and he stirred something in you?"

Snap focused on the floor. "Not necessarily..."

"You called him 'heroic,' my dear, but you're mistaken. He did not love me. I knew that, of course, and understood he'd marry for money and social position, yet at the time, I paid that no heed. And I forgave him his cruelties because the baron's grip made him a desperate man. But he is no hero."

Snap didn't know what to say. The dowager's words pricked like thorns, but didn't pierce deeply enough to disturb her faith in Captain Hart.

"Shall we continue our walk, dearie?" Lady Davenport took Snap's arm and glided down the hall. "A graceful woman is to appear like a specter, floating as if her feet don't move at all."

"Wouldn't that be alarming?"

"Droll child. Bend your knees slightly, and you'll find it easier. Chin up."

Snap followed her in-law's example, though she inwardly cringed.

As they reached the end of the hall, Lady Davenport executed a weightless turn and still holding Snap's arm, embarked on another ghost-like lap. "He's to marry Lopey Whitlocke. You must have heard the rumor."

"What?" cried Snap, stopping dead and dislodging her arm from the woman's grasp.

"You were so enamored of him as a child…"

"Have they a date?" Snap interrupted, panic rising.

"June twenty-second at Westminster. I'm sure we'll get an invi—"

"But that's the day of my come out party!"

"You can still go; the servants are perfectly capable of—"

"Aren't you jealous?" Snap demanded. "Or do you

The Baron of Bad Behavior

despise him for throwing you over?"

"No one 'throws me over' anything," Lady Davenport said coolly. "I simply understood his restless spirit and let him fly away. I'm rather shocked things have gone this far with Lopey; the gossip is he put the notice in the papers himself. That's a very different Captain Hart from the one I knew."

Snap scarcely heard her. It was imperative to find Gareth and steer him away from this disastrous marriage. He absolutely must see he should wed no one but herself.

"Would you show me how to glide one more time?" Snap said.

With an obliging smile, the dowager moved down the hall, her arms elegantly bent like a ballerina's, her slippers whispering over the parquetry. "And we walk like this. And we greet our husband thusly."

Instruction on husband greeting was a lesson lost. Snap tiptoed away, then scampered out of range.

After closing the door to her room, she dove into the clothes press, digging furiously in search of trousers, shirt, vest, and boots: articles of clothing she'd used in Exeter whenever she needed to look like a boy for unescorted escapades. A discreet knock interrupted her search.

"My lady, I just—"

She looked up at the sound of someone clearing her throat to find Mrs. Pennal, the housekeeper with a stern, displeased expression on her long horsey face.

"Miss Widcomb will not be assistin' you today, my lady," Mrs. Pennal said in her thick Welsh accent.

Snap straightened. "Why ever not?"

"'Tis not proper for a kitchen scullery to overnight

become a lady's maid." The woman's jaw settled like a boulder in a stone wall. "The whole staff is in an uproar about it, and I'll not have the household disrupted because of—"

"I'll go down and explain the situation to them," Snap replied, resting a comforting hand on Mrs. Pennal's concrete shoulder.

"The staff is entirely too busy to stop and hear your sermon, my lady, especially Miss Widcomb. In fact, Miss Widcomb is engaged in peeling a sack of onions and gutting a boar. Therefore, I shall send Malloy up to assist you. She has been the dowager's personal lady's maid for many years and has agreed to take on the extra effort of attending you."

The heat of outrage burned Snap's cheeks. "Now look here, Mrs. Pennal," she said, raising her chin and stiffening her back, "as sister to your mistress, I believe it is my prerogative to choose who I shall invite into my dressing room. I would ask that you kindly refrain from making those decisions for me."

Instead of lowering her gaze and shuffling away, as Snap had every right to expect, Mrs. Pennal grew in stature until she loomed so large all light was blocked from the windows.

"Your sister warned me about you, my lady," the housekeeper said, as her lids lowered to a concentrated squint, "and she is in full agreement about the duties of Miss Widcomb. Now, if there is anything you require, I'm sure Malloy is capable of performing it. Otherwise you may wait upon yourself." Executing a military turn, the housekeeper marched to the door and, giving Snap one last warning glance, clicked the latch shut.

"Don't bump your horse face on the stairs,"

mumbled Snap, as Mrs. Pennal's footsteps receded down the hall.

Back at the clothes press, Snap dug deeper, and then decided to give Malloy a taste of her future by dumping the entire contents on the bed. To her dismay, the masculine items she'd packed, right down to the white cravat, were missing. Mama must have whisked them from the trunk just before it was loaded onto the coach.

"Lud, lud, lud!" How could she sleuth out Gareth's address if she couldn't pretend to be an errand boy?

There came a scratch at the door. "My lady?" said a thin, crackly voice.

"Come in, Malloy."

The door swung open, but Malloy remained on the threshold. The dark strands of her mousy hair had been coiffed so strictly the tooth marks of the comb could be seen. Between each tortured tendril, glimpses of her sallow scalp showed. The only lively thing about Malloy was her pale piercing gaze, which darted about Snap's room like a rat racing from one crumb to the next.

A natural born spy. Snap disliked the woman even more.

"Mrs. Pennal said you could do with some help, my lady," Malloy said, dropping a low curtsey.

Snap gestured at the pile on the bed. "All this needs to be cleaned up." Turning her back on the maid, she went to the desk and dug around until she found a beaded reticule.

"Going out?" Malloy asked.

Snap whirled about. The woman still stood in the doorway, her silvery eyes alight with greedy curiosity.

"Aren't you supposed to be busy tidying?"

"If you were going out, Lady Davenport might want to know where you'd gone is all," Malloy said, not moving from the doorframe.

"Well, I'm going to the drawing room," Snap replied, unable to keep annoyance from her tone. "You may rush down and tell my sister of my plans, if you desire."

Irony was wasted on Malloy. "No need for that," the lady's maid said, taking her first step into the bedroom. "So it's just to the drawing room you'll be going?" The silvery glance flicked to the reticule.

Forced to abandon the silk bag, Snap huffed with vexation, and swept toward the door. "You'll have plenty enough to do here, Malloy, so you needn't worry about my whereabouts. And if I'm going somewhere of interest to my sister, I'll be the one to tell her. Do we have an understanding?"

The lady's maid gave her a strange half bob of the head, then watched with that keen stare as Snap pivoted to close the door.

Chapter 13

Rather than come in the front door of the Cock & Bull Tavern (Cock & Balls if you read its desecrated sign), Gareth sneaked around the rear and surprised Tommy Taylor at his table in the back.

"Feckin' Mother a' Mary!" Tommy cried. "You scared me half out o' me wits."

A half hour at most had passed since he'd collected his pay and the man was already spittle-slicked and bleary-eyed. Bloody blast it—he'd got to Tommy too late; his pockets were sure to be empty.

"You got the pound, eight pence?" Gareth growled.

Tommy had the decency to look ashamed.

"Three weeks in arrears, boyo, and Beam Murphy on the way. For the sake of the wife and bantling, I put him off for a bit, but if you don't care that your family's starving, why should I if your hands are broke?"

Tommy's unfocused eyes filled with terror. "If you'd found me but a moment earlier, I'da had the blunt, but—"

"Timing's not my bloody problem. Get it today or Beam'll have your guts for garters."

Tommy lurched to his feet and gripped Gareth's sleeve. "You gotta help me, Cap'n. Without me hands, the wife'll leave me and take my son with her." Tears swamped his eyes. "My son, Cap'n. Please."

For an inveterate swill tub, Tommy wasn't a bad

sort. When there was work on the docks, he took it, he never clouted his wife as the others did, and only stole when hunger pinched too hard to resist.

Gareth turned his back on the fellow. Addressing the tavern crowd, he said, "Who's to lay sixpence I can make it out of this hell pit without touching a toe to that gin-soaked floor?"

Heads rose, followed by a rumble of interest. A good twenty-five feet with nothing to stand on had to be traversed from the last table to the door. Every man sized up the distance then gathered to lay their bets.

I left these shenanigans behind in the shipping lanes and the army. What the devil's got into me? Then the answer came clear and bright as a church bell: Snap. This was just the sort of hijinks he'd boasted of when she was a child at his bedside. But why impress a rum-looking gal who isn't here to watch?

Nevertheless, when the crowd gathered, and all eyes were on him, he hopped from a complete standstill onto a table, leapt eight feet to the next, which hugged the wall, and was about to vault to the third, which was closer to the door, when seeing their odds decreasing, the onlookers yanked every stick of furniture to the middle of the floor. Satisfied they'd blocked his progress, they shouted good-natured obscenities.

"You haven't beaten me yet," Gareth said, laughing.

He removed his boots, stuck his stockings in the top, and left them beside him on the table. Then he backed to the chair rail running the length of the wall. By putting his heels on the tiny ledge and leaning out to place his hands on an overhead beam, he inched down the length of the room. When the chair rail ended he came to a dead stop.

The crowd elbowed one another and loaded him up with a fresh round of insults.

"You think I won't make it to the door?" Gareth said, beads of sweat stinging his eyes.

"Don't see how you can," said a shaggy fellow.

"Care to up the ante?"

Coins chinked into a bowl held by the designated bet collector.

When the wagering ceased, Gareth dropped his hands from the beam, fell forward into a somersault, and rose to a handstand.

As the inhabitants of the Cock & Balls roared in disapproval, Tommy Taylor shouted, "He said he'd not touch foot!" Gareth hand-walked to the door, kicked the latch with his toes, and only stood when his palms hit the cobblestones.

With a low grumbling growl, the Cock & Balls patrons parted with their coin, but once all were accounted for, Gareth was pleased to see he'd collected over a pound and a half.

"I'll pay your debt to Wadsworth," he told Tommy, "and I'll deliver the rest to your long-suffering wife. If there's any justice in the world, she'll keep your mitts off it."

Again, a rumble of dissatisfaction filled the tavern; with that kind of coin Tommy would have surely paid for a round.

"Oh, be thankful," Gareth told them, as he left the gloom of the tavern for the afternoon sunlight. "I just spared you a gin headache that'd lay you out till midday."

Gad, Snap will love this tale! Gareth caught

himself. *Nay, keep this exploit to yourself. Maybe tell Lopey.* But he knew he wouldn't; Lopey was not in the market for a man who could walk a chair rail.

****

The last of Malloy's suspicious gaze disappeared as Snap shut her bedroom door.

Lud, the woman is irksome.

She walked toward the staircase. That awful feeling of defeat knocked timidly at the entrance to her mind. Without so much as a how-dee-doo, she dismissed it.

A set of boy's clothes. That's all I need. That can't be too hard to obtain... She reached the top of the stairs and paused a moment, too deep in thought to step down. *It will take money and stealth, of course. A lot of stealth with old Malloy on guard.* Thrumming her fingers on the newel post, Snap decided her first task was to throw that sneaking peeper off the scent.

She thumped down the steps, making sure each footfall was loud enough to echo through the house. With emphatic clumping, she entered the drawing room and stomped around its perimeter just to give Malloy something to get bored with. Spies always listen a few minutes to make sure their quarry has settled.

The distinctive swish of Mrs. Pennal's stiff skirts approached. With an audible thud, Snap dropped into a chair at the card table, and taking a deck, shuffled loudly so Mrs. Pennal would hear, peek in, and see her preparing to play solitaire.

The instant the housekeeper's footsteps receded, Snap took off her shoes. Tiptoeing to the drawing room's arched entrance, she assessed the distance to the cloak closet—her father's cape was a reliable source of money. To get to it, she'd have to traverse about forty feet without a single console table, cabinet or chair to hide behind. Taking a deep breath, she hurtled into an all-out sprint. A few strides into her mad dash, however, she heard voices. Upstairs? Downstairs? Malloy? Truss, Pennal, Ellie, or anyone else in the family?

Heart pounding, Snap scooted back behind the door frame. But the voices came no closer. *Now, now!* She leaped from behind the arch and raced full tilt for the closet, stepping lighter than a ghost on the marble floor. A few paces from her goal, the knocker clanged on the front door. Startled, Snap tried to stop, but her stockinged feet slid, and she careened past the closet door, halting just shy of the window.

A regal-looking woman waited in a carriage as her footman stood at the entrance. Truss approached, coming rapidly up the stairs. Skittering for purchase, Snap grabbed the closet door handle, then muffling the latch with her hand, slipped silently inside just as Truss's tread reached the hallway.

"Hades' brother!" she mouthed silently.

The dark wrapped her like a soft, safe blanket, and in it she smelled wool, the tang of mold, and dust. It was the intoxicating scent of attics, basements, abandoned barns, and adventure.

The footman announce that Lady Pemneux desired an audience with Countess Eleanor Davenport.

Anyone with a title got taken to the saloon, not the drawing room, thank heaven, so even as Lady Pemneux fussed her way through the front door, Snap felt around the pockets of the cloaks hanging on hooks at the back of the closet. Empty. Mama's sister May lived in the colonies during the American Revolution, and she'd sewn coins into the hem of her cloak in case the house was commandeered by either the British or the rebels. That money, she said, spared her many hungry weeks, and it kept her cloak from flying open in the wind. Papa adopted the tactic, and as a result, Snap had survived many financially dry spells. The best part was that Papa never seemed to notice his hems were lighter, or weighted with pebbles.

Even with her eyes adjusted to the dark, she couldn't distinguish Papa's heavy charcoal from the other cloaks. It seemed like she'd felt a million hems before she finally found one with lumps in it. She shook the coins toward a secret rip next to the stitching at the back. It took a lot of coaxing and digging to get the first coin out, which disappointingly turned out to be a button. She'd put it there in February when she was desperate for licorice.

The next object felt more promising, but it was a flat stone. Had she run out the supply? Two more buttons and a nail later a shilling finally dropped into her palm. A second shilling gave her hope she could outfit herself properly, and then, prize of prizes, an entire guinea squeezed through the tear.

Silently slipping her boots back on, she plotted her passage to the roof, down the drainpipe, and through back alleys to find a lad who would sell his clothes. Once she were outfitted as a messenger boy, she could find Captain Hart and warn him of the doom awaiting him if he married anyone but herself. It was an adventure worthy of her—one employing all her skills, her wiles, and her physical daring. A zig of excitement chased down her spine.

Quickly she stuffed the buttons, nail and pebbles back in the cloak's lining, then turned her attention to the hall. All seemed quiet. Ellie would be serving Lady Pemneux tea, but had Malloy finished putting the clothes away? Malloy...she had to get rid of that harpy and have Lizzie reinstated.

Stewing over Malloy, Snap stepped into the hall at the very moment Lady Pemneux rounded the corner with Ellie and Truss on her heels. "Oh, you startled me," said Snap, pretending to be looking at herself in a mirror inconveniently located too far to the right to catch her reflection.

Lifting a brow, Lady Pemneux fixed her with an icy smile. "You must be Lady Nefertiti Albright."

"Yes, my lady, that is correct," Snap said, dropping a curtsey. "It is a great pleasure to see you again, Lady Pemneux. We met at your divine ball."

"Humm...I don't remember you at all. Your sister says you're well behaved. Is that true?"

Ellie focused a wild, imploring look at Snap.

"Oh, yes," Snap said sweetly. "My favorite activities are embroidery and playing the pianoforte. Sometimes I read books, but never on Sundays. Oh, and I pray a lot...to the Lord above." That was true—she was always asking him to deliver her from tight spots such as this.

The corners of Truss's mouth twitched, and Ellie, who stood just behind Lady Pemneux's right shoulder, stifled a giggle.

"In view of your sisters' unorthodox courtships, your deportment has been of considerable concern to us."

Snap blinked, pretending to be shocked at the

doyen's words. "That's perfectly understandable," she said nodding in serious agreement. "My sisters, I'm afraid, used up all the high spirits in the Albright family, so I am left meek as a lamb."

Ellie rolled her eyes, but the sun came out in old Pemneux. She beamed.

"Well, child, I had come today to question the countess about your suitability for our establishment. Since you're cognizant of my position in Society, you understand how important her assurances are to your future. Having met you personally, I feel confident there will be no scandal."

With a submissive glance at the floor, Snap replied, "Of all my sisters, I'm the least likely to come to shame. I abhor music, theatre, or outdoor activities of any kind, and, you'll be happy to know, even though I am an Albright, horses scare me."

Truss coughed, but before Snap could catch Ellie's reaction, Lady Pemneux's gloved hand touched her cheek. Gently, she lifted Snap's face to meet her gaze.

"Precious girl," she said, her steely eyes soft with affection, "you remind me of myself at your age."

Snap flapped her lashes. "I shall consider that the highest compliment ever paid me."

With a contented smile, Lady Pemneux retracted her hand, and reached into a reticule in which she fished for a few seconds, then withdrew a small rectangular card. "It is with the greatest pleasure that I bestow this upon you. I hope we see you often, and that you find a suitably soft-spoken member of the elite to take as husband." As if it were a medal for bravery, she offered the card.

Snap suddenly realized her right hand held three

stolen coins and Ellie would know exactly from whence they'd come. A rush of terror closed her throat. Pretending timidity, Snap wrung her hands, thereby transferring the loot to the left. "Are you sure I'm worthy?"

Lady Pemneux's beam brightened. "Of course, child, now take it."

Written across the top of the card and underlined, were the words, Ladies' Voucher, Almack's.

Chapter 14

Before ol' Pemneux's bulk disappeared into the coach, Ellie had Snap by the hand and was dragging her down the hall toward the drawing room, which possessed sliding doors one could close. That did not bode well.

Instead of closing that door and turning on Snap with rage firing from her eyes, Ellie covered her face in a terrifying show of grief. Snap's heart plummeted; she could practically feel it pooling around her feet.

Staggering to the far end of the room, Ellie clung to a peach drapery, her entire body trembling. A sob rent the air, and Snap nearly drowned in guilt.

"Oh Ellie, I'm so, so sorry." She rushed to her sister, and was about to pat her back, but there in her hand were the three poached coins. How she hated them now! They were hot and moist in her fist, and their edges were sharp. She imagined them cutting into her flesh, and knew she deserved their punishment. "I couldn't tell old Pemneux the truth, could I? It just seemed you wanted me to play the innocent."

A tear hit the parquet, and Snap thought she'd die of shame. "I'll catch her and apologize," she pleaded. "Look at me, Ellie. Please, or I'll start crying too."

Ellie's shoulders went from trembling to shaking then she burst into loud, snorting laughter, and nearly tore the curtain off its rod. "Oh my word." She turned and gripped Snap's shoulder trying to keep from collapsing. "I tried, I honestly tried to convince you I was crying, but you are too funny. 'Afraid of horses'… 'Meek as a lamb'…"

A bubble of laughter pushed aside Snap's woe. "Oh Ellie, you shouldn't have tricked me. I was so worried you were upset."

After lurching to a sofa, one hand pressed against her stomach, Ellie plopped into its upholstered depths. "I ought to be mad. It does you no good to see me chuckling at your deceptions, but honestly…" She stopped as a fresh gust of laughter caught her. "You only told that old battle axe exactly what she wanted to hear."

The sisters nearly fell off the sofa in their hilarity. Until the coins dropped on the carpet, and the guinea, glinting gold as a lamp in a window on a dark night, rolled onto the parquet, circled, and fell on its side with a clatter that could rival church bells.

"Oh, how did those get there?" Snap said, leaping off the couch and snatching the coins.

In the second it took Snap to retrieve the evidence, Ellie's expression changed to confusion. Gone was the laughter that had put them in each other's arms. Unable to look at her sister, Snap moved to a side table.

"I'll just put these here so your husband will see them when he gets home. He must have lost them in the cushions." She stacked the coins neatly with the golden guinea at the bottom, then sneaked a glance at Ellie.

Dimples of disappointment framed her sister's mouth. "That is not Hugh's money."

Employing a careless, casual tone, Snap replied, "Oh, I wonder who lost it then? There are so many people coming and going…"

Ellie folded her hands and brought her knees tight together. Her disapproval shifted into anger. "This is exactly what we've been telling you, Snap. Fibbing about money is what a child does. Sebastian will be telling me such stories soon, and I'll be able to see through them as easily as I can see through yours. You must grow up, Snap. This is completely unacceptable in a young lady about to enter the marriage mart."

"If you call me Nefertiti Albright and shake your finger at me, Ellie, I shall scream." Snap slumped into a chair opposite her sister.

"Sit up and tell me where you got that money," Ellie barked.

Snap scrambled to think of a reasonable excuse but came up dry. "Out of Papa's cloak."

"You have your own money," Ellie replied. "Why did you raid Papa's linings?"

"Because that horrible, horrible Malloy you sent to spy on me was watching my every move, and I needed money from my reticule, but I knew she'd ask why, so I had to steal."

Ellie sat back and took a deep breath. "If I asked you what you plan to do with two shillings and a guinea, would you tell me?"

Biting her lip, Snap weighed the pros and cons. The pros won, though. Lying to Ellie was unbearable, and her sister was right, it was time to show a higher level of maturity.

"Boy's clothes," she admitted. "Mama took all mine from the trunk before I came to London."

Her sister sighed. "You can't have boy's clothes here, Snap. If you were ever caught in them, you'd be ruined, and absolutely no one would want to marry you."

"Pish. What am I going to do with a reputation?"

Ellie didn't respond, in fact, she didn't even look at Snap—just stared off into space as if she were searching for something. "Do you remember what Papa used to tell us about going to a foreign land?"

"Learn the culture," Snap replied instantly; those words were used whenever Papa talked about Egypt or the Romans, which was constantly.

"Well," her sister continued, "London is a foreign land. You have to abide by the culture in order to fit in, and if you don't, the consequences can be terrible."

"But I don't want to marry someone who expects a quiet wife. I don't want to be someone's brood mare, sitting inside, pretending to embroider just to make people like Lady Pemneux happy."

"Every man at Almack's may not want to marry a docile lamb; someone who's 'afraid of horses' and 'abhors outdoor activities.'"

Ellie smiled so gently, Snap's will cracked in two. "All right, I'll go to Almack's and be a perfect lady. I'll dance well, but not too well; and drink lemonade, but not too much lemonade; and I'll be a model of propriety. But, promise me, Ellie, that you'll call off Malloy. That harpy is unbearable."

"Malloy can do your hair and dress you."

Snap was about to object, but Ellie held up a hand for silence. "But Lizzie may accompany you on outings."

Snap rushed to her sister and gave her a tight hug. "I adore you, and I'll never make you regret this decision."

Disentangling herself, Ellie held Snap at arm's length, her blue-eyed gaze piercing to the soul. "Of course I won't regret it," she said. "Why would I regret it?"

Frozen like a rabbit, Snap replied, "You won't. That's the whole point."

****

Sauntering along the crowded streets, Gareth was happily reliving his victory at the Cock & Bull when he caught wind of a change in the St. Giles rookery. A cluster of grimy men, aprons stained and shirt sleeves rolled high, turned to watch him stride by. Their faces were pinched with worry. A woman raced around the corner, a hand clutching a tattered straw bonnet to her head, when a hatchet-faced lass stopped her.

"Is she dyin'?" she cried.

"Let me by," said the woman in the bonnet, shoving her assailant aside. "Ozzie, you got your cart?"

One of the men split from the cluster and grabbed a pile of rags from a rickety wheelbarrow. The others joined in, clearing the wheelbarrow and dumping the contents on the cobblestones.

"Watch me things, Nate," Ozzie called as he and the rest of the men swiftly followed the woman in the straw hat.

"You gonna stay and see to her, ain'tcha?" An ancient crone peered up at Gareth with black, steely eyes as her gnarled and filthy hand laid hold of his sleeve.

"See to whom, and why should I?" Gareth exclaimed, jerking his arm away.

"She's one of your own, is why!" the crone shrieked. "Keep 'em here, ladies. He wants to leave our

Maudie to die."

"I'm no whore master, and I know of no one named Maudie."

"You knows 'er, and well too. Ain't her pa owing the baron?"

A sick feeling tightened Gareth's stomach. "Is she Maudie Rose?"

"Fetch a surgeon," a man bellowed as the wheelbarrow rattled around the corner, a dusty pack of children streaming behind.

A crowd formed around the conveyance, which thickened as doors opened and onlookers poured into the street. The crone dragged him into the horde, elbowing a path through the bodies.

"Make way," she screeched. "Let 'em see 'er!"

It was worse than he feared. Maudie Rose, the prettiest flower in all St. Giles, lay in the wheelbarrow gasping with pain, blood pulsing from wounds to her face. Her perfect skin had been slashed, once down the left cheek, once down the right; her brow and eye forever disfigured by the blade. These were the marks of Baron Wadsworth, a destructive signature writ large on the surface of the one thing of beauty in this godforsaken place.

"Oh Maudie Rose," he said, his throat so tight he could barely speak. He took her delicate hand and her fingers fluttered against his.

"My papa didn't owe till three weeks yet," she whispered.

"I know, I know, and I would have covered for him if he were late. The baron must want his payments faster from the rookery, Maudie Rose, so he cut you to scare the lot."

She looked at the crush of faces, the weeping women, the men taut with horror. "I'll not be married now; no more than a beastly slut." Tears diluted the blood, then overwhelmed it, clearing a trail from her ruined eye into the tendrils of her blood-soaked hair. "May God take me now. Please take me now, my Lord."

He clutched her hand more tightly. "Maudie Rose, I'm marrying a countess. Don't despair, I'll get you a place in her household."

But there was no relief in the girl's eyes. She knew what he couldn't admit: that a countess would never allow such a damaged creature in her sight. At best, Maudie Rose would work in the scullery or out on the hay fields—employment that would first torture and then defeat her delicate frame.

Her father shoved his way through the bodies and dropped to his knees beside the cart. "My girl. My beautiful, beautiful little Rose."

Gareth pushed all the money in his pocket into the man's trembling hand. "Get her a doctor," he said, backing away.

"Spend it on my grave, Papa," Maudie Rose whispered. "Not a pauper's grave… please not a pauper's with bodies piled on top of me."

Chapter 15

Snap shimmied down the drainpipe nearest her bedroom window as Lizzie waited in the garden. She considered what Ellie had said. Fitting into the culture of London was of utmost importance, absolutely, and that's why a set of boy's clothes was so vital. How could she go about town on her own without pants and a vest? Society wouldn't allow it. Therefore, if she were to track Captain Hart, the only respectable way would be to do it as a boy, and since the whole point of being in London was to find a husband, her actions were fully justified.

Jumping to the ground next to Lizzie, Snap whispered, "I must make one point very clear—we cannot be caught in men's wear or my reputation will be ruined."

Lizzie looked at her as if she'd gone daft. "Then it's best we stay in dresses and not leave the property."

"Pish to that," replied Snap with a wave.

Then moving with the stealth of a mouse in a larder, she darted across the lawn and ducked behind a row of shrubbery edging a brick wall that circled the garden. Lizzie followed.

Keeping low in the bushes, the girls came to a wooden gate bracketed by a trellis of roses. Conveniently, the opening couldn't be seen from the house. As they peered at Park Lane through the gate's peeling white slats, Snap said in a low voice, "Now remember, we want at least one boy my size."

"What about me?"

"If I have an outfit, it will be easy to buy you one."

Lizzie's brow furrowed. "Then why don't you just buy 'em for the both of us?"

Sighing, Snap shook her head. "And just how is a lady supposed to walk into a haberdashery and buy herself a jacket and cravat? Honestly Lizzie, you don't know a thing about how such actions are viewed."

"You could say they're for a brother."

"But that would be lying, wouldn't it?" She gave Lizzie a disapproving look meant to quash further comments, so the maid limited herself to rolling her eyes.

Across Park Lane's broad stretch, a nanny pushed a pram on the sidewalk skirting Hyde Park. Behind her strolled two gentlemen sweating in dark wool and black top hats, and beyond them, a young lady and her maid lingered under a chestnut. But there were no boys, nor were there likely to be the kind of boys who'd be willing to sell their clothes.

"We'll have to go to either Piccadilly or Oxford Street," said Snap.

Lizzie jerked her thumb toward the south. "You'll get better quality on Piccadilly."

"Then we're off to Oxford."

Throwing her hands in the air, Lizzie gave her that "you're daft" look again. "What're you looking for, a chimney sweep?"

"Close to a chimney sweep, but not quite as grubby. We don't want to be caught, and if we're in filthy, but not too filthy, clothes, no one will pay us any mind. We'll be able to go anywhere and do anything we want."

Swept up in the vision of absolute freedom, Snap unlatched the old gate and pushed. A dreadful squealing issued from its rusty hinges. She winced at the sound, and looked between the roses to see if anyone— especially Malloy—had poked their nosy selves out the mansion's windows. *Not a one, thank goodness.*

Through the gate, she set a brisk pace toward Oxford Street with Lizzie trailing behind, until a familiar voice stopped her.

"Come look at this, Snap," said her father.

He peered over his glasses, studying something in the road. Lizzie cut Snap a look of terror, but Snap gave her a small reassuring shake of the head.

"What is it, Papa?"

"Look where I'm pointing," he said, indicating Park Lane's beautifully kept path.

She willed her eyes to see, but couldn't find anything out of the ordinary.

"There's a slight bump in the road."

"Oh." And there it was—an almost imperceptible rise that bisected the thoroughfare, lifted the sidewalk a fraction, and disappeared behind the wrought iron surrounding the park.

"Come, come, come," he said, stepping into the road without bothering to acknowledge an oncoming carriage. The horses threw their weight to their haunches and with a tremendous jangling of harness, managed to avoid hitting him.

"Sorry, my lord," cried the driver, whose tone didn't match the impatience on his face.

Snap gave him a meek smile of thanks, then she

and Lizzie scurried across the street.

Lord Albright had his face poked between the iron rails as far into the park as the fence would allow. "Just as I thought," he said, his pitch high with excitement.

She studied the area where the mound continued into the tree line. Nothing grew on it but a few shabby shrubs.

"It's an ancient wall, isn't it Papa?"

"I'm guessing Roman, and it extends into our garden then makes an abrupt right under the herb bed. If we dug deep enough we'd find metal arrowheads, pot shards and possibly bones."

"Mrs. Dibble won't understand if you sacrifice her herbs and vegetables in the name of science, Papa. You'd better get permission from Ellie."

"We'll excavate along the left side of the wall first," mumbled her father, withdrawing his head from between the iron bars. "That's where the garbage dump is most likely to be." Pushing his glasses back on his nose, he looked at Snap as if he'd just noticed her. "Are you off someplace?"

Only the slightest twinge of anxiety stirred in her. "I thought ol' Lizzie and I would find a young man and buy his clothes."

"Ah, I see," said her father, nodding at her even as his gaze returned to the mound. "Well, best of luck then, and when you're back, find a shovel and help me in the yard."

"I could start right now," said Snap, as he moved toward Park Lane.

"No need yet. I've got to map out where we're digging first."

"But I'll help when I get back, Papa."

He didn't turn, or nod, or wave in acknowledgement before he disappeared behind the gate.

Lizzie looked at her wide-eyed. "He don't care about you getting boy's clothes?"

"If he heard he would care," said Snap, walking toward Oxford Street. "But now that he's got something to excavate, I could tell him I'm planning to walk naked before the Prince Regent and he wouldn't raise a fuss."

"I'd get a blistering good whack with a birch branch if my papa were alive to catch me in the kinds of doings you get up to."

"Well, your upbringing was different from mine. When we were children, we were allowed to behave like wild things. Papa wasn't supposed to be an earl, just a scientist, and Mama got so involved in his work, she never taught us the niceties of Society. And Uncle Sebastian, who had the title, well, he didn't care a whit what anyone thought. He led a notorious life, dashing about with women, riding hell-bent-for-leather, and worst of all, pressuring the church to help unwed mothers. You can't imagine the scandal! Then he taught every child on the estate how to ride astride, swim, fish, and build a campfire. I even know how to snare a rabbit, just like you, Lizzie."

"That's fine, but can you skin it?"

"If I had a mind to."

"And there's your pa with the shovel in the garden, and you skinning some beast right next to him."

Snap giggled, and Lizzie allowed herself a pleased grin.

"If I were caught by such as Lady Pemneux peeling back the fur on a rabbit, can you imagine the uproar?"

Snap said. "It was bad enough in Exeter. As it was, my sisters weren't invited to parties. And, you know what, Lizzie? In town, women hissed at us as we passed. As if learning to swim and ride were our fault. Peggity, my oldest sister, she cried every time. Ellie just loved horses, so it didn't bother her too much, but Claire, who tends to be shy, she retreated to the local midwife, Jenny Martin, and took up the healing arts."

Lizzie kicked a stone, sending it rolling down the wooden walkway. "People are meaner than cornered badgers."

"This whole London *ton* is a fearsome group," Snap agreed. "But I suppose that's the difference between the upper and lower classes. You'd get a terrible beating, but I'd be shunned."

Lizzie thumped the stone again. "Oh, I'd get the same, plus a whipping. The difference is, I could move one town over and no one would chase my history. You, they'd suspect something was up, dig out the scandal, and have it in the morning papers."

It hadn't occurred to Snap that her reputation was mobile. "So even if I went back to Exeter, you think they'd hear about something I did in London?"

With that "you must be daft" lift to her brow, Lizzie answered the question.

Snap was about to respond when out of the corner of her eye she spotted a lad in torn breeches, a coat with a hole at the shoulder and a broad-brimmed hat of indistinguishable origin. Grabbing Lizzie's hand, she breathed, "We've found him."

****

Awnings hung over the sidewalk on Oxford Street, each sheltering another vendor selling fruit, vegetables, flowers, pots, pans, and sundries. Dogs basked in the sun, and harnessed horses stood tethered to boys who lay propped against crates, playing ball and cup. Though their target weaved in and out through the crowd, Snap made a beeline down the center of the cobbled street, keeping the lad's broad-brimmed hat in sight.

"You there!" she called, but he just kept walking. "Oh, young man!"

If he turned, Snap didn't see, because just then a woman and a barefoot child shot in front of them, carrying a basket of lavender and carnations.

"Please kind lady, buy my posies," cried the little one. "Oh, do! Please! Poor little girl! Do buy a bunch, please, kind lady!"

"Oh lud," said Snap, diving a hand into her reticule. "Take a shilling and excuse me." She tossed the coin as she ran past the flower girls, but she'd lost sight of the broad-brimmed hat. Increasing her speed, she yelled, "Lizzie, do you see him?" When she got no response, she whipped around only to have the barefoot child barrel into her.

"You forgot your posies, kind lady." The urchin loaded three bouquets into Snap's hand.

"No, no, I don't want them."

"But you paid for three." The child pushed them back into Snap's possession.

Two more vendors raced into the street. "And I've got some ribbons'll please you, kind lady," said a woman.

"Mine's in different colors," said the other. "And I got three starving babes what needs caring for."

Trying to get away, Snap shouted, "Lizzie!" and at

last saw the maid dart around two butchers and a sundries vendor who'd blocked her path.

As they took off in the direction they'd last seen the lad, other merchants stirred, excitement rippling down the avenue faster than they could run.

At Regent Street, Lizzie whooped, "Got 'em!"

Their quarry had made the mistake of pausing outside a bakery where a display of cakes must have arrested his attention. In the next second, Snap swooped in on his right and Lizzie on his left.

"Eh, what's this?" The lad backed away in alarm.

"No, no!" cried Snap, barely able to catch her breath. "Please let me speak to you."

"I didn't pinch nothing. You got the wrong man."

Before he could run, Snap snagged his sleeve. Tattered and worn, the cloth tore, leaving the cuff dangling over his hand.

"Aay! Destruction of private property! Destruction of private property."

Heads turned, stall-keepers glared; the entire street seemed to erupt in displeasure.

And then the boy was off, shouting, "Destruction of private property!"

Lizzie stepped close, whispering. "God's teeth, we're in the St. Giles rookery."

In the excitement of the pursuit, Snap hadn't noticed the stench of human excrement, the huddles of grimy-faced children, the chickens clucking in the street, the men leering, and the snaggle-toothed women laughing with scorn. She had failed to heed the culture of London, and she prayed they wouldn't pay a price for her mistake.

"We gotta go." Lizzie shifted her knife to her left

hand and took Snap's arm. Eyes down, they stepped over a stream of sewage oozing through the cobblestones, when Snap's arm was nearly jerked from its socket. A filthy youth of about ten had her reticule in his blackened paws.

"Let go!" she shouted, yanking back. If the little cur got her money she'd never find Captain Hart.

Behind her, Lizzie screamed and her grip was torn from Snap's arm. "I'll cut you, you little chittiface!"

"She's got a knife!"

"Beat the hoyden bitch!"

Snap couldn't help her friend. A sea of smirking, greedy lads circled as she clung to the strings of her reticule. The little boy tugged harder.

"Get behind," an older lad directed, and suddenly Snap was falling, her shoulder crashing on the rocks, sewage splashing into her face, the bouquets of flowers exploding in a cascade of petals.

Two others shoved the little one away and grabbed the reticule, pulling so hard, they dragged Snap across the muck-filled street. But she wouldn't let go, not if it meant she'd never see Captain Hart again. And then a boot slammed down on her arm. Lights of agony dazzled her eyes and she wailed as the reticule left her grasp. Somewhere nearby, Lizzie shrieked in pain.

If Lizzie dies, it would be my fault. For the first time in her life, Snap wished she weren't quite so impulsive. Lying in the gutter, a dozen jeering faces whooping and catcalling, she brought her knees to her chest and bellowed, "Let her go!" then she struck with the full force of her legs, toppling one buck.

The crowd scrambled back.

They had Lizzie down, and while one searched

under her dress for a hidden purse, another, flashing her knife in his hand, kicked her in the stomach.

Crawling toward them, Snap yelled, "Leave her alone! For God's sake, leave her alone!"

A roar, loud as a coach-and-six and angry as a fighting cur, rent the air. A lad hurtled into her path, falling hard on the road. Behind her, fists whacked against flesh, curses pierced the air, and screams of panic rose as the melee gained in intensity. Then, as quickly as the fracas began, the wretched boys dispersed, scrambling away in every direction.

Gentle hands helped her sit up, and then a pair of canary breeches squatted before her and Gareth's hazel eyes, sharp with concern, looked into her own. "Are you all right?"

Such a massive lump of gratitude filled her throat, she couldn't speak. She nodded, but held up her arm. A deep scrape seeped blood, and the limb was red and quickly swelling.

"Poor Armalaid."

The name was so funny, she couldn't help smiling. He moved to help Lizzie, and that's when the tears came.

"I never thought I'd see you again," Snap croaked.

"Did they hurt you badly?" he asked Lizzie.

She sat up and covered her face with her hands.

"Oh Lizzie, did they take your knife?" Snap asked.

Instead of answering, the girl folded her arms over her knees and buried her face. Her shoulders shook with grief.

"Sap-headed jackanapes." Gareth grunted.

In all her life Snap had never felt so terrible. She slid over to her friend. "I'll buy you a new one," she said, touching Lizzie's shoulder.

"My papa give it to me. Now I got nothing from him." And then her whole body convulsed in a sob.

Tears sprang to Snap's eyes. "Her father's dead," she told Gareth.

"You, you poxy louts," he shouted at the sullen adults eyeing them. "Not one of you helped these young ladies from Kid Bowman and his bastard band? See where that'll get you next time you're in hock to the baron."

He gestured to a massive block of a man who raised a fist and growled. Snap recognized him as the bruiser who cut her brother-in-law with a piece of glass. A murmur of fear rattled through the onlookers, and shame-faced they ducked back in pubs, or scuttled into their ramshackle stalls.

Gently Gareth helped the girls to their feet. "Sorry about your knife," he said. "Let's get you both somewhere we can clean you up. There's pestilence in this rookery that can kill from a scrape."

"Go shake those ruffians, Beam," Gareth instructed the huge beast. "Get the knife back."

Beam grimaced, dumb and mean, then lumbered off after the pack of jackals.

They'd walked less than a block, when Snap heard the clop, clop and rumble of an approaching coach.

"Bloody hell," Gareth cursed, and shoved them behind the door to a miserable tenement.

"What's happening?" cried Snap.

"Hush now." He held his finger to his lips.

The coach slowed, and then the clop and rumble halted just outside. Someone had kicked a hole in the door's lower panel. The girls squatted and watched, while Gareth stood silent and grim behind them.

An emaciated man sporting a gold-tipped cane, a pink vest, and a brown velvet tailcoat, appeared from the depths of the conveyance. The black pupils of his eyes glinted, sharp and deadly in his skeletal face.

"Where's your ma?" he barked at someone Snap couldn't see.

"She ain't here," answered a child, though boy or girl, Snap couldn't tell.

The cane slashed through the air with a whooping sound that ended in a crack followed by a tortured scream.

"Oh God, he's beating—" Snap cried.

But before she could finish her sentence, Gareth had his hand over her mouth. "If he sees me with you," he whispered urgently, "he'll ruin you."

Another horrific whack followed, and then the cane clattered to the ground as the man convulsed in a spasm that nearly felled him. And that's when Snap recognized the fiend—Baron Wadsworth—the man who plagued her family for possession of the Fitzcarry pearls.

"Bloody cur!" wailed a woman from an upstairs window. "Keep your bandy mitts off my kinchin!"

The outraged mama's footsteps echoed down the hall, and Gareth dragged Snap and Lizzie back, flattening them against the wall as the woman raced past, slammed open the door, and ran into the street. Through the opening at the hinges, Snap saw the woman bend to grab Wadsworth's cane. With lightning speed, the coachman applied the horsewhip to her, opening a slash in her cheek. She dove out of view toward her child. The baron, having recovered himself, adjusted his pink vest as the whip continued cutting through the air, landing with deafening cracks, and moans of anguish.

"The money, Mrs. Hauser," he said.

A shilling, three ha'pennies, and a farthing rolled toward him. "It's all I got."

The whip stilled. "Your husband is a good-for-nothing noose anchor," the baron spat. "Tell him I'll be by tomorrow for the rest."

No one moved on the street or behind the door until the coach rattled away. Snap shook with terror, but her hands didn't tremble. The shaking was inside, and she wondered if it would ever cease.

Mrs. Hauser came into the hall, hunched over a tiny boy with an angry lump on his forehead. Gareth moved out of her way, and she cut him a look of pure resentment.

"Where was you?" she hissed.

"Protecting the young ladies," he shot back. "Where were you when that band of filch pockets were tracking them? Nobody gets my assistance until this one's knife is returned." He jerked his head at Lizzie. "Spread the word."

A look of panic softened the woman's glare. "But the baron wants his blunt tomorrow."

Gareth shot back a hard look. "Then you'd better act fast."

Her hand reflexively clutched the child's shoulder, but she didn't speak, just nodded, and made her way up the stairs. The back of her dress had been sliced to ribbons. Red welts showed through the remaining threads.

"Do you mean you would have stopped the baron if

we weren't here?" Snap asked.

Gareth cleared his throat. "Something like that."

Her heart sank. What a wretched adventure this had turned out to be.

"The knife ain't that important," said Lizzie.

He ushered them into the street. "She's had worse. Besides, it's rookery justice." The corner of his lip twitched, and he looked miserable. "You'll get your knife back, and I'll give her extra before he gets to her again. My bl—uncle. That spawn of the devil should hang…"

His hand went to the small of Snap's back as he steered them toward a narrow byway. The shaking stopped, but then he removed his hand, and the shaking started again.

"May I hold your hand, Captain Hart? she said. "I'm trembling."

He looked away. "Wouldn't be proper."

"May I hold your arm then?"

Shaking his head, he answered, "No."

That familiar pang of hurt arrowed through her, the same hurt she felt when Papa bustled by as if she were of no more importance than a side table. She looked to the ground in case her eyes reddened.

"You can walk close, though," his voice rumbled.

She tucked in beside him, and there, with the heat of him warming her, their strides matching, her hip and arm fitting like a puzzle piece to his, a silent shout of joy chased the last shiver from her body.

Chapter 16

Within minutes of arriving at Lopey's Belgravia town house, the hostess had Snap and Lizzie soaking in tubs of hot water. A footman was dispatched to tell Lady Albright her daughter was safe, but would, with permission, remain for dinner. Gareth walked the length of the Rococo parlor and tried not to imagine what Snap looked like with hot water sluicing between her creamy breasts, the steam rising to pink her cheeks. Devil take it, he had to stop. Such thoughts were for topping fellows with titles and riches and fine reputations that would rub off on the little hellion.

His pacing was interrupted by the sound of someone clearing their throat. Snap stood between the room's gilded double doors. She had wrapped herself in a teal and gold chinoiserie banyan that so overwhelmed her it dragged on the floor, exposing the finest white ankle Gareth had ever laid eyes on.

"What the devil are you doing in that get-up?"

She shrugged. "I found it on a hook in the bathroom. The servants are cleaning my dress, and I couldn't bear to just sit there, so…"

With a smile that *plinked* his veins like a harp, she waded into the room and settled on Lopey's favorite chaise. Even draped in that ridiculous mountain of cloth, Snap's slim figure and youthful gaze shattered the images he'd cherished of Lopey resting seductively on that same piece of furniture.

"Get up!" he demanded.

Snap's lower lip folded, and she swung her legs to the side, affording him a glimpse of knee that tightened his belly. "Whatever for?"

"Because that's Lady Whitlocke's seat."

She leapt up at that, then looked about helplessly. "Where then?"

Hooking it with a boot, he hauled over a tufted silk hassock from its place by the fire. "Sit on this."

As she settled, those arresting pools of blue caught him. "Will you sit with me?"

He grunted, and lowered himself into a gilded gewgaw at the far side of the furniture cluster. By God, if her father saw them even this close, the man would have a right to shoot on the spot.

"I'm ever so sorry you had to rescue us," she said, looking heartbreakingly contrite.

If he didn't beat back his emotions, he'd be at her feet, comforting her, losing himself in her scent, the feel of her slim fingers, and the light of the afternoon sun twinkling in her eyes. "What were you doing in St. Giles, anyway?" he said severely. "You could have disappeared in that hell hole. Believe me, there are men angry enough at the aristos, they'd have done you serious harm if I hadn't happened along."

"My goodness, you're cross," said Lopey, entering the room. "It isn't as if she intended to visit the rookery."

"Don't be so sure..." Gareth muttered.

After giving the bell pull a good yank, Lady Whitlocke settled on her chaise and studied Snap through the lenses of her lorgnette, taking the girl in from tip to top. "You found my son's banyan," she said with a touch of ice. "How clever of you. But my fiancé did ask a question, and I'm curious to know the answer. How did you come to enter St. Giles?"

Her words signaled a challenge. One well-bred woman against the other, entering the equivalent of a street brawl. Sweat prickled Gareth's brow.

Snap's clear blues widened slightly; she stretched her legs until her pink toes poked from under the hem of the banyan, then withdrew them in an obvious effort to stall. Gareth sat forward and rested his elbows on his knees.

"Where's Lizzie?" she said finally.

With a vague wave Lopey answered, "She's down in the kitchen enjoying the company of my servants and being taken good care of."

"Oh," said Snap, biting her lower lip. "Well, we went down Oxford Street seeking a young man who would sell us his clothes."

Lopey made a faint strangled sound.

"You see, if a young lady wishes to go on an adventure, she really can't in London without a lot of fuss and bother—footmen and lady's maids and the like. But if she's got a good set of breeches and a wide-brimmed hat, she may move about at will."

Gareth was about to lecture on dangerous men and the need for young ladies to be escorted, when Lopey got the first word in.

"That's an astute observation, Lady Nefertiti," she said. "A widow is supposed to enjoy freedoms not granted others, yet there are no clubs at which I can dine, no theatres I can attend alone, and I risk censure if caught with interesting, unprincipled characters." She trained a warm gaze on Gareth. "Being a woman is not an adventure, but a lesson in patience. Feminine birds, even those housed in a gilded cage, wear the more somber feathers, I'm afraid."

That Lopey ever chafed at her lot came as a surprise to Gareth. "What would you like to do that you haven't done, my love?"

"A hellfire club," Snap interrupted.

"Something outdoorsy," Lopey said. "Perhaps a boxing match."

"What's all this about boxing, Mother?" Finnegan sauntered into the parlor.

For the first time, Gareth noticed how tall and angular the lad looked, and how an impressionable young lady such as Snap might think him handsome. A creeping heat tickled the back of his neck.

"Oh, hello there," Finnegan said, casting an approving glance at Snap. "Is someone going to introduce us?"

"My son, Finnegan, the fourth Earl of Whitlocke," said Lopey. "Lady Nefertiti Albright."

"Most people call me Snap. It's from the Christmas game, Snap Dragon. I always snatch the most raisins from the burning bowl of brandy. But I imagine Lady Nefertiti is more appropriate."

Finnegan pressed his lips to Snap's hand, then flipped his tails and sat in the chair closest to her. "Well, Lady Snap, you've got on my banyan. It suits you."

The girl blushed, and a pang of some unknown emotion pulsed down Gareth's spine. Before Snap could reply, Gareth cut in.

"Your mother was saying she'd appreciate a bit of

outdoor adventure."

"And a boxing match would suit, Mum? Rather scandalous, I'd say."

Lopey pursed her lips. "And I wish it weren't."

Grinning, Finnegan wiggled his fingers as if to conjure a change of setting. "What would make you happy, a jungle in darkest Africa, a wind-swept mountain peak, or the spray of the ocean's salty deeps?"

"My son is a poet." Lopey tilted her head toward Finnegan. "But if you must know, your last image sounds rather pleasant. What do you think, Captain Hart, would you take me sailing?"

"It's been a long time since I captained one of my father's ships," said Gareth. "I'm not—"

Snap lurched forward on the hassock. "That's a splendid idea! I adore boats, and I could show you all sorts of ways to hide as a stowaway, Lady Whitlocke."

Before Lopey could respond, something crashed into the window. Her lorgnette dropped to her waist. Swiftly she rose and looked into the garden. "A bird," she said in alarm.

Looking deeply disturbed, Lopey sought Gareth's gaze, but it was Finnegan who gained his attention. The lad was looking at Snap in a way that caused a surge of temper.

With his gaze still locked on Snap, the fourth Earl of Whitlocke slapped his thighs. "It's settled then. I'll rent us a yacht, and we'll take our chances on the high seas."

****

Racing down the back hallway at Mayfair, Snap called, "Mama, Papa, look at the barouche that delivered me. Come quick!" Not a peep issued from her father's study, so Snap tore open the door to find her parents hunched over the usual pile of books and parchment. "Look out the window!" she cried, dragging her mother from her chair. "Papa, you come too!"

Just as they reached the window, the red spokes at the rear of the carriage flashed between garden shrubs. Two footmen in full livery sat straight and elegant on a rumble seat at the back.

"It belongs to the fourth Earl of Whitlocke. I met him today, aren't I lucky?"

If Sofia Albright or her husband had a comment, it was silenced when Snap's sister Claire came into the study.

"Oh my goodness, Claire!" Snap screamed in delight. "You just missed it. I was driven home in a barouche and four, and guess who it belongs to? The Earl of Whitlocke! Look at my arm, Claire. I was mauled by a band of brigands!"

"Sweeting," her mother exclaimed, "who attacked you, and where?" She tapped her husband's shoulder, drawing a reluctant glance from the man. "John, Snap was attacked."

Keeping a finger on his place in the text, he gazed momentarily at his daughter. "Well, she seems none the worse for it."

"Oh Papa," said Snap, his disinterest squeezing her heart. Then taking Claire by the arm, she dragged her toward the door. "Come upstairs and bandage me. Mama, you come too."

Snap sat propped against the pillows on her bed with her mother and sisters arranged about the coverlet. Elderly Sport, a spaniel, snoozed on Ellie's lap.

Leaving out any mention of Gareth, and attributing her rescue from the criminal gang to Finnegan, she recited the day's adventure. "And as soon as he can rent a yacht, we're going sailing!" she concluded, not mentioning that Gareth would captain the vessel.

"What a stroke of luck," said Peggity. "Now you'll simply marry Lord Whitlocke, and spare us the expense of a come out ball."

Snap wrinkled her forehead. "Miss out on dancing and Champagne? Not me."

"Don't forget to keep your arm in the salt water," Claire instructed, gently pulling the scraped limb back into the bowl.

"Besides," continued Snap, "there may be other gentlemen who are even more suitable. You wouldn't want me to marry the first man to show interest... would you?"

"I did," Claire and Ellie answered simultaneously.

"So did I," added Peggity, "and I wish I hadn't. So, Snap has a point."

Mama rested a hand on Snap's foot. "Where did you say you were walking?"

"St. Giles rookery."

"God's teeth, Snap, what were you doing there?" Ellie said in exasperation. "It's terribly dangerous. You could have been killed."

"Lizzie and I lost track of where we were going because we were deep in conversation." That was partially true. She and Lizzie had been talking before chasing the lad with the broad-brimmed hat. When fibbing, Snap found it best to stick close to the truth.

Her mother shifted on the bed. "Whatever would an earl be doing in a rookery, that's the thing that concerns me. It's lovely you met him, Snap, but I really need to know more about this young man before I'll let him take you out to sea."

Unease pierced Snap's elation. Should her mother make inquiries, she'd learn that Lady Whitlocke and Captain Hart were engaged. That knowledge would vastly reduce Snap's chances of seeing him again. Desperate to nip her mother's concerns in the bud, she waved a dismissive hand,

"Pish. Mama, the earl is a poet. They go all sorts of unexpected places seeking inspiration."

Claire lifted Snap's arm from the bowl and began drying it. "Men who have ruined their good sense with gin dwell there, Snap," she said quietly.

"There are also opium eaters, pickpockets, and all sorts of riff raff in those neighborhoods," added Ellie.

Mama shook her head. "I'll have Mrs. Gower ask after the Earl of Whitlocke. She'll know if he's a man of good character."

Claire, Ellie, and Peggity simultaneously swiveled to stare at their mother in amazement.

"She won't find out a thing," said Ellie. "Poor Peggity married that dreadful Rupert, Duke of Hanesford, and Mrs. Gower encouraged the match."

"And when I wanted to leave before my darling Flavian's mad ward could harm me, it was Mrs. Gower who persuaded me stay," added Claire.

"And the only time Mrs. Gower could have been helpful by escorting me on the boat to the St. Leger horse race, she panicked at the water's edge and wouldn't budge." Ellie put her hand reassuringly on Snap's knee. "If scouting's required, I'll have Hugh do it. He'll find out about this Earl of Whitlocke."

A lump of fear settled in Snap's stomach. "I promise he's right as rain, Mama. In fact, now I recall the poem he wrote about the rookery. One of the lines was... 'And though the street 'twas ere so smelly, from the depths of the rookery's belly, came a maiden sweet as jelly—'"

"Well, then he's a dreadful poet," interrupted Ellie.

Snap shrugged, a little hurt. "I thought it had a nice ring to it."

Claire's shoulders shook with silent giggles, Mama's brows were knit in perplexity, and even Sport had his ears back.

A little angry now, Snap said, "Even if he's not the finest wordsmith, that doesn't mean he's a dissolute rogue. And even if he were a dissolute rogue and a terrible poet, if I loved him would you forbid my marriage? Besides, his mother will be with us on the boat, so what could he possibly do to me?"

Lady Albright looked as if she were formulating an argument, so to distract her, Snap flinched, pretending Claire touched her wounded arm in some agonizing spot. "Ouch," she groaned. "Oh, I'm in pain."

"Poor, poor sweeting." Her mother leaned forward and brushed the hair off Snap's forehead, which Snap hoped was a little hot and sweaty.

"Mama," she said in a quavering voice, "do you think I should have a new frock for the outing? One that matched my bonnet? I'd like to make a good impression on the earl. He's exactly the sort you'd want me to marry, isn't he, Mama?" By forcing her eyes not to blink, Snap produced a tear.

Ellie rolled her eyes, but their mother's concerned expression deepened. "My darling, the man you marry will be the man who makes you happy. If he's an earl, then more doors will be open to you, but all your sisters married for love, and I want the same for you."

Awash with gratitude, Snap put a hand to her heart. "Do you mean that?"

"Am I the sort to wish her daughter a miserable life?"

"But you mean anyone I love?"

"It's a trap, Mama," said Peggity. "Don't promise anything or she'll marry a fishmonger."

Before her mother could change her phrasing, Snap threw her arms around her. "Oh Mama, I do adore you so."

****

Lopey trailed a finger along the gilt frame of a chair in her private parlor, an intimate room festooned like a circus tent with green striped fabric draped from the ceiling. A dozen beveled mirrors lit the interior with flattering natural light.

She peered closely at herself in one of those mirrors, as if checking that her expression was sufficiently thoughtful. There was silence until she said, "That bird…"

Gareth suspected another of those "ill omen" talks. Dropping his head in his hands, he mumbled, "And we're off to the races… What about the bird, my love?"

"That was a pigeon who broke its neck on my window; it's as if it died trying to warn me of something."

"Pigeons often mistake glass for open sky. You mustn't—"

"And yesterday two clouds met forming the face of a man with a hook nose."

"What does a hook nose conjure? Lord Prendergast has a hook nose. So does Lady Pemneux, yet you keep their company."

"But these clouds were ugly; usually I see archangels or chubby piglets." She moved to the chaise beside him, took his hand and let her lorgnette drop. Fixing luminous mouse gray eyes on him, she said, "Would it be too much to ask, my darling, that we postpone our wedding until—"

"Until when?" He should have known this was coming. Bloody bird, bloody, bloody clouds.

She bit her lip. "July, perhaps?"

"After the Season? When everyone's packed up and safely in the country? Are you ashamed of me, Lopey? Because I can do some packing of my own if it would suit you—"

"Oh, how you do fly off the handle, my dearest. No, no, though nature may throw a thousand obstacles in our way, we'll hold the wedding whenever you wish. Please… It's agonizing to have upset you." A hand went to her heart as the other reached for him.

Ignoring the gesture, Gareth settled back in his chair and put the tips of his index fingers to his lips. Did she or did she not display a reassuring level of contrition? Should he let her get away with delaying their wedding? "You haven't upset me—not in the least," he said coolly. "But whereas I wished to acquire a special license and marry posthaste, you insist on having the banns called."

A puddle of shame, Lopey fell back in her chaise and worked her mousy grays into a state of abject pleading. A tear dribbled down her cheek, which she allowed to run to her chin and *splat* on her silk gown.

Her unhappiness left no impression on his heart. *What a cold, unpleasant thing I am.* She had an immense fortune; she possessed an interesting mind; and her looks were far from gone. All he'd ever wanted—money, prestige, respectability—his ambition demanded a response to that one fallen tear. Gently, he took Lopey's hands.

"I want to make you my bride," he said. "You're everything I've longed for."

"Forgive my silly superstitions, will you, darling? Imagine being afraid of birds and clouds—I'm mortified. Truly." She straightened his collar, her fingers lingering against his neck, her gaze seeking absolution.

He should kiss her. He should cup her face in his hands. He should smile. But he didn't, and the moment passed. Instead, she smoothed his lapels and gave his chest a tender pat.

"The church bells shall ring for us, Captain Hart, and I will be your fortunate bride."

Just as Lopey said the word "bride," a vision of Snap barged into his thoughts. How deeply her tears had upset him as she lay on the cobblestones in St. Giles. He'd gone into a frenzy, throwing those young heathens about. He wasn't a fighter...not ever...yet he'd bloodied every one of the poxy filchers.

Don't think of her. It was Maudie Rose who sent you mad. Not Snap. No, not Snap... Absolutely not Snap.

Chapter 17

Gareth looked so dashing at the wheel of the yacht, Snap knew she'd never see such a blood-tinglingly handsome man again as long as she lived. Oh, she'd known as a child that he was good-looking, but now... now his physical beauty pitched her over the moon.

His legs were parted, boots at the edges of the steering platform, black Byronesque curls unpomaded and ruffling in the breeze, arm muscles straining the fabric of his jacket, and his piercing hazel eyes fixed on the Thames. The man was everything she'd dreamed he'd be and more...so much, much more.

She prayed he would notice her frock. The skirt and bodice were blue and white striped cotton trimmed with pink ribbon, and Mama bought her a parasol to match. The gown's high hem revealed an embroidered white petticoat, and upon her head she wore a simple straw bonnet decorated with pink and blue flowers. The ensemble was not for a little girl—its low bodice showed her breasts puffing like twin snow caps. She struck a pose, arms spread along the safety rail with her body swiveled toward Captain Hart so he would notice her *décolletage*.

Snap adopted the facial expression Lopey had had as they approached the waterfront. It was a faraway, mature sort of look, with a hint of worry in her eyes.

A full minute passed, however, and Gareth said

nothing. Snap suspected it was because he was angry with Finnegan. Finn had delayed their departure by almost an hour. The lad forgot their outing today, spent the night at White's (or so Lopey said), and had to be fetched and dressed before they could set sail. As a result, Gareth was steering due east into the morning's blinding sun through an obstacle course of boat traffic on the Thames.

"At least the day is fine and the wind isn't too strong," Snap said, placing herself strategically in front of him in a new pose she anticipated would have the maximum effect: chest out, fingers interlaced.

"Move aside, I can't see the first mate signal small craft," he barked.

She stepped left. "Did you know you're marrying Lady Whitlocke on the same day as my come out party? I'll be eighteen on June twenty-fifth... and marriageable."

"That's an interesting fact."

"I thought you might want to delay—"

The first mate cried, "Anchor line at starboard."

Gareth tweaked the wheel. "Not now."

Abandoning her spot in front of him, she went to the rail, and peering over the right side of the vessel yelled, "We're closing at about three cable lengths, but you'll get by without a scrape." His look of surprise was supremely gratifying. "You didn't know I stowed away on fishing vessels, did you?"

"I should have guessed you'd do something that maggot-pated," he replied, trying to look severe, but he was impressed and amused.

She could see it in the crinkles around his eyes.

"Don't you think dawdling just a little on the date

of the ceremony would be…a good thing to do? I don't want my party to overshadow yours."

He made no comment, but his lips drew into a tight, determined line.

He's not going to budge. Snap sighed, but then brightened. All he needs is a different approach.

"Do you want to know where I hid on board?" she said, squinting at the shore as if she'd prefer to watch it glide by rather than speak another word.

"If it doesn't distract me from the river, I'll hear your shenanigans." Rising on his toes, he shouted to the first mate, "Signal that dinghy to wait. He thinks he can pull by, but he's dead wrong."

"Aye, aye!" came the reply.

Delighted, Snap sidled close to him just as she had as a child. "I curled up under the net on a trawler, and they didn't know I was there till we were a mile out to sea." She laughed. "Jack Nasty Face pulled that net back and nearly lost his sea legs. Oh, what a ruckus! All about how 'women bring ill luck because the sea is a jealous mistress.' I said if they didn't quit their belly aching, they'd scare the fish away. That shut their gobs. By day's end they had a hold full of mackerel, and the captain declared I could come aboard anytime I wanted."

"You're lucky they didn't use *you* as bait."

She laughed. "First of all, Captain Hart, despite what you think, sailors aren't such a hardhearted bunch, and second of all, even they knew I'm not easily deterred once I've taken a notion to something."

For a moment, he went still.

"Why in God's name would you want to spend a day on a mackerel trawler?"

Snap bit her lip to suppress a giggle. "Because of you."

He jerked the tiller and the schooner jolted to the left before he got her straight again. "Little liar, I'm no fisherman."

She put a hand on his sleeve. "You told me the most wonderful stories about being at sea; how whales leaped in the air and blew plumes of spray; how the ship nearly capsized in a storm and the sail dragged in the ocean, getting so full of water you thought you'd never right her; and the time Four Fathom Pete got pitched into the Channel with the anchor rope caught to his leg, but you dove in, cut the line, and hauled him to the surface. Oh, I had to get on a boat after that."

Just as Gareth's mouth opened to respond, Finnegan rounded the mast and joined them. "You can speak to me now, Lady Snap. I've finished my verse, and it's written with you in mind."

Snap clapped her hands. "How flattering!"

"Allow me to recite it," Finnegan said, his face radiant with pleasure.

"For he through Sin's long labyrinth had run,
Nor made atonement when he did amiss,
Had sighed to many, though he loved but one,
And that loved one, alas, could ne'er be his."

"It's lovely, but I thought you said you wrote it? Isn't that Byron?"

Gareth snorted.

"It's not," replied Finnegan, his eyes a bit wild.

"Oh, but it is. In fact, it's in the first canto of "Childe Harold's Pilgrimage." You were testing me, my lord, and I'm afraid you failed to catch me out."

Finn croaked uncomfortably.

"You men," Snap *tsked.* "Captain Hart is shocked I know starboard from hull, and you're shocked I know Bryon from Whitlocke. All men think women are dull as headless chickens."

"Never," cried Finnegan. "One glimpse at your luminous gaze, and I understood the heavens had wrought a soul with a brain like a planet."

Gareth quirked his lips. "Like a planet?"

"I meant that her mind is forever spinning and floating above the fray."

"Ah, spinning and floating," said Gareth, not even trying to suppress a smile. "I can see that."

Snap huffed. "I understand perfectly what Lord Whitlocke is saying, and I think it's a charming compliment." She settled her most dazzling smile on Finnegan. "Thank you, my lord."

Chin high with pride, the poet glanced at Gareth in triumph, but the captain ignored him, keeping his eyes on the river.

"Clear sailing, sir!" shouted the first mate.

"All hands on deck. Hoist the sails," Gareth bellowed.

A mad scramble ensued, with a dozen sailors darting every which way, ropes rumbling through pulleys, and sails *thwap, thwapping* as they caught the wind. Snap clutched the rail, elation zigging to every limb.

A cry of consternation caught her attention, and a cluster of sailors rushed to the bow. "The jib's caught on the bowsprit," one shouted.

"Get on it then," Gareth called back.

It won't be mature or ladylike, but a man's weight on a jib-boom? Before a single sailor's muscle could twitch, she dashed to the front of the yacht, shouldered through the seamen debating who would risk the climb, and jumped onto the upward tilting beam. Clutching the guide ropes, she tightroped past the jutting breasts of the figurehead, and out so far nothing but the Thames lay beneath her.

"Eh, eh, miss!" a burly sea salt barked, but Snap paid him no heed. The thrill of adventure had her in its clutches.

"My God, get her off there!" Finnegan yelled.

"She'll drown her bloody self!" another sailor cried.

Lopey screamed, and the whole deck flew into a frenzy, yet Snap moved on until she reached the jib-boom, a narrower wooden spar secured to the bowsprit with iron turnbuckles. She dropped to crawl, spray slapping her cheeks and wind kicking her dress. Her bonnet flew off and clung to her neck by the chin strap. The treble of shouting rose to a screech, but Gareth's voice was not among them, and that made her laugh. Only he could appreciate how marvelous it was to ride above the water on a stick of wood.

Snap stretched out on the delicate pole to distribute her weight more evenly. With ankles and knees gripping tightly, she hauled herself up its slight angle. The sail was caught by a rope fiber wedged in a grommet at the very tip of the needle of oak. Just as she had dragged herself to within six inches of her goal, a wave hit the hull blasting a gale of wet into her face. She blinked and laughed with joy.

As her perch creaked ominously, she reached for the frayed line and yanked it hard. The cord stuck in the grommet like a willful cat on a warm lap.

Lud, I should have brought a knife. She jerked again with all her might.

"Forgot something, sailor?" a voice called.

Snap looked to the deck in time to see Gareth swing onto the bowsprit. He winked, then clenched a knife between brilliant white teeth and walked up the beam. Excitement skittered through her, loosening her knees and making her hands numb so she had to grip extra hard to keep from falling. His black Byronesque curls writhed in the stiff breeze, and his eyes flashed merry and bright. Oh, she simply had to make him marry her!

He got within reaching distance, drew the knife from his chompers, and grinned. The air crackled with the heat of that grin. "You've no more brains than a turnip with its roots in the air," he said.

She laughed and swung her legs, pointing her toes so he'd note her trim ankles, which were indecently exposed due to her skirts being hiked by the boom between her legs. "Pish," she said, thrilled when his gaze flicked down. "Don't you think you'd better hand me that knife before we're blown off course?"

A sly smile crooked his lips. He squatted, took her ankle in his warm, calloused hand and gave it a little shake, half-caress, half-censure. "Outrageous miss," he said, only his voice was liquid as honey—honey in a rough, waxy comb.

Snap gasped, and that sly smile broadened into something knowing, and so masculine every ounce of her self-possession poured like droplets into the Thames. He knew it too. With a snort, he loosed her ankle and yanked down her skirt.

"They'll be talking on shore before we set anchor if

141

you expose yourself that way." He gave her the knife. "Don't cut yourself, madcap, or the blood'll ruin your dress."

The thrill of him made her shiver. As she applied the knife to the rope fiber, she pressed her bosoms together and twisted her body so he'd be sure to see.

Shaking his head, he retreated down the bowsprit. "Get about your work, before I drag you off that boom and teach you how a young lady should behave."

Desire arrowed through her heart, into her stomach, down her limbs, and into her most private region. She nearly lost her balance.

Spiffft, the fiber broke and the sail dropped, canvas slapping and shuddering in the wind. At that moment, the bow tipped into the trough of a wave so big she could practically touch it, and when the boat rose on the swell and the water banged hard sending spray raining over her, she filled with a crescendo of power and joy.

He lusts for me!

****

The vixen's taking forever to climb off that bloody bowsprit. Not out of caution, either. Picture perfect— the wind blew her dress tight against her thighs and billowed like a flag behind. Tendrils of hair, pale as dried grass, blew across her pink cheeks. Her red lips, and blue eyes were so bright with joy he felt his soul fly to her and bury itself in a kiss.

"Did you know," Lopey said, abruptly slamming his soul back in his body, "birds by the flock lifted off from shore as you were conversing with Lady Nefertiti."

What his fiancé meant by that he couldn't tell, but her expression was grim, and when she glanced at

Snap, that expression tightened.

Not such a marvelous idea to marry precious Finnegan off to this earl's feral daughter after all, eh? Well, the lad's a twit. When Lopey and I are married, I'll see Finnegan wed to a quiet, practical gal, someone who can keep the finances and who doesn't know bad poetry from good.

As Snap navigated off the bowsprit, a twinge of sadness hit him. Pluck to the backbone in her, yet well he knew, the lad didn't exist who'd love her courage. Just a school of selfish dolts bent on indolence. They'll expect her to cater to a propriety dictated by hens with no imagination. It sickened him.

Snap jumped onto the deck and greeted the crowd with a grin and a bow.

"What the hell were you doing?" shouted Finn. "You could have been killed!"

She shrugged, the light in her face dimming slightly. "Oh pish. I did just fine, didn't I?"

Lopey pressed a hand to her breast. "Really, you mustn't do that again, my dear... Clearly you weren't aware that your ankles... Well, they were seen."

The sailors leveled disapproving glances at Snap before drifting away; the rank and file expected decorum in their betters, and woe to those who failed to meet those expectations.

Her grin melted into stiff-mouthed defensiveness. "Oh, do stop frowning, Lord Whitlocke," she said, aiming her anger at Finnegan.

The lad stomped his foot. "It's very wrong of you, you know. It's not what's done—not what's done at all."

Snap's fingers went to fists, and Gareth braced for

a tirade. Instead, she somehow controlled herself.

"Pish to you." With a shake of wind-blown curls, she marched to beside him at the helm.

Clearly, she expected sympathy, and in point of fact, he was. The picture she made on the boom was the prettiest sight he'd ever seen, but it wouldn't help to say so. "It's a fine thing you did, but only a daft—" he began.

Cutting him off, Snap said in a strained voice, "The weather is perfectly charming today, is it not, Captain?"

"Climbing about may be a lark to you, but—"

"Look at that sun," she added, a bit louder, "It's bright enough to burn the eyes out of Satan."

"But apparently not out of daredevils," he mumbled.

Color flared in her cheeks. "The very moment the last guest leaves my come out party, I'll be as subdued as an old ox. Lady Pemneux will appear positively kittenish next to me, but just for this day, I'd like to enjoy this outing as well as light conversation with willing participants."

She struck that pose again—the one that made her look like a cartoon image of Lopey—hands clasped, eyes focused on nothing. It drove him crazy.

"Who do you think you're fooling with that nonsense? If I weren't steering this craft, you'd be pirating a passing ship."

She was supposed to be insulted, but instead, a grin blasted across her face. "Is that why you adore me?"

"Adore you, wench? Stealing hats that cost me a fortune, getting into scrapes in St. Giles, scrambling up bowsprits. I'm afraid to contemplate the trouble you'll be in next."

She met his annoyance with a merry titter. "Shall I surprise you?"

"God spare me!" he barked.

Chapter 18

The launch dropped them on the Isle of Sheppey at the mouth of the Thames. As the footmen laid out the picnic, Snap gazed at the enticing vista of marsh grass blowing first one way then the other as the sea breeze shifted. There were shells everywhere on the sand— thousands of pretty ones, most of them unbroken—and the beach curved to a spit of beach that begged to be explored. *Is it proper for an earl's daughter to collect shells? Surely even Lopey couldn't resist such marvelous shapes and colors?*

With nary a backward glance, Lopey took Finnegan by the arm and walked him west along the beach, making it clear Snap was not invited.

So much the better. I'll have free rein to show Gareth we're perfect together.

Conditions could not be better for her campaign. The damp scent of salt and sea reminded her of Devon and her home at Exmouth. The mackerel there were probably running thick as molasses on a day like today. Even old Jack Nasty Face would grin.

Gareth was instructing the servants to move the picnic back so the tide didn't wash everything away, and yelling at the sailors for clunking the basket of china down too hard, and generally keeping things organized, so Snap stayed close to the action. And then a sailor carrying a table over his head shifted off the path from the launch and nearly brained her. If she hadn't ducked she'd have had a fine blue bruise on her forehead.

"Sorry, my lady," the brute said, but there was nothing sorry about him.

Then an auburn-haired swabbie with pale blue eyes gawked at her—an openly suggestive expression on his skinny face. Her first instinct was to throw sand in his eyes, but instead, she glared back.

"You're going to trip if you don't mind your feet," she barked.

"Yes, my lady," the swabbie responded, walking backwards to keep his gaze on her.

A flush of outrage turned the world red. Damn his insolence! Sailors and servants alike strolled by, barely concealed smirks on their faces.

"Get on, you cursed numbskulls," Gareth shouted, "You'll speed things up or you'll learn to walk on water if you want to get home."

The men instantly cut her a wide berth and bent to the work of establishing the luncheon.

Gareth applied the slightest touch to her back, guiding her away from the picnic.

"In all my born days I've never experienced such impertinence," Snap said, just loud enough so the miscreants could hear.

"They think you were out of line."

Snap gestured toward the yacht. "All I did was climb a simple, straight-forward flying jib-boom they were all afraid of."

"Young ladies don't climb."

Snap planted her feet in the sand. "Nobody in Exmouth minded my climbing."

"You were a child then. In London, you're supposed to act like a marriageable debutante, and husbands don't want wives who scale trees faster than their offspring."

"But you do—you don't mind my adventuring."

Gareth froze, then lifted an admonishing finger. "Chit, you need to get me out of your head. By heaven, if you're hearing wedding bells looking at me, then I know a nice pile of straw in Bedlam that'll keep you comfortable. I'm marrying Lopey, and even if I did have eyes for you, which I don't, your papa would come after me with a dozen swordsmen, the Lord Mayor of London, and a hanging rope."

"Pish," said Snap, "my papa doesn't give a fig about who I marry."

"He would if they read my name at banns. Now, leave me alone to arrange the victuals." He turned to walk away.

"There's no one else to talk to," Snap said, catching his sleeve. She cocked her head toward Lopey and Finnegan, who were quite far down the beach.

"Whitey," he called, motioning to the footman, who trotted over. "If you head that way," he said gently, pointing Snap toward the spit, "there's an inlet around the curve where egrets roost. Whitey, grab a bucket so the lady can fill it with shells and stay out of mischief."

She waggled a finger. "Leave me to my own devices, and you may find me atop the highest dune. This is just a warning."

His eyes fired with good humor. "There's a church on this island. If I see you on its steeple, I'll not be accountable for the attitude of the men on the sail home." He folded his arms across his chest.

"And if I find that church and scale that steeple, I'll summon you to my side, Captain Hart, whether you will or no."

He huffed. "Don't be surprised if I send Finnegan instead."

"Ha!" Snap started down the beach. Waving a hand, she called over her shoulder, "Finnegan Whitlocke'd break his noggin on a sand dollar, and you'll be drowned in shame for having killed an earl just to spite me."

She was rewarded with the rumble of his laughter.

****

For as long as he lived, Gareth knew he'd never forget Snap riding the boom, wild with joy and poised like a pirate princess spying for bounty. By God, the chit knew nothing of decorum. How could her parents let her loose on London with so little training in the feminine arts? He shook his head and tried to keep the smile from his lips. Vixen. Her feral ways will stir the blood of every buck who lays eyes on her. Just as certainly, the *ton* will come down on her like a cudgel, blast their hides.

He finished giving orders to the men just as Lopey and Finnigan returned from their walk. She must have noticed Snap's absence.

A blanket had been spread for them on the sand. Back propped against two thick pillows, Lopey reclined Rococo style, leaning a tad more on one hip, the naked toe of her right foot peeking seductively from under the heavy ruffle of her hem. She wasn't wearing glasses, so she couldn't be making much headway on the leather-bound treatise she held pinched between pointer and thumb, her remaining fingers fanned picturesquely. *Harnessing the Cosmic Energy of Household Apparitions.*

A flare of annoyance struck him. Her pose had to be uncomfortable, and that damn frilly dress must be stifling in this heat. Snap wouldn't bother with such niceties, and bloody hell, he had to admire her for it. Immediately he felt contrite. Ever since the first widow lured him to bed on his sixteenth birthday, he'd invited the posturing of older women, even encouraged it. That Snap barged in like a blast of spring air was hardly Lopey's fault. He stroked his fiancée's cheek with the back of his knuckles the way he imagined a lover in one of her paintings would. A pleased smile curled her lips, but she pretended to keep reading.

Finnegan sprawled beside her, an air of discontent radiating like heat from a coal. "Are we supposed to just lie here?"

Lopey turned the page.

"I've got sand in my stockings, Mother."

She tilted the rim of her bonnet to block the sun, but her gaze remained on the text.

"It's near my knee, and I'll go mad if I don't get it out." He dug a finger under the buttons of his breeches and scratched hard. "Mother, it's killing me."

"Compose a rhyme about it, my darling," Lopey said without glancing from her book.

"Sand is not grand when it leaves you unmanned," said Gareth.

Lopey tittered, but kept to her reading.

Petulantly, her son rolled to his other elbow and gazed up the beach. "Where is Sna—Lady Nefertiti?"

"I pointed her toward an inlet down the beach,"

Gareth said, distracting Lopey by pulling down on the spine of her treatise until she had to look into his eyes.

"Naughty boy," she mouthed, then wrestled control of the book.

Finnegan glanced at the footmen. "You let her go off unescorted? There are pirates, you know."

Gareth shot the lad an amused smirk. "She's chaperoned. Besides, that bucket of wild oats would join their thieving band and lead them all to the gallows."

Lopey tittered again.

"Well, there's a dim view," Finn replied, scrambling to his feet. He glared down at Gareth. "I'll go fetch her."

"What, and fight those pirates single-handed?"

Patting Gareth's hand, Lopey said, "We'll send a servant."

It occurred to Gareth the chances were high Snap would be doing something gossip-worthy. It was bad enough that the story of her jib-boom adventure would get out, but heaven only knew what she was doing down the beach.

"I'll go," he announced.

Lopey gripped his arm. "Stay," she said, her lower lip protruding in a pout.

"No, I'll go," Finnegan said, stepping off the blanket.

"Absolutely not!" his mother nearly shouted.

The servants routed curious glances their way.

"You may get lost, my darling."

Finn flashed her an impatient look. "I'll walk straight down the beach and back. How could I get lost?"

"All my menfolk want to abandon me," she complained. "And we were having such a lovely time together. Let Bernard and Alexander go." Her hand fluttered toward a pair of footmen standing by the table.

Gareth took in Lopey, the picture of domesticity, with her book and pear-shaped bottom nestled in the dip of the blanket. Yet, the thought of Finnegan in a hidden spot with Snap grated on him. Clearly Lopey wouldn't want her son cantering after a harridan the lad could never tame.

Gareth leaned close to her ear and whispered, "The young lady's unpredictable. We might not want the servants to see…"

Her eyes widened, and she gave a slight, alarmed nod.

As he walked away, he tried to keep his strides even and unhurried, but the moment his concentration slipped he found his pace quickening. Blood surged painfully in his veins, and it wasn't out of fear for her safety. Snap was probably up to all sorts of nonsense. No doubt she'd filled the basket with little gifts from the sea, and her feet were likely bare, her ankles in plain sight, and her dressed tucked high in its waistband. Would her hair be loose? Would her eyes reflect the ocean? In spite of himself, he broke into a trot.

As he crossed the spit, he saw Whitey wading on the other side, the basket clutched in one hand and his attention fixed on the water.

"Where is she?" Gareth shouted.

The footman jumped, nearly dunking himself in the shallows. "She told me to catch crabs," he blurted.

"Is she near?"

"To tell the truth, Captain Hart, she got away from me."

"Then why in bloody hell aren't you looking for her?"

Whitey grinned. "I'm a Devon man, Captain, so I know how things are with her. She's all right. The girl—I mean, Lady Nefertiti is resourceful."

Gareth grunted, then scanned the landscape for signs of her. Nothing. He broke into a run, and having covered about a quarter mile, he found an inlet hidden by marsh grass.

He wouldn't have found it except its waters ran darker over a moss of seaweed clinging to the ocean floor. Black mud embankments cut between marsh grass so tall it took a trained eye to spot the inlet's path. Ergo, it was the perfect hideaway for Snap to do something ghastly. It wasn't until he waded far up the tight waterway that he spied her.

When he did the shock caused him to lose his footing and plunge to one knee, soaking himself to the hip.

Chapter 19

When Snap saw the look on Gareth's face she remembered she had on even less than when he'd seen her at Julian von Eck's studio—at least then she'd kept on her shift. She squatted in the drink, hiding her naked body to the chin.

"Bloody hell! Where in creation is your dress?"

He'd never looked so angry. Bowsprit climbing was one thing, but apparently bathing *au naturel* was intolerable.

"Don't fret. It's safely on the bank."

"How are you going to put it on when you're soaking wet?"

"I was nearly dry before you forced me back into the water."

Powerful as Poseidon, he churned through the water, a towering wave of a man capsizing her reason. "You're muddy," he said, glowering.

"There are sand crabs in the flats."

Gareth grunted. "So Whitey informed me. Put your face in the water and scrub."

Once she'd flicked the droplets from her eyes, he said, "Look up." Shaking out his handkerchief, he wiped her right cheekbone with rough, abrupt strokes. "Botheration, your pale skin makes it look as if I'd beaten you."

His touch wasn't soft, but it caused a delicious

tingle all the same.

"And you can't stay submerged all day. Stand, but cover yourself. I am no gentleman."

Wrapping her arms about her breasts, she rose slowly dripping from the stream, teasing out the moment, as Gareth kept his focus strictly on the water. Then she turned her back to him.

"Oh, dear God," he murmured under his breath.

Was he looking at her bottom? How much could he see? And should she curve her back just a tad to enhance the view?

"Where did you drop your gown?"

She started up the inlet, but he pushed past her. "Just tell me. I'll lead the way."

They waded about fifty yards to a spot where the high mud bank formed three easily-mountable steps. "My frock is to the right."

With eyes averted, he stepped from the stream and held out a hand to help her traverse the slippery mud. The feel of his fingers gripping her own sent heatwaves colliding with the chill of evaporating water on her skin. She shivered.

"Button it," he commanded, peeling off his linen jacket.

The sight of his broad back hidden only by a thin linen shirt made her breasts feel heavy and tender, and there was pressure between her legs—something between an itch and a fever. As they moved to the top step of the mud bank, it came to her that before this moment, she'd wanted Gareth as someone to accompany her on feats of daring. But this was an entirely different kind of wanting…and it both electrified and mystified her.

She'd left her clothing draped on the marsh grass. In one swift scoop, he handed her the shift, which she wrapped around the lower half of her body.

He cupped her neck, the corded veins on the back of his hand, the dusting of dark hair at the wrist, and his callused thumb and forefinger brought the handkerchief to her chin. This time, he applied the dampened cloth gently, stroking her skin as if it were fine glass. The sultry sun hummed with heat, unseen gulls cried above the sand, and the air hung heavy with salt and sea. Something magical was happening. She could feel it.

Their breathing synchronized and mingled in the savory air, and she felt their bodies commune one to the other—his, molten as warmed butter passing through the fabric of his coat and her shift. He pulled her closer and rubbed a flake of mud from behind her ear. She touched his hand, and his breath hitched as hers came more quickly. She caught his liquid gaze, held it, and let her longing burn from inside to tangle with his need…

"I am no gentleman," he growled, the war in him playing out on his features. A breeze fluttered the black curls across his brow, and then, as if submitting to a queen's sword, he lowered his head near hers. Then hesitated.

She stilled—letting him choose her—breaking him with her youth and beauty, praying the flesh of the scoundrel would vanquish the conscience of the man. The strain caused him to shut his eyes. And when their lips touched, all the world, gulls, sea, mud, salt, and marsh grass, exploded in a burst of light.

The slick wet of his tongue bumped against her lips. She pushed the tongue back with her teeth because he couldn't have wanted it there. Tongues weren't part of kissing.

He reared back and looked at her with surprise.

"What is it?"

He bit his lip and buried his face in her hair. Tremors convulsed his chest.

He's weeping. It must be the thought of losing Lopey. Victory hummed in her veins.

She went for another kiss, but he held her at arm's length, a big, confounding grin stretching his cheeks.

"What's got you Cheshire catting?"

"I'm going back to the picnic."

"To tell her?"

Gareth wrinkled his brow and the grin disappeared. "Tell who, what?"

"You've thrown Lopey over for me."

He looked away, regret pinching every feature. "What a hash I've made of it... Forgive me, Snap, but that can never be."

"But you kissed me!"

"I shouldn't have. Not ever."

"Mrs. Gower, my chaperone, says if a man kisses a woman and they are alone then he has to marry her."

"I'm sure she meant, have 'relations' with her."

"She meant when he loves her!"

The green drained from Gareth's eyes. Taking a deep breath, he turned his back. "Get into your dress, Lady Nefertiti. Lopey will be anxious for us."

Church bells rang in the distance. Each clang shuddered through the break in her heart. The gulls cawed louder, and the ocean pounded the sand with a firmer din, as if all of nature were determined to echo her pain.

He kept his eyes focused on his bare feet as she dressed. "Ach, little girl, you're going to make a fine wife for someone someday."

"Oh, shut your gob, and stop calling me 'little girl.' Just button me up." She proffered her back.

He turned her to face him. "Lady Nefertiti Albright, daughter of the Earl of Alphington, Tweaksend and Surry, I am leagues below your station, I've no fortune or future, my reputation is bleak at best, and your father will never give his consent. Believe me, there are better men than I to wed you. Now, let me finish these fasteners before Finnegan rounds the bend."

****

By God, I've lost my sanity. Why'd I kiss her? A bloody muddle, a hash, a stupid blunderous thing to do to a young... Lopey. She's the perfect wife, she's got money, social position... Clementine. Laura.

He jerked a little hard on Snap's ties as he made a bow of the last fastener. "For the life of me, I don't know how you got out of this contraption alone."

"There are a great many things you don't know about me."

"Humm." He nudged her toward the inlet. "I do know your mother would be appalled to learn you were bathing stripped to the skin."

"Oh pish, my mother would scarcely blink. She never bothered at all till Papa became earl. In fact, no adult paid the least heed to me until you."

She picked up a clam shell, shot him a bitter look, and hurled it into the marsh grass. "I haven't thought of a single man since."

"You haven't met any other men."

"I've met Finnegan."

"As I said…"

"Oh, stuff a boot in it." She strode away.

At the bank of the inlet, she kept her back to him. Tendrils of her hair fluttered from a loose *coiffure* that had eased halfway down her neck. In one hand she held the ribbon ties of a straw bonnet, which she swung back and forth with jerky agitation. The stream stopped her. No one in a gown could wade down it without a soaking.

"You may carry me," she said in a clipped tone, "or we can wait a few hours for low tide."

God's teeth… What would his body do if he touched her…? He harrumphed and studied the water.

Snap pivoted, her eyes bright with challenge.

The distance to the beach through the marsh grass would take them forever in bare feet—too many shells and that sharp grass could slice your pads like a tomato. His gaze returned to the inlet, then back to the bank.

"God's teeth," he growled, "none of your trickery."

Steeling himself, Gareth clambered into the water and held out his arms. Light as a leaf, Snap jumped into them and tucked her head close to his.

With a half breath, half whisper, she said in his ear, "I am in your arms; don't pretend I'm not."

"One more word and I will dump you in the drink."

He sent up a prayer of gratitude to the cold water, because the feel of her snug and soft against his body steamed his blood. The worst of it was, she fit so perfectly—like a custom pair of hessians—the roundness of her bottom, the delicacy of her arm slung across his shoulders, the tickle of her corn silk hair against his cheek… As hard as he fought them, images of her pinked *derrière*, her breasts, pale as froth on a mug of stout, and heaven help him, that small brown mole in the center of her back. Damn his eyes, every fiber in his body thrummed at the recollection.

Sloshing resolutely through the water, he said nothing, yet beads of sweat formed on his brow as Snap's warm breath caressed his neck. Heat passed between them, brought on by more than the welter of the sun, and with each step, that fire grew.

To dampen his ardor, he pictured his wretched uncle Wadsworth, twitching and swinging his ostentatious gold-tipped cane, but then he caught her scent: tangy salt mingled with loam, vanilla, and roses. His chin eased toward her hair.

The minx must have sensed his rising desire, because she gave the tiniest stroke to a spot just behind his ear. He swallowed. He blinked. His skin fevered. He was going to kiss her again. It couldn't be helped.

Snap closed her eyes, her breath going shallow in anticipation, and then she tilted her sweet mouth toward his. And that's when the marsh grass dipped, giving him a full view of Lopey ambulating across the sand with Finnegan at her side.

He plunked Snap onto the bank, and viciously whispered, "By the way, you kiss abominably."

Chapter 20

Truss opened the front door the moment Snap descended from Lopey's carriage. Exhausted, her damp shift chafing, her lovely dress filthy with a streak of bowsprit dirt down the front and patches of mud everywhere else, all Snap wanted to do was sink into a tub and soak her discouragement away.

Only one kiss! It wasn't enough—and he'd come so close to kissing her again. Until Lopey and Finn came along.

The woman had waved from the beach, and Finnegan bolted toward them like a dog to a bowl of meat. Without a backward glance, Gareth waded away, leaving Snap to fend for herself amongst the mudflat's sharp shells, razor grass, and pinching crabs.

"Let me carry you now," Finnegan said. So, instead of into his arms, she jumped on his back. His disappointment was palpable all the way though shirt, vest, and jacket.

Lopey gave her a knowing look after her son put her down. "I saw a portent of something, my dear. Little fish leaping out of the water and the shadow of something big chasing them. Whatever do you suppose it means?"

All Snap had thought to say was, "It's supper time?"

Now, back in the confines of Mayfair with little

chance to see Gareth again unless she could think up something extraordinary, she tossed Truss her shawl. "I'll need a bath. I'm a mass of sand," she told the butler, peeling off her gloves.

"Of course, my lady," Truss replied. He looked behind her, then back with a questioning gaze. "And Widcomb?"

"Widcomb?" Snap was confused.

"Your chaperone." He said "chaperone" as if it were the most dubious title imaginable.

Lawkes, I forgot Lizzie!

The girl had agreed to linger at Gunter's Tea Shop instead of going sailing. "Even lookin' at water makes me vomitous," she'd said.

Snap certainly hadn't wanted ol' Malloy to accompany her. That magical kiss would have been impossible under the nose of that high stickler.

Blurting the first thing that came to mind, Snap said, "Lizzie'll be toodling along in a minute, Truss. I sent her to run an errand for me."

"I see." But it was obvious from his tone that the butler didn't see at all, or perhaps saw too much, since all the shops were closed at this hour. "I'll inform Malloy of your desire for a bath."

"My bath, ha, ha, ha," Snap said, her feeble attempt at a laugh sounding as if it were rusted iron scraping on rusted iron. "Let's hold that for the moment. My directions to Liz—Widcomb were quite complex. I'll just check to make sure she follows them correctly."

"Of course." The butler's lower lip dimpled with skepticism.

"Yes," Snap reiterated, drawing her gloves back on and reaching for her shawl, "very, very complicated."

****

Lizzie sat near the back of the confectionary, eleven empty ice glasses in front of her. She looked slightly green. "They don't let you have a table if you ain't ordering," she said in lieu of hello.

"You could have walked Berkeley Square."

"And what if you come for me, and me not here, what then?"

At that moment a waiter with a forelock of tangerine hair pomaded into poorly made Byronic curls arrived at the table. Looking first at Lizzie for confirmation, he addressed Snap. "Milady, it's one pound, three shillings for the miss's tab."

Snap's jaw dropped.

"I tried everything in the shop, didn't I, Mr. Stainton?"

He didn't wink at Lizzie, but he did twinkle. "That's the truth."

Snap passed Lizzie a dark look, then, digging into her reticule, she scraped out a few coins. "Well, all I've got are three crowns, two shillings," she said, glaring more fiercely at the maid. "I didn't budget for one pound, three shillings' worth of ices."

Mr. Stainton twinkled again. "That's all right. You can send the miss back tomorrow with the difference."

"Humph," declared Snap, as Lizzie and the tangerine gleamed at one another. "Are you quite done or do you desire another ice?"

Her annoyance had zero effect on Lizzie, who met her comment with a pair of raised brows that said, is that you chastising me for unladylike behavior?

Snap stomped out of Gunther's and didn't even look back to make sure Lizzie was following.

"Slow your pace," cried Lizzie, waddling heavily and holding her stomach.

"If you're going to be in service to me then there are a few things I need to make clear."

"Such like?"

"Well, you're not to flirt with young men. It's not the thing."

"So it's all right for you to be ahoy-ing with a sea captain all day, but I'm to keep my gob shut and talk to no one?"

"We weren't 'ahoy-ing,' and I went escorted by Lady Whitlocke and her son, so my conduct was unimpeachable."

Lizzie slanted her a glance. "If 'unimpeachable' means you were up to no good, I'd agree."

Snap shot back her most disapproving expression. "I ask that you not speak to me in that familiar tone."

"Bosh. Besides, ain't you toffs supposed to set an example for us simple folk? I'd—"

Snap halted with a sharp little cry and put out an arm to stop Lizzie. "Baron Wadsworth," she said, as if the name had been punched from her gut.

"There's that blighter what stole my knife!" Lizzie cried, bolting straight for Wadsworth and a lad talking with him.

"No!" screamed Snap.

And in that moment, Wadsworth pivoted and pinned her with a look that grew brighter as he focused on the one distinguishing attribute of every Albright: blonde hair, pale as corn silk.

The lad scampered away, Lizzie, holding her stomach, was hard on his heels, while Wadsworth shuddered in some dreadful spasm, and then sauntered, swinging his gold-tipped cane, towards Snap.

"Bless my soul," he cooed. "if it isn't the Earl of Twickenham's daughter. Those flaxen tresses give you and your kin away, I'm afraid."

Frozen with fear and revulsion, she couldn't think of a reply. This man, in his relentless pursuit of Mama's necklace, the Fitzcarry pearls, had caused her family infinite trouble. Ellie was nearly burned alive in a horse barn, and he'd tried to have Mama murdered by Peggity's dreadful first husband. Unprompted, Snap's hands rose as if to ward him off. He captured one in a fawn-colored glove and twitched violently. A malevolent blast shot up her arm. She shrieked and yanked away.

The baron burst into happy spluttering gurgles that left dots of froth in the corners of his mouth. "And how is your family?" he asked when he'd spent his mirth.

"Very well, no thanks to you."

"And your mama, is she faring well?"

"My mother is as far from the grave and from giving up the Fitzcarry pearls as the ocean is from running out of water."

Wadsworth convulsed in hideous mirth.

She was about to brush past him when Rascal, in a storm of black and white canine enthusiasm, bounded over and planted his paws on her hip. From around the corner strolled Gareth with the pug and spaniel at his heels. Wadsworth eyed her, then Rascal, and finally Gareth.

To her horror, a delighted grin curled the corners of his fleshless mouth.

Chapter 21

"You have some interesting friends," Baron Wadsworth said, lying on a blood-red divan in the front room of his apartments.

Gareth shrugged and moved a backgammon piece. "As do you, Uncle."

"I have enemies and people who owe me money. You, however, have friends…and admirers. Admirers with access to the Fitzcarry pearls."

God's teeth, how Gareth hated this kind of talk. His bloody uncle was obsessed with those damn pearls. The villain had very nearly turned him into Ellie Albright's murderer just to get his hands on that strand. Blast, blast, blast! If only Rascal hadn't put his damn paws on Snap—behaving like a bloody duck hound pointing to a kill. Now, it was too late. Now, his uncle had her in his sights, and heaven help Snap and her family, there was nothing Wadsworth wouldn't do to catch his prey. The knot in his stomach pinched harder.

And one thing is certain, my uncle'll have me on the rack and screaming to force me to steal it.

"Why are you so bloody bent on getting those pearls? If they're stolen, they can't be worn because everyone in England and the Continent would recognize even a single bead from that necklace."

Wadsworth sniffed. "A certain lady in Paris desires them, and I—"

"Don't tell me you're still courting Marie Eugénie Floquet? There couldn't be a more rapacious—"

"I am also 'rapacious,' as you so uniquely label admiration for things of beauty. That is the core of the friendship I share with Madam Floquet. She wants the pearls, and I will get them for her."

Wadworth's expression hardened, brooking further conversation.

"Move your stone already," Gareth grumbled.

His uncle peered at the backgammon board, then neatly shook out two dice, and moved a checker onto his home board.

Gareth sucked air between his teeth, and reached for the dice cup.

"You can help me, nephew, especially with your knack for the fairer sex."

Gareth sat up to keep the bile from his throat. "I've never put my 'knack for the fairer sex,' at your disposal before, and I don't intend to now. You're on your own with whatever scheme you're dreaming up."

Gareth hit a blot on Wadsworth's home board, and set his uncle's stone on the bar. Now it was the baron's turn to be upset.

Gareth kept his focus on the game, but he heard the uneven jerk of the dice as a tremor shook his opponent. It took the bony bastard a moment to regain his wits enough to move a stone, but when he did, he hammered Gareth's only unprotected game piece, sending it to the bar.

Your niece is quite well these days." Wadsworth pronounced "niece" with a long hiss, dangerous as an adder's warning.

The muscles in Gareth's back contracted, joining

his stomach in dread. Wadsworth's wolfish gaze lit with delight.

"Perhaps I forgot to mention that I'm thinking of moving her into my home in Devon for the summer months. Your sister objects to the arrangement, of course, but you know how persuasive I can be."

The feckin' devil was threatening him with his darling niece, Clementine, the prettiest, sweetest thing the whole bloody line of Harts had produced since the first Hart rutted with whatever wanton would have him.

He's bluffing. Laura and Clementine are well hidden.

However, the blackguard wanted a reaction, the more violent the better, and Gareth wasn't about to give him the satisfaction.

"I have served you well, Uncle," he said with icy calm, "I have squeezed ha'pennies out of starving widows, and sent Beam Murphy to beat, harass, and strong-arm rich and poor alike." He slid a backgammon piece down a triangle, protecting a strategically placed stone. "Your end of the bargain is to leave off that child and my sister. Have you forgotten?"

Instead of responding, the man hummed a little tune and kept his gaze on the board. "I've paid you for your efforts."

"A meager living, at best," Gareth spat.

"Admit it, darling boy, you enjoy playing Robin Hood to my Sheriff of Nottingham, and the work keeps you spry. Employment behind a wooden desk with a feathered quill could hardly suit you."

"Leave her with my sister or I'll hang for your murder, Uncle. I do not lie."

"We're a serious young thing today, aren't we?"

Wadsworth rolled his eyes into his head, exposing an expanse of white struck through with blood vessels. A beatific smile played about his lips, and it was all Gareth could do to keep from punching it into mush.

"Our agreement was that I wouldn't go near her," Wadsworth said, his voice light with triumph. "Clementine and Laura will go to Devon, while I remain here."

Gareth's leg kicked involuntarily, jostling the backgammon pieces. "That is if you find them."

"Cardiff, nephew. You've got them in a farmhouse at St. Fagan's."

Muscles clamped to the breaking point, he fought to rein in the desire to choke this man until he lay still and blue. "If Clementine is taken, you can expect me to go to the magistrate."

"Dear boy, that's quite a rousing speech," Wadsworth said, his eyeballs rolling down to fix on Gareth. "But there isn't a magistrate in England who'll touch me, as well you know. The Prince Regent promised eternal gratitude for the secrets I gave Wellington about Napoleon's troop movements. There would be no Waterloo without that essential tidbit, and that's a bankable mark in my favor. And then there's my dear friend Minister of Police Joseph Fouché who placed France's network of spies at my disposal. They made it so much easier to find my dear niece and her charming child.

"Your infamy is growing, Uncle. The prince may have lost his charitable feelings for you."

The baron giggled. "I've given the prince a great deal of latitude collecting his gambling debts. He's eternally grateful. Besides, do you imagine poor Laura can defend her child from a dozen of my men? Could you, nephew? Clementine will be on my guest list in Devon until I have the Fitzcarry pearls. Who knows," he added, crossing a leg, "she may inherit them someday."

Throat dry, Gareth rasped, "You'd rather swallow them."

Wadsworth giggled. "How well you think you know me."

"If you've some charitable part you're hiding, I wish you'd reveal it now and leave my niece free. That little girl has done nothing to you."

"Harsh, harsh, harsh." Wadsworth laughed. "She would enjoy the smells of the sea and the warmth of the Devon sun. There's no harm—"

"She is eight years old, and without her mother—"

Gareth swallowed his words, barely able to keep himself at the game table. Every inch of his body strained to rip down the walls and his uncle along with them. But all he could do was breathe. Breathe, and hold his temper. Devil, devil! The man had him trapped. Years and years of blackmail, he'd endured to keep his family safe from this monster, and now this.

Fingers stiff with rage, Gareth reached onto his uncle's side of the backgammon board and straightened the pieces. "Tell me what you want, and cease this charade; I've no stomach for it."

Taking his time, Wadsworth indulged in a deep, tolerant sigh. "The Albright girl is pretty, so I'm sure you won't mind spending time in her company. Win her trust. Her come out party is in a few days—"

"No!" Gareth stood so violently an end table shook, rattling a shepherdess figurine, a framed picture, and a Chinese vase into a frenzy. "I am marrying Lady Penelope Whitlocke that same day, and I will not endanger my courtship or marriage by being seen with Snap Albright."

" 'Snap,' is it?" His uncle hooked a checker with a boney finger and drew it into place. "Clementine will laugh and laugh when she hears that name."

Gareth wanted to scream, to rip the fine paper from his uncle's walls, to smash the inlaid furniture, and hurl each priceless gold statuette, porcelain figurine, and ormolu clock against the room's white marble floors. But more than anything, he wanted Baron Wadsworth dead. Only the man's blood staining the Persian carpet could cool his wrath.

"No more, Uncle," he said, his voice deep with his desire to kill. "Once the pearls are yours, you will deliver Laura and Clementine, and then we are through. Come near me, and I'll cut your face and then your wretched heart, if there's one big enough to stab."

Chapter 22

Late the next evening, when the night sky lay thick as velvet and the wings of crickets rubbed their perfect note, Gareth gingerly separated the rain-laden fronds of a weeping willow as he spied into the lit windows of Hugh Davenport's Mayfair home. As anticipated, Snap's silhouette appeared in the lamp light. Her bedroom did indeed overlook the garden.

After removing a glove, he dug around in the exposed earth beneath the willow until he found something hard. He picked the object out with a nail, and drew back to hurl it at the window. The object, he realized just before it left his hand, was round and thin. Deciding it might be a shilling, he stuffed it in his pocket and scratched about some more. Quickly, he came in contact with another mass possessing the same coin-like contours.

Someone must have lost a purse.

A third and then a fourth coin met his fingertips before he found a suitably jagged stone. Snap had disappeared from the window, but he tossed the pebble anyway. *Tink!* It hit the glass. He lobbed a second and third pebble then found two more coins.

By the time he'd dug out another stone, Snap, in her nightdress, not even covered by a robe, appeared at the window.

"Chirp, chirp, chirp," cried Gareth, trying to sound

like a mockingbird.

"That's a ghastly bird call," Snap announced. "Whomever you are, you ought to haunt someone else's garden."

"Hush," he whispered. "By the willow. Chirp, chirp, chirp!"

"Truly, that is the least convincing— If I must shoo you away, be warned, I will."

Too surprised to move, he watched in fear and admiration as she climbed out the window, swung onto the drainpipe and shimmied to the ground.

Shadowed by trees, all he could see was her pale negligee, like a disembodied wraith wavering in the starlight.

"Chirp again, intruder," she demanded.

Before her voice could alert the household, or more urgently, her father, he sprinted to her side and put a hand over her mouth. In an explosion of tigress-like moves, she clawed his hands, jabbed his ribs, and twisted her wrists free. Only when he had her pinned hard against him and nearly shouted his name did she cease struggling.

"Lawks, you nearly got yourself killed."

He chuckled but didn't let go of her. Thinner than the fashion, she was all bones and sinew, and energy and warmth. He ought to let go. Especially because she leaned against him, fitting into his chest like a key in a lock. If he didn't stop holding her, he'd do something regretful. With a little shake of her shoulders, he put six inches between them.

"Why are you climbing down drainpipes in your nightdress when you think there are strangers about?"

"Curiosity."

She said it blandly, as if thieves and killers didn't exist in London. He huffed in frustration. "Well, you mustn't."

"But you wanted to see me or you wouldn't have tossed stones and chirped like a…a… man who wants to get someone's attention."

For the first time in his life, Gareth felt outgunned. "Where can we talk?"

"In secret?" She stepped back. "Didn't you vow never to see me again because of Papa?"

"That was my wish—for your sake."

"Then I'm glad your wish didn't come true."

Treating him like a puppy on a leash, Snap pulled him toward the far corner of the garden where a rose bower framed a marble bench.

"What must we talk about?"

Damn and blast it, the excitement in her voice was unmistakable. By God, he wanted to kill his uncle.

Even in the dark, her eyes shone with admiration. For her safety, he wanted that light doused. It was time she learned how deceitful the world could be—how crushing it was to all the best instincts of the soul. Above all, she had to understand who he was and what his real intentions were.

"Baron Wadsworth wants the Fitzcarry pearls," he announced brutally.

"Of course he does." She nodded. "But he can't have them. Mama doesn't want to sell. And please don't growl at me. I despise it. If I remember correctly, and I do, the last time you used that tone you told me my kiss was awful. It's not a nice timbre at all."

"I use it because I am in deadly earnest."

He faced her on the bench, and their knees

knocked. She opened hers just wide enough for him to slip his left knee between. The feel of her hard little bones made him swallow, and for a moment he couldn't remember why he was here gazing at her shimmering eyes. Taking a breath, he recovered himself.

"I'm to steal them. My uncle... My uncle is not a man to be trifled with. It's not my desire to hurt or disappoint you, but he is threatening my eight-year-old niece. We have but three days before I marry, so for my niece's sake alone, we must see each other as much as possible." He took a deeper breath, stealing himself for her reaction. "Baron Wadsworth instructed me to win your trust, then pilfer the necklace at your party."

Instead of shrieking, or at least holding a hand to her bosom in shock, Snap leaned forward eagerly. "Where shall you take me?"

"Gad, woman, aren't you the least bit upset?"

She shook her head. "About the pearls? You'd bungle it."

"I'd do no such thing."

"Oh pish, you're no kind of thief."

He bumped her knee as a distraction and simultaneously slipped a ribbon off the end of her flaxen braid. Dangling it before her nose, he waved it snake-like, and waited for her reaction.

"A ribbon is as far from a string of pearls as a badger is from a rhinoceros. Now, what are you planning for me? I should like to see a house of ill repute or a gambling den."

"Bloody—no!"

"But you know all about them, don't you? Haven't you led a wicked, wicked life?"

It took a moment for Gareth to retrieve his jaw. "I

haven't been the noblest fellow in England, but I haven't been a total rakehell either. And regardless, I'm not about to risk your place in society by escorting you to scandalous scenes."

Snap shifted her knees, leaving cold where there had just been warmth. "If Papa can't know, and Lopey must be kept in the dark, and the *ton* mustn't see me, and unsavory places are out of the question, I should like to hear Byron recite poetry."

"I'm afraid he's incl—"

Her hand rose to hush him. "All the world is mad for Byron. If you cannot take me to hear him, you may tell your uncle to stuff your niece in an oven, for Snap Albright will have none of you." She stood to walk away, but he caught her arm.

"Byron is the worst debauché in England. A young lady, especially one who is yet to come out, must not be seen in his presence."

But Snap wasn't listening. She dusted the back of her nightdress. "I don't care what you think of him, Captain Hart. In three days, you shall be too married to take me, and I shall be too occupied by dull lords, to be asked. Therefore, facilitate my worship of England's greatest poet or suffer your uncle's consequences. The choice is yours."

Chapter 23

The harpsichord *plinked* an elaborate *arpeggio* before Monsieur Tatu, the dance instructor, halted the minuet lesson for, Snap estimated, the four-hundred-and-eighty-seventh time. Her heart wasn't in it. Papa promised the minuet at the start of the dancing, yet with only two days to her party, he hadn't attended a single lesson. She pressed her lips together. No doubt, he'd got himself involved in some Roman conquest thing.

"No, no, Lady Nefertiti. You rise on the foot, thus, and down, two, three, four, and up, and then down. And you circle with grace, *comme ça?*"

He sidestepped, crossing beribboned slippers one before the other, revealing twisted, yellowed teeth in a strained attempt at a smile. His discolored chompers, Snap noticed, contrasted sharply with a white, elaborately-tied cravat snugged against his throat.

"Is there a more entertaining dance we might open the ball with? Something with dash?"

She had been dropping hints about learning the waltz throughout the lesson, but Monsieur Tatu refused to catch on. As for the minuet, she didn't bother to copy his steps because she knew them by heart, however, he grew so deliciously frustrated she couldn't resist botching them.

"You are so lucky, Monsieur Tatu," she said, intentionally stepping on her own toe. "As a man, you may dance any dance you wish or see Lord Byron any time you like, or—"

"Oh, but I could not! *Par exemple*, zee poet is performing out of doors, but alas, only invitees may go."

"When?"

"*Demain soir*."

Tomorrow night! Quick action was needed—Captain Hart had to take her, then renounce Lopey and marry her instead. There were so many arrangements to be made, so much to accomplish in so short a time!

The instructor elegantly dipped, crossed feet, and held out a hand for her to take. Instead, she circled, deliberately clenching her fists and hunkering into the stance of a fighter judging the best angle for a knockdown.

"But this is wrong," Monsieur Tatu cried in despair. "You look as if you wished to wrestle me to the floor!"

The Dowager Lady Davenport rose from a gilt chair tucked in a corner of the ballroom. "First impressions are vital, my country starling," she announced, her regal bearing giving her the authority of a field general. "The first dance of a come out ball is always the minuet—"

"But a waltz is so much more exciting," Snap pleaded, "and it would—"

"Do not mention that fatal contagion in my presence! You absolutely must follow form if you're to make a proper match; therefore, the minuet is essential."

The finality in the dowager's voice put an end to Snap's argument, though she would have liked to mention that some dull blade who worried about propriety was hardly the sort of fellow she intended to marry.

"But the minuet is a thrilling dance," Lady Davenport said encouragingly. "Why, it's every bit as entertaining as the waltz, is it not, Monsieur Tatu?"

"*Oui*, every bit and more!" the dance instructor chirruped. He gestured to the harpsichordist, who resolutely hit the keys once again.

Snap raised her arms as if they weighed a hundred stone apiece and stomped out the first few steps. She noted with satisfaction that Monsieur Tatu's face reddened and that his breathing changed to distressed huffs. He looked as if he were about to cry.

"It is like this, my chickadee," the dowager said, sailing across the marble floor.

Monsieur Tatu's yellows made a glorious appearance in a smile of true delight, and off they went, mincing over the marble to the lilting tinkle of the harpsichord.

As the dowager sank into a deep curtsey with her gaze downcast in a modest pose, and Monsieur Tatu swept into an elaborate bow, and the musician concentrated on a flurry of delicate notes, Snap ducked through the door and bolted below stairs.

Swinging into the kitchen, she said breathlessly, "Lizzie Widcomb, cease slicing those apples; I have a far more important job for you."

****

Gareth bit into a triangle of toast in the morning room and flipped a page of *The Times*, when, with a barely audible clearing of the throat, Lopey's butler caught his attention. A scrabble of claws ensued as the canine heap under the table rose to sniff the butler's trousers. A silver salver descended in front of Gareth, displaying a poorly folded note.

Before he could read the missive, the servant whispered, "The maid who delivered it asks if you've found her knife. She said you'd be cognizant of her meaning."

"Tell her the weapon is just out of my grasp for the moment, but I will retrieve it soon."

Nodding sagely, the butler went to the door and closed it in a slightly savage manner as the dogs attempted to follow.

The note, hastily scrawled, was from Snap, begging Gareth to come "immediately."

"Anything of interest?" asked Lopey, dropping a spoonful of jam onto a buttered scone.

He folded the note neatly and slipped it in a pocket.

"Just another aristocrat wanting to delay payment to the baron."

With *The Times* in hand once again, Gareth was drawn to a brief announcement that St. Lawrence Jewry church was about to undergo renovations that would close its tower. The view of the city from there was quite lovely, and Snap silhouetted against silver clouds...

"Did you ever see the vista from St. Lawrence at Guildhall?" he asked Lopey.

She lowered her teacup. "I should think not. It's a stronghold of the Church of England, and I'm strictly Catholic. Besides, they say in all of London, the fog lifts last around its bell tower—that's hardly a good sign, wouldn't you agree?"

"Hmm." He was about to ask for the source of her

information, when something banged hard against the window.

"Another bird!" she said, rising so swiftly the china rattled and her napkin slid to the floor. After opening the window, she poked her head out then drew back with a gasp.

"What is it?" asked Gareth.

"It's not a pigeon this time." Her voice rose in alarm. "It's a crow."

He threw the newspaper on the table and went to her. Lying on the stone walkway was a crow, motionless, its neck bent awkwardly, its lustrous black feathers tight to its body. A wooly ball of fear clogged his throat at the expression on Lopey's face. Horror pinched the corners of her mouth, and her mouse gray eyes reflected every phantasmagorical conclusion her odd beliefs could muster.

He held her shoulders and stroked down her arms, desperately trying to calm her. "This happens every spring—"

She stopped him with a sad shake of her head. "It won't work, my darling." Tears escaped down the wrinkles framing her eyes. "We must postpone our wedding until nature's portents improve. The warning signs are everywhere."

Gareth rubbed his chin hard. Bloody hell, Wadsworth could slash his niece's face to ribbons by the time every flying beast quit migrating into Lopey's windowpanes.

"Two days before the date and you wish to cancel…because of a bird? When then? When shall you declare before God your commitment to me, and I to you?"

"My dearest, Parliament will be seated again in October. Would you be willing to wait until November?"

"That is past ninety days from now, Lopey. Our license will be void." Trying to check his agitation, he shook out a handkerchief and gently blotted the tears from her face. "I honestly feel our time is now. Who knows what may happen before October—I could be killed, you could take another lover—"

A hand went to her breast. "But I wou—"

"My sweet turtledove," he interrupted, "I wish to be your husband now, not when every feathered creature in England leaves for the winter."

Her lip trembled as her gaze drifted back to the crow. Before she could utter another objection, though, he pecked her on the cheek.

"I'm off. Please don't worry, darling Lopey. Even nature can't stop the union of two people meant for each other.

Not one more bird, he prayed, as he bolted out the door. Not one more blasted bird.

****

Snap grabbed her prettiest spencer off the bed (the green silk jacket with tucks everywhere), and had it on before Lizzie could help, then she tossed the maid a bonnet, looped her reticule around her wrist, and raced out the door.

In tandem, they pounded down the stairs. It was critical to make it out the front door before questions were asked; Gareth could already be waiting for them.

Just as they hit the bottom, her nephew Sebastian flew around the corner and hurled himself full force into Snap's skirt. "Uppy!" he cried, bouncing up and down, his pudgy arms thrust toward her.

"The moment I get back," she promised.

"Uppy," the child demanded again.

"Where's your nanny?" she asked, hoisting the blue-eyed, blond-haired cherub and settling him on her hip. "Someday," she whispered in the boy's ear, "Captain Hart and I are going to have a baby, and you can teach our little one how to be adorable, too." Following three kisses, she blew a raspberry on his cheek, sending him into a gale of giggles.

"Sebastian?" called Ellie.

"Oh no, it must be nap time. I hate naps, don't you?" To distract her nephew from their impending separation, Snap waltzed and twirled toward her sister before lowering him to the floor.

"Uppy," Sebastian pleaded, his grief-stricken gaze shooting a hundred arrows into Snap's heart.

"You look as if you're about to go somewhere," Ellie commented.

"Not far. Just a jaunt around the park."

"Snap, there are a thousand details to discuss."

Surreptitiously, Lizzie twitched her gaze toward the door.

"But I thought we'd settled everything for the party."

"Uppy!" Sebastian cried.

Snap patted his head, and focused her most earnest expression on her sister. "You're so much better at these decisions. Couldn't you do it for me, please?"

"Uppy, uppy, uppy!" Sebastian jumped up and down, reaching for Snap like a supplicant to God. Tears filled his blue eyes as his wail rose both in pitch and decibel.

"Lud, when is that nursemaid's leg going to heal?" Ellie swept up her weeping babe, and kissed his damp face. "Auntie Snap will play with you after your nap, won't you?"

"On my honor as a gentleman," Snap replied, offering a formal bow before heading toward the door.

As Ellie disappeared up the stairs, Snap and Lizzie scampered toward the door. But just as Snap's hand was inches from the knob, a "Hallooo," from Mrs. Gower, a cousin who served as matchmaker and chaperone to the Albright family, stopped her.

"There goes our escape," Lizzie whispered. "And the captain's likely waiting."

"Come visit," Mrs. Gower trilled from the saloon. "You'll have to bring yourself here. I'm too flummoxed to travel."

Snap closed her eyes in frustration. *Am I never to escape!* "Tell Captain Hart, I'll be there shortly," she whispered to Lizzie.

Cutting Mrs. Gower a look, Lizzie replied *sotto voce*, "You'll need the luck of ten cats and a king to escape from that one." Then she slid out the exit.

"How lovely to see you up and about, Mrs. Gower," Snap said, confident the chaperone had an ailment ripe for discussion.

"It's my arms this week. They've gone all a-wobble, I'm afraid."

Snap planted herself on a divan opposite the woman and folded her hands neatly. "Tell me about your arms; how you do suffer, poor Mrs. Gower."

"If I try to hold them up—do you see? Do you see how they wobble?"

The limbs behaved like any other arms held out

straight as a gate, but Snap clucked sympathetically. "They're waving like flags! Have you taken willow bark?"

"You won't catch me downing witch's brews."

"Claire says willow bark works wonders with pain, but I know something that's just as effective." Snap rose from the divan and went to a sideboard upon which glittered a row of cut-crystal decanters. She selected the one labeled "Sherry."

"I think sherry would work best," Mrs. Gower said, a slight tremor in her voice, intended to depict the delicate state of her arms.

Secretly, Snap rolled her eyes. Not a day went by without Mrs. Gower dosing herself with sherry. She returned with a snifter filled to the brim.

Following a fulsome gulp, Mrs. Gower glanced impishly at Snap. "There's precious little time before your come out, so, I want you to carefully picture the sort of dashing young buck you'll desire in the marriage bed."

Heat rose in Snap's cheeks—Mrs. Gower could be so earthy at times. "I've found him," she said, "But Papa doesn't think he's suitable."

"Oooo, that's not a good start."

"Which is why you must help me convince him."

Mrs. Gower drained the glass. "A little more, dearie? My arms are so painful and unsteady."

Snap returned to the sideboard, refilled the snifter, and brought the decanter back with her.

Following three unseemly gulps, Mrs. Gower gave a contented sigh. "And who is the gentleman who's captured your admiration?"

"Honestly, I'm afraid to say his name in this house,

but you've done so well by my sisters…" Quietly Snap whispered, "Captain Gareth Hart."

"Oh, he's a hellish fine rogue." Mrs. Gower beamed. "But all the world knows he's mad for gals my age."

"I believe I've changed his habits. He adores me—though he's refused my proposal."

"Oh, my dear, let him bend the knee. It builds gratitude in a man."

That's fine to say, but he may be married before he realizes he bent the knee to the wrong woman. Still, Mrs. Gower could be a valuable ally.

"Shall I pour?"

"Just add a drop. It's for my nerves."

She topped off the glass.

"Captain Hart has every attribute I seek, and I've loved him since I was a child. Absolutely no one else will suit."

"Lawks." The chaperone tipped her glass and took a hearty swig. "What a long time to pine for a man. But I fear you're headed for a fine battle."

"Oh, Mrs. Gower, I can't tell you how much I appreciate having you champion my cause. When will you speak with Papa?"

"Did I say I would?" She looked bewildered.

"Yes. Just now."

"I have to think." She tapped her temple. "Your father disapproves, you said? Maybe… maybe… What about your mother?"

"She wants me to marry for love."

"The Season is… There's long list of eligible bachelors—" Mrs. Gower mumbled.

The sherry was taking effect.

"But I'm not interested in them, and it would be a blot on your reputation if you failed me. Now that I've found him, you must convince Papa. You did it for my sisters." That was hardly true, but in moments of desperation…

A blurry smile stumbled onto Mrs. Gower's lips. "Aye, but it's your first Season; plenty of time. Plenty of time…"

"No, I have no time at all."

The woman blinked, her eyes resting at half-mast. "Hart… Hart…"

"Will you promise to help?"

Blearily Mrs. Gower slid Snap an expectant look, and then focused on the sherry.

"Promise?"

"Of course, child."

After emptying the decanter, Snap lifted the snifter to Mrs. Gower. "Thank you. I know I can trust you."

As the glass neared the chaperone's lips, Snap pointed at the window. "What a stylish landau."

Mrs. Gower pivoted in a woozy arc, and Snap dashed for the door.

Chapter 24

"Well that's a surprise; they're already renovating," Gareth said, looking from the hack at the façade of St. Lawrence Jewry church.

A thick bramble of scaffolding reached clear to the bell tower, and workers shoring up the building's crumbling white wall, occupied a series of platforms all the way up.

"Hey there," he called from the hack's window, "Is the tower closed?"

A no-neck laborer with a rag over his mouth, nodded, and dumped a few shovels full of mortar into a massive bowl.

"Let's watch," said Snap, jumping from the conveyance.

Every worker's gaze shifted to her—a blast of sunshine with her smile and bright blues. He and Lizzie followed, trailing Snap as she ambled through the mess of bricks, timber, and tools.

Two days to the wedding...

Gareth wondered if it was wise to leave his fiancée alone. Who knew what signals Mother Nature might send? Then a breeze ruffled Snap's pale green frock. It clung to her legs, and his heart lurched.

Gad, how can anything be so pretty?

The no-neck laborer secured the bowl of mortar to a pulley, and cried, "Comin' up," then hoisted it to a pair on the fifth tier.

The laborers were so busy tracking Snap and Lizzie, however, they lost their grip on the bowl and sent it swinging.

"Ay, ay, you gollumpuses!" shouted a wiry fellow from the highest platform. He shot an angry glance at Gareth, then scrambled down the ladders.

"Lads, we'll break now," he bawled as he passed them. "You'll not keep your wits till the circus leaves town." He flashed another scathing look at Gareth and the ladies.

The men swarmed off the scaffolding, winking and flexing their muscles.

"Will you be gone long?" Snap inquired of the wiry fellow.

"'Bout an hour." He grunted.

"Oh, dearie me," she replied, the picture of disappointment.

Immediately, Gareth went on the alert. Snap had a look in her eye—a look that said she was thinking of doing something that ought not to be done.

"Well, I hopes you'll wait for me, rum duchess," said a youth in homespun as he passed Lizzie, "I'll be happy to show how we lay on the lime." A lewd grin stretched his cheeks.

"Stuff a sock in it," the maid snarled.

Gareth took a few menacing steps toward the fool. "Sod off, and make it quick."

As the youth followed the others around the corner of the church, he gave an innuendo-packed nod to Lizzie, then trotted to catch up.

Snap emitted a satisfied huff, then went to the foot of the construction, walked an arc around it, and appeared to carefully study the scaffolding. "If I race you to the top of the tower and win, will you grant me a boon?"

"God help me," he said. "What sort of 'boon'?"

"You know what I'd do if I was you?" Lizzie interjected. "I'd say no to that bet."

"You hush," Snap admonished.

The maid raised her brows knowingly and pinched her lips between thumb and forefinger.

The tower reached a good sixty-five to seventy-five feet in the air, Gareth guessed. Ladders connected the platforms, and the whole scaffold was held together with ropes and cross-hatched poles. All he had to do was get to the ladder first and prevent Snap from passing the rest of the way up.

"It's a dangerous climb and I—"

"So true. A young lady should not ever climb so high, but I'm going to whether you warn me off or not." She offered a sly twinkle.

Of course, he could wrestle her to the ground and prevent her, but Snap was the sort who would sneak back without him. "Then name your boon, my lady," he said, sketching a magnanimous bow.

She clapped her hands in delight. "Did you know Lord Byron will be reading tomorrow at an outdoor venue?"

Gareth laughed. "As much as you long to see our greatest living poet, it's impossible to take you to that event."

A golden smile creased Snap's pert pink lips. "You're going to say women aren't invited, but I don't view that as an obstacle. With the right clothes, I make a very convincing young man."

He pressed his temples. "You do realize the day after that, I'll be marrying Lopey and Society will be getting its official look at you."

She cocked her head and fixed him with a coquettish grin. "Those are indeed the facts."

He took a deep breath, glanced at the tower, knew she didn't stand a chance, and shrugged. "Fine."

Lizzie shook her head in vigorous alarm, but Snap quashed her with a threatening glare.

"You haven't seen me climb," Gareth assured the maid.

"And you ain't wise to her shenanigans."

He chuckled. With his boot heel, he drew a faint line in the grass. "Shall we race from here?"

Snap lifted her skirts and put a slippered foot to the mark. Gareth went next to her and slid his right toe up to the line.

"Lizzie, you say 'Go,'" Snap commanded.

In response, the maid sat on a pile of timber. "I'm thinking I shouldn't."

"Oh pish, just say it."

"Take your marks," the maid announced begrudgingly. "Get set..."

When she failed to say more, Snap eyed her severely.

"Go," Lizzie whispered.

Gareth bounded forward, heading straight for the ladder. Quicker than lightning, he achieved the first platform and was pleased to note he hadn't as yet heard Snap's footsteps behind him.

The next ladder he took two rungs at a time and looked back to see if she followed. Nothing. But directly below, Lizzie's face was red with effort, though he couldn't see what she was straining against.

Galloping across the platform for the third ladder, he stopped suddenly as Snap shot past, hands gripping the pulley rope, her feet planted on either side of the mortar bowl. A wild, victorious smirk flashed by as she soared up the side of St. Lawrence's.

Blast her vixeny hide.

****

Eight chimes hung in the bell tower. Snap counted them as she waited for Gareth to climb the rest of the way up the scaffold. Rapturously she watched as he ascended, his grin widening each time their gazes met. Her heart beat so rapidly, her blood zinged so swiftly, she thought she might faint with excitement.

When his broad shoulders filled a cut in the tower's stones, she stepped back in awe. Instead of climbing in immediately, he stood on the low wall, held the lintel with one hand and crooked his muscular arm above his head. The fabric of his navy jacket strained to contain bulging muscles. Sweat beaded on his brow, and his breath came hard as he took her in. A merry twinkle in his eyes morphed into a drop-lidded look so lustful she couldn't breathe.

He didn't say a word. Not a syllable. In one stride, he covered the distance between them, wrapped an arm about her waist and jerked her close. He was going to kiss her! His look carved a path to her *décolletage*, his hand clasped her side from rib to hip. He tipped her back, she arched, pressing her bosoms against the stitching of her bodice, and then, just before his lips met hers, he pulled her up, flipped her over his knee and swatted her bottom.

"You," he said, letting her go, "are a scamp, and I

ought to give you a real spanking."

"Shall I hold onto a bell as the blows fall?"

He laughed. "Oh dear God, what am I going to do with you?"

"Kiss me."

"I'm engaged to another woman."

"She doesn't suit."

"And who ever does?"

"Me."

The playful hints of green left his eyes as the brown deepened to seriousness. "You're too late, you're too young, and you can't provide what I need."

"I'll be of age tomorrow and I come with an enormous dowry."

He shook his head, and there was sadness and regret in the gesture. Taking her hand, he singled out her index finger and tapped her nose with it. "I need Society, and you are not Society. You'll never be Society, my little Exmoor pony."

"Marry me all the same," she whispered, her soul proffering itself like a hapless creature on an altar.

Slowly, reluctantly, he released her finger. "That's not going to happen." He turned toward the internal ladder to the tower. "Time to go."

"Wait!" Snap caught his sleeve. "Now you're angry. I won't come down if you're angry."

"I'm not."

"But it's there in your eyes." She snatched his hands, and led him deeper into the belfry. "Let's do something fun, and I promise not to propose anymore. Teach me to waltz—absolutely no one will—they say it's too *risqué*, but you're a marvelous dancer—the Dowager Lady Davenport swears to it."

He looked at her incredulously. "There's a massive gap in this floor. Do you want to die flattened on the floor of the nave?"

"Pish, I'll be safe in your arms."

She raced to the farthest bell, and with her fingernails, tapped out the tune to the Sussex Waltz. And oh, Heaven be praised, that smile returned and mischief glinted in his eyes. She tapped louder, and louder still, until he laughed outright.

"You're a wicked little siren." He leaped easily over the gap, and snatched her hands from the bell.

She stood close and put her palms on his shoulders.

"The dance begins apart."

But Snap didn't let him go. "I'm not interested in that part. What are the steps when we twirl together?"

For a moment, he looked as if he'd resist.

"Please," she begged.

"So the price of losing the race is dance lessons and Byron?"

She nodded happily. "Now where do my feet go?"

Those powerful hands, roped with veins, square at the wrist, and creased with use, rested on her shoulders. Snap gazed deep into his hazel eyes, noting with a rush that a ring of fawn surrounded the pupil. The color gave way at the edge of the iris to flecks of yellow, green, and a hint of blue.

"Look at my feet," he said, tilting her head down. "I step forward with my left, while you step back with the right." His grip on her resumed, and he nudged her foot back. "Then we slide to your left and close with feet together."

"Ahhh."

After a few faltering tries, the waltz's three-quarter

time seeped into her muscles. He quit calling the steps and hummed the Sussex Waltz, turning her in a circle, and then another and another, until they were flying around the bells so close to the gap she felt the breeze on her ankles.

The pace grew faster, and Snap threw back her head, laughing with exhilaration, and suddenly she was airborne as he lifted her in a wide arc over the gap. She screamed with delight, so around they went again, and he lifted her higher, her slippers grazing a brass bell as he brought her down to the wood once more. Elation stole her breath, strangling her shrieks of joy.

In the distance, Lizzie yelled, "No rascality, you hear!"

He slowed then, halted, and guided her to a neat turn under his arm. "And that, my sweet hellion, is how to waltz."

Instead of releasing her hand, his wicked grin dissolved and something tragic and longing filled his gaze.

Your place is with me.

She wished she could say it out loud without driving him away. She tightened her grip, and his fingers lightly squeezed hers back.

Looking at the sky beyond their stone nest, he said, "I wish…"

But at that moment, a shout came from outside. "Ay! it's me rum duchess, waitin' by the church. Let's say we get the vicar and make a night of it, eh?"

The laborers were back.

Chapter 25

Snap gave the bell pull a good yank and returned to her dressing table where she thrummed her fingers on its polished surface, thinking, thinking. "Quickly, Lizzie," she called just as footsteps ceased outside her door.

Lizzie burst into the room, slightly out of breath. "You're up to something. I could tell by the force of the clang."

"You enjoyed Gunter's, did you not?"

"It were a sight more entertaining than that peawitted fool at the church." The maid paused, squinting suspiciously: "What'd ya want with Gunter's?"

"And there was that charming young man—the tangerine waiter who plied you with every sweet in the shop at great expense to me—you'd like to see him again, yes?"

"Tangerine?" Lizzie's lips thinned.

Snap pivoted in her chair and waved a one-pound note in the maid's direction. "Buy yourself a giant ice, but ask your paramour for the use of a pair of trousers, a jacket, shirt, vest, and shoes."

"He ain't my paramour, and he's about five times taller'n you."

"It's a full pound, Lizzie. Imagine what fun you and Mr…?"

"Stainton."

"You and Mr. Stainton could have with it: the show at Astley's Amphitheatre, Vauxhall Gardens, Drury Lane…"

"I'd see Ranelagh Gardens, but I wouldn't touch toe in Drury Lane."

"Why ever not?" But as Lizzie's mouth opened to reply, Snap raised a commanding hand. "Never mind all that. I shall give you this princely sum, but only in return for a set of men's clothes. Will you ask him?"

Instead of taking the bill, Lizzie folded her arms. "Your come out party's a day hence. Ain't it time to learn to be ladylike instead of boy-like?"

"Oh pish, there's nothing I don't know about all that prissy folderol."

Lizzie's left brow rose.

Snap lifted both brows. "English servants are supposed to be deferential and excessively loyal."

"And English ladies are supposed to be mannerly and quiet, so we're even."

They glared at one another.

****

Gareth slowed his mare but kept her at a collected trot past the Earl of Davenport's Mayfair abode. The home's white limestone and black trim windows were awash in afternoon sunlight, and Park Lane bustled with high steppers drawing handsome barouches. In each was arranged a colorful display of ladies in ostrich topped bonnets.

He was pleased to note that Lopey's sporty red-wheeled gig stood out from the crowd. The carriage's excellent construction and the fineness of the horse—a gleaming chestnut—were reminders of his fiancée's largess. Of course, Snap might have an equal portion. No, no she wouldn't—a sizable dowry, perhaps, but not multiple estates, not an established house in Belgrave Square.

He studied the mansion's windows and wondered what her room might be like. Were her nightclothes adorned with lace, or simple and straightforward?

A little of each. His groin tightened.

Ugh! Dragging his unruly brain from her bedchamber, he forced himself to list her worst qualities: she's reckless and impulsive. She prefers adventuring to running a household. That means the poor sod who marries her, will have that burden added to the list. She'll do well charming natives in exotic locales—expeditions he, fortunately, no longer desired.

Yesterday's romp up the tower was purely nostalgia-based, amusing, but far from how he wished to spend his days. Clementine and Laura, safe in the protection of the husband of a powerful and wealthy woman. Uncle Wadsworth banished forever and powerless to blackmail him. With all Lopey's money, he'd be a man of leisure. That meant evenings at White's, gambling like a gentlemen instead of collecting their bloody debts.

I can't wait for the morning's wedding bells. No, I can't...

Just as he steered his horse down Hereford Street to be out of view from the Davenport home, a boy in an absurdly large hat, a forest green jacket, trousers, and canary vest leaped into the gig and shouted, "Trot up!"

The chestnut sprang into action, the gig's movement nearly tossing Gareth off the back.

"Damn your eyes!" he shouted, about to shove the

urchin from its perch.

And then the little scoundrel peeked from under the hat, training a pair of glorious, seductive, and mischievous blues on him.

"Damn your eyes," he repeated, unable to suppress a surge of desire. "Damn your eyes…"

****

Four footmen surrounded Uncle Hassan, who greeted his guests in the drive outside of a relatively modest Tudor home. His short, paw-like arm circled above a substantial paunch in a gesture of welcome.

"We're out in the field. Follow the cut grass," he said. The man was chinless—a puffed wattle quivering beneath full lips, his head tilted high, giving him the aspect of an animal sniffing the air.

If a beaver could walk upright, it would look like Uncle Hassan.

"Will you introduce me to your young friend?" the beaver asked.

"Of course, Uncle Hassan," Gareth said, gesturing at Snap. "This is…is…"

"Melrose Carbingle." She shook Hassan's paw.

With obvious difficulty, their host stifled some sort of strong emotion, but Gareth emitted an explosive guffaw he turned into a cough.

"He's my cousin," Gareth said. "Here to recover from a bout of madness." He took her arm and headed toward the grass path. "Melrose Carbingle…"

"The name came to me in a flash."

"He knows you're a woman. Those clothes are so long you look like something drying on a line."

"All the better for your reputation as a rake."

"Not if Lopey gets wind of it."

Snap halted. "You want the pearls, yet you don't want me to be seen in public, and the likeliest way for Lady Whitlocke to learn about tonight is if Finnegan, who after all is a poet, tells her. Ergo, I have concocted an excellent disguise."

****

Gareth grunted. As ridiculous as her outfit might be, he couldn't help but notice she looked irresistible in it, her pink cheeks and lakes of blue gaily peering out from under that horrendous hat.

Oh, to smother her in kisses, to lower her onto white sheets and... He beat his thigh until the pain brought his thoughts under control.

"Are you all right?"

"Leg cramp."

They walked on.

"Is Uncle Hassan on your mother or father's side?"

"Neither. He's a man who likes his friends to call him uncle."

They entered an evergreen forest sparsely lit by oil lamps dotted along the path.

"And from which side does Baron Wadsworth hail?"

He took a deep breath. "Mother's. The man was born a twitching, wretched monster, and he hated her concern more than he hated his parents' disgust. If Mother found him after a fit, stiff and unconscious, she'd stay till he woke. Yet the rotter would screech till she fled. 'No one can love an abomination,' he told her. "I'll take the scraps God cursed me with and serve them cold.' So, though she alone cared for him, when she needed help, he..."

****

Before Snap could learn more about the villain who sought to steal her family's greatest treasure, the trees cleared, revealing a line of bonfires illuminating a rock promontory. Black shadows cut the rock's jagged surfaces, restless light caught its plains, and nothing seemed substantial. It was as if fairies, witches, and warlocks might lift the scene by the tips of their wands and loft it to the clouds.

A shiver slid down her spine. As they came nearer, she heard voices. The silhouette of a crowd of men in dark coats, reared dark on dark against the rocks. There were no women. None. She could barely contain her excitement.

"Thank you." She found Gareth's hand and kissed each knuckle. He didn't draw away. "A million times, thank you."

He tried to linger at the back of the crowd, but she escaped and pushed to the front just as George Gordon, Lord Byron himself, appeared on a ledge six feet up the side of the promontory. Wild applause erupted. She clapped too. Her heart mushroomed until it hurt.

Before the great poet uttered a word, a hand pulled her behind a short fellow in a tailcoat.

"Stay unobtrusive," Gareth whispered, "or your backside will pay for it."

The gravity of his threat gave her delicious goosebumps. She pressed close, letting his body heat her rump. He didn't step away.

"I stood in Venice, on the Bridge of Sighs," Byron read in a sonorous voice. "A palace and a prison on each hand: I saw from out the wave her structures rise, as from the stroke of the enchanter's wand."

In her lifetime, Snap never expected to see a man

quite as romantically attractive. Byron's black curls banked above a high forehead, his long pale cheeks sinking into eyes dark with emotion. There was nothing friendly about her hero—his focus was inward—so that her mind hummed with longing to shift his attention to herself. She sighed, thinking she could happily stand in this crowd all night and listen to his verses. Gareth gave her a little shake.

Ah, he's jealous. He senses when I'm not thinking of him.

Deep into the fourth canto of "Childe Harold's Pilgrimage", distant bells tinkled.

"From thy Sire's to his humblest subject's breast

Is linked the electric chain of that despair,

Whose shock was as an earthquake's, and oppressed

The land which loved thee so, that none could love thee best."

Byron shuffled the page to the back of a pile in his hand. The tinkling grew louder, and then a goat bounded into view, taking a place on the promontory beside the great poet. Another and another of the animals collected about him, tilting their heads in curiosity, listening as he read on, as if they'd been summoned by the devil in exchange for the music of his words.

Silhouetted against the moonlit night, the scene was so magical, tears rolled down her cheeks. When she wiped them away, Gareth rested a hand on her shoulder. His fingers absentmindedly stroked her neck and curled a strand of her hair, yet even his touch couldn't distract her from Byron's figure. The bonfires cast gold and shadows across his troubled brow, the goats watched like the forces of indulgence that dragged the poet into the depths of despair.

"Farewell! with Him alone may rest the pain,

If such there were—with You, the moral of his strain."

Byron swept the sheaf of papers high with a flourish, then bending into a bow, he swung them back and accidently dropped them. Most of the composition scattered on the ground in a shower of white pages, but many swept skyward on the updraft caused by the bonfires. As if they too were pages, the goats sprinted away, leaping from rock to rock, springing and brandishing their horns in a dance of delight.

Before she could rein herself in, Snap clambered onto the outcropping and hand-over-hand, headed for the nearest page. Once she'd secured it in a vest pocket, she climbed higher, past the light of the bonfires, deep into the shadowed cracks and crevasses of the cliffside, collecting the precious verses as she went.

High on the cliff and inches from capturing a page, the wind tossed it back into the sky where it whirled to the peak of the promontory. Determined to retrieve the page, Snap studied the cliff's surface for her next move.

A crack so deep the bottom was obscured, blocked her climb. It ran about three feet across but presented a sheer rockface on both sides. In fact, she couldn't find a single, reachable hand or foothold. Leaving her vantage point on a narrow shelf, she descended about ten feet to find another path, but conditions were even worse. The promontory appeared unscaleable.

Never having met a rockface she couldn't conquer, Snap scrambled back onto the shelf to see if she'd missed something, when movement below caught her attention. Through the dark rose a darker being, a man moving quickly, efficiently, as if he'd mounted this crag a thousand times. Snap's heart fluttered, beating faster as Gareth drew himself onto the shelf with her and stood so close, his breath tickled her hair. Would he scold? Would he insist she go down?

Before a word could pass his teeth, she blurted, "There's a page I think landed on the top. There may be others."

"Ahh. But a bit madcap of you to go sprinting off like that. The audience may want to know the mountaineer, and Mr. Carbingle, your disguise is… lacking."

Snap twisted her lip. "But it's *Byron*."

He rested a hand on her back. "Irresistible, eh?"

She nodded.

Turning his attention to the crack, he assessed it a moment, then put a hand on her shoulder. Sure he would call off the hunt, she was startled when he said, "Steady me."

Leaning on her, he eased off his boots and stockings. Carefully he extended a leg across the chasm until his bare foot lay flat against the rock surface. Easing himself into position, he put his back flat against the near wall of the crack, and with a nimble lurch, braced his other leg on the far wall. Now, suspended above the chasm, he pushed up with his hands. Maintaining pressure with one leg, he took a step.

In a state of fear and wonder, Snap watched as he rose up the crack to the summit, hooked his elbows over the edge, levered his body onto its surface, and disappeared from view. "You're the pirate!" she shouted.

He peered over the edge. "Hush, or they'll all come bounding after us."

"We met at Lady Pemneux's ball," she whispered. "I was the young lady in the reflecting pool."

His laughter rumbled down the crevasse—butter and honey—just like she remembered.

"You shimmied to the roof of the portico the same way, except between pillars. Not a farthing was pillaged that night. My sisters said the only event I missed was the ballroom getting hotter."

"Sorry to disappoint. It was a bad night for pirating."

"It was a dreadful deception. I'm coming up to chastise you." She bent to untie her laces.

"It's not a climb for novices. Why don't you start on something that won't kill you?"

"But you could talk me through."

"I can, but I'd rather not watch you plummet to your death."

Having removed her stockings, she planted a foot on the far wall. "I trust you, even if you're not a pirate."

Chapter 26

The instant Snap was within reach, he caught a fistful of her collar and held on, but the lithe little thing navigated the transition from chasm to summit perfectly. "You're quite the summiteer. I didn't know a woman existed who would try such a stunt."

"I'm not afraid of heights."

It occurred to him that Lopey had probably never scaled anything higher than a footstool. "Your talent is quite extraordinary."

Snap smiled. "Those are very nice words coming from a nonpirate."

He forgot to reply. She stood so straight and fearless he could do nothing but admire her. A long minute passed. Even in the dark of night, her eyes sparkled with mischief.

"Do you want to kiss me again?"

"No." Though the true answer was a resounding yes.

The little rantipole aimed a piercing look. "I don't believe you."

He didn't feel like adding another lie. Instead, he scanned the rocks. "Where do you think those verses landed?"

She found two while he collected a page that tried to hide itself in a tight fissure.

As she slid the sheets into her vest, a gust of wind

skipped up the promontory and took Snap's oversized hat with it. Gareth lunged to catch the errant *chapeau*, but, hopping and dropping on freshets of air, it disappeared below. With the next stiff breeze, hanks of Snap's hair escaped their pins, creating a tufted, lopsided mess.

"Lud, what a bumble broth," she said. "I can't saunter through that crowd with my hair in disarray. They'll spot my sex in two shakes." She searched her scalp for pins, then attempted to fasten the boisterous locks into a semblance of order.

"Cease, cease," he said, as the construction formed a nest of ragged ends and lumps. After removing the pins, he combed his fingers through her tresses, gently separating snarls strand by strand.

"That feels lovely. Lizzie tugs too hard. I wish you were my lady's maid."

"Your father would still recognize me in a dress."

Chuckling softly, she leaned against his chest, then slid down the length of his body to perch on a rock outcropping. "Sit behind me, please. I want you to keep taming my hair."

This is a mistake. If Lopey found out...

But the feel of her lustrous mane, the breeze, the sensuous peace of this moment... He sank to the ground and lifted her heavy locks, letting them flow through his fingers. She moved his legs to sit between them and slid back close to his chest.

"Someday, I'll visit the Far East. Have you been there?"

"We sneaked into Siam. Officially, trade with Europeans is prohibited, but Father made a secret arrangement to buy silk. They paint with gold, intricate patterns so tiny it seems impossible a human hand created them. They use elephants to build their temples, and the people are finely featured. It's very beautiful."

"Would you like to return?"

"Oh, yes," Gareth said. "I mean no. No, I'm past all that."

Far below, the bonfires burned, and a handful of musicians strummed guitars. The music rose in muffled notes, velvety and sweet, and the audience shifted about, their silhouettes breaking the firelight.

When his arms grew tired, he rested them on her shoulders and caressed her throat and cheek, but only dreamed of planting kisses in the fragrant hollow beneath her jaw.

"We need to stay here until they leave," she whispered.

Closing his eyes, he brushed that hollow with his lips. "Yes."

****

As the gig bounced over loose stones on the way back to London, Gareth struggled to remain somber despite Snap's avalanche of delight. He harrumphed and grunted as she prattled on with unrepentant bliss. Repeatedly, he tilted his hat her way to hide a grin.

"Raptures, that's what I'm in," she gushed. "Wasn't it beautiful so high up? How I adore a mountain top. And Byron was magical—such a handsome, tortured soul. But you, you're my pirate, which is so much better even than Byron. No wonder I went mad for you the night of the ball. Do you know, all I saw was a little of your mustache, yet somehow I must have sensed you. What did you see of me? Did you think about me?"

"You were naught but a blur of white."

That was a bit of a lie. Her gown was a light smudge on dark water, true. But when she raised her skirt, imagination filled in the view.

"Don't you think we should come back tomorrow and explore that outcropping? Perhaps a sheet of his poem was lost. We could present it to him with the rest of the canto. We could pack a picnic and watch the goats in the field. Ask Uncle Hassan, he's very fond of you."

An inward groan nearly escaped as she playfully pulled him around to face her in the swinging light of the carriage lamp.

Your wedding is only a day hence.

"Uncle Hassan's only vaguely fond of me, and I promised Lopey I'd be by to check her ledgers and discuss last-minute wedding details."

"Don't go on about it," said Snap tucking closer still, her warm body causing his blood to thrum. "Magical nights are rare gifts that shouldn't be spoiled by thoughts of chores."

"Marrying Lopey is not a chore."

He willed his body to shift away on the gig's seat. It failed to respond.

Holding his arm, she turned so her breast brushed his biceps. "Lady Whitlock's ledgers are safe on the shelf, and the baron would be so much happier if you kept my company."

"I'm not risking my very imminent marriage for his sake. And it was foolish of me to let you risk injuring yourself clambering all over rocks—especially so near your come out party."

Snap laughed. "Oh pish, why would I want to

marry a man who can't stomach a few scratches on his bride? And, why would a man who can captain a ship and steal horses from the enemy want to spend his days counting Finnegan's money?"

He winced. "Once Lady Whitlocke bears my ring on her finger—"

"But if we were together, we could use my dowry to travel and make our fortune in exotic lands. We could import horses like the Godolphin Arabian and gallop across the Devon moors. Byron would visit us and bring his pet bear. And at night, when poet and bruin are asleep, I will lie my head upon your shoulder, like this." She pulled the waves of her hair to one side. "And I'll let my cornsilk locks fall across your chest, like this, and—"

The bulge in his nether region, which had been threatening an appearance all evening, leaped to full height. His hands rose to pull back on the reins to slow the horse…to truly kiss her and feel the softness of her skin against his lips, to…

Clementine. Laura.

Abruptly, he shoved Snap away. "Learn this: adulthood demands sacrifice. We cannot host Byron because we will nev—"

"Pish to that. There may be unpleasant things one is supposed to do: glide when you walk, fold your hands like a schoolmarm, stop climbing the drainpipe— you can submit to all of them without dying of boredom. Everyone says if I don't grow up I won't be acceptable to Society. Well, I think sitting around a stuffy drawing room talking about who you know and how much they have is the most unpleasant thing of all. If that's what adults do, I'm not going to bother." She turned away and stared furiously at the night-blackened landscape.

"Everyone in England—nay, everyone in the world—wants to be in British society," he thundered. "Devil take it, I fought a war to raise my rank; I courted widows for money and access; I spend every ha'penny Lopey gives me on lacey cuffs and fitted jackets; and all you have to do is stay away from drainpipes? You silly little chit, you have no idea of the gold you want to cast aside."

She whipped around, and from the lamplight on the gig her eyes ferociously glittered. "I'll never be acceptable, and neither will you. Except I'll be climbing mountains and drinking wine with Lord Byron while Lopey entertains Lady Pemneux in the parlor. And when you enter, they'll stop talking—both of them."

He jerked the horse to a stop. "Get out of the gig," he said, through gritted teeth.

"It's dark out, and I don't know how to get home."

"You spoiled little hooligan, get out!"

He gave her a push, but she clung to the back of the seat. "I won't go."

Beyond determined, he peeled her fingers off the railing one by one, yanked her across his knee, and then landed a few mighty smacks to her trouser-clad bottom.

She scrambled off in the only direction he'd allow: the dark, dirty road.

"I'll show you," she screamed. "I'll be sailing to Siam, and you'll be Lopey's fat accountant!"

Bursting with cold-hearted rage, he twitched the reins, and the horse broke into a trot. An instant later, Snap raced to the animal's side, then, holding onto the harness collar, she vaulted onto its back and took control of the reins.

With a cluck and a kick, she had him desperately clinging to the gig as it bounced precariously behind a horse in full gallop.

Chapter 27

The next morning, the bloody morning before his wedding, Springer, Rascal, and Mimi lay in a lump at his feet as he entered yet another pile of receipts into Lopey's bloody register. It had been a terrible slog since bleedin' sunrise. The embroidered vest he'd ordered for the wedding went missing from the tailor's, and Snap's remark about becoming a fat accountant nagged him so much he kept losing his place and having to start over. The humiliation she'd subjected him to—unable to control his own carriage horse as she rode it hell-bent-for-leather all the way to London.

Hell and damnation, he'd lost his place again!

He shifted a dog off his boot and stared hard at the ledger. One-hundred-eighty-four pounds, thirty-eight pence for rye seed to the Norfolk estate, add in forty-three pounds... The exhilaration of climbing those rocks and the feel of Snap's lithe body, her hard little bones and taut muscles when he'd given her that spanking...

"Devil take it!" he exclaimed, realizing he'd lost his place for the umpteenth time.

She was wrong, of course. Life with Lopey was exactly what he'd dreamed of: money, respectability, the finest clothes, horses, clubs, and above all, the power to keep Laura and Clementine safe...

I can't wait to be leg shackled.

Rocking back in his chair, he stared out the window. By God, Snap had bested him though. Made him look a regular idiot with his horse barreling into the stable yard... And that grin she planted on him, full of teeth and triumph. A laugh caught him by surprise. He looked for the perpetrator, then realized he was the one chuckling. He fought off a mouth-stretching smile.

Rascal planted two paws on Gareth's thigh—tail wagging and liquid eyes begging for a game of fetch.

"She doesn't know me at all, but she got me good, didn't she?" he said with a full-throated laugh as he tousled Rascal's fur.

His distracted state of mind wasn't because he was fond of Snap... He was, but she was a menace to everything he'd sacrificed to achieve. That didn't mean she had no desirable qualities... He swallowed. Desirable qualities that gnawed at him. The itch was like some deep addiction, terrible for his health, yet irresistible. It had to be because the mad little thing was always up to something amusing. Snap's company was akin to watching a Punch and Judy show. Just a trifling diversion in an otherwise normal day. He chuckled again.

Rascal whined and rested his snout on Gareth's knee. He was about to abandon the register and succumb to the dog's blandishments when the door opened.

"What are you so merry about?" said Lopey.

He lied. "Ach, the dogs. You know how they can do silly things."

She raised her lorgnette. "No, if it were the dogs, they'd all be standing, but only one is standing and the rest are lying down. Furthermore, they're looking at me. No, decidedly you were not laughing at something they did." She lowered the eyepiece.

Unwilling to explain, he changed the subject. "Who have you set out roses for in the front hall?"

Lopey gave a slight shrug. "Lady Dalrymple-Ross. She adores the smell of roses."

"She's visiting today? I've always wanted to meet her."

He waited for Lopey to invite him now that they were betrothed, but she dipped her head and fingered the gold edge of her lorgnette. At that moment, a starling slammed into the window. The lorgnette dropped and Lopey cut him a stricken look. His heart sank.

"Ah, well then," he said, turning to the register and dipping his quill. "Enjoy her company, my darling, I've got to get back to these sums."

She remained in the doorway a moment, as the back of his neck heated, then she quietly closed the door. A moment later, a tap sounded at the window. The dogs rose as one, every nose pointed toward the sound. He scarcely heard it. Was that how it would be in his marriage, his socially significant wife entertaining the high and mighty as he skirted the periphery? Would it be as Snap predicted?

"Damn and blast it!" he growled as the numbers blurred into columns of black.

Tap, tap.

Gareth didn't look up. Once Laura and Clementine were secure, life with Lopey would have its compensations—she was a calm, intelligent, if eccentric, companion, rich beyond measure. Whether he could chum around with every titled gent at White's or not, didn't really matter. What did matter was love—No, mutual respect. Mutual respect was what mattered... that's what led to happiness.

The tap sounded again, but this time so loudly that the glass rattled in the sill. Mimi stood on her hind legs to see, Rascal barked, and Springer did both. Disturbed by the commotion, he caught Snap's red-cheeked face peering in.

"Great God Almighty, what the devil do you think you're doing?"

"Open the window."

"Hold onto something! Bloody hell, it's four stories up." He yanked open the window and grabbed her by the collar, dragging her over the sill.

She untucked her skirt, which she'd hoisted between her legs and tied with string at the waist. "I wanted to let you know I can't go mountain climbing today," she announced.

"I never said I'd take you in the first place."

"Mama says I have the final fitting for my gown. *The* gown. The one for my come out. So I can't go."

"We weren't going."

"But you must come see my dress and tell me what you think. You know all the fashions, and what suits and doesn't suit, so you must let me know before it's too late."

"Why would I know the first thing about ladies' fashion?"

Snap put her hands on her hips. "Are you saying you won't come?"

He shook his head in disbelief. "Tomorrow is my wedding day. And even if I were to come, how am I supposed to offer my opinion? Knock politely and expect your mama to usher me to the sewing room?"

"You're in a dreadful mood today. Have you all noticed?" she said, addressing the dogs. They replied by whacking her skirt with their tails.

"If I'm the least bit out of sorts, it's your fault," he growled.

"Pish. If anyone should be put out, it's me. You spanked me, after all."

"As if you didn't deserve it."

"Because I said you'd never be accepted by the swells? Lud, nothing makes people madder than the truth."

He would have yelled, he would have stomped his foot, if Lopey hadn't just proved the wench correct by closing the door on a visit with Lady Dalrymple-Ross. Instead, he sat back in his wooden chair at the desk and closed the ledger that tracked Lopey's fortune, all of which would be Finnegan's someday.

"What kind of disastrous scheme have you cooked up so I can see you in this new gown?"

With a little hop, Snap planted her pert behind on the corner of the desk. "There's a tree on the park side of the house. All you have to do is enter through the garden gate, which is quite hidden, sneak through the shrubbery, then shimmy up the tree to the roof. I'll meet you there."

A bark of laughter broke his stunned silence. "You are destined for Bedlam. A grown man does not climb trees for rooftop assignations with young ladies. Especially captains in the British Army with a wedding to attend in the morning."

Instead of frowning, objecting, or at least abandoning her spot on the desk, Snap fixed him with eager eyes and leaned close, hands clasped in excitement. "You'll adore it on our roof. I wouldn't ask if I didn't think you would. It's like being atop the promontory. The park is so pretty, it goes on for miles, and you can spy on the riders and nannies. I've even seen couples doing the most shocking things. Please come. The seamstress will be there at three, we eat dinner at five, so you should arrive at seven because Papa and Mama and the rest of the family linger at the table blathering about the Roman conquest and Parliament until I'm mad with boredom."

Gareth folded his arms. "I won't be there. Don't expect me."

She slid off the desk, and bold as brass, gave him a peck on the forehead. "I do so value your opinion. Who knows what damage I could do to my reputation without your help." Then, with ghostly grace, she drifted toward the door, accompanied by the gentle rustle of her silk dress, and her slender fingers enclosed the handle.

He bolted from his seat, snagged her by the waist and hauled her to the other side of the room. "You can't go out that way, Lopey's downstairs."

Snap looked confused. "I could tell her I came to see Finnegan."

"And flew in the window? Besides, she'd know you were lying."

A wild gleam lit her blues. "You feel guilty about me."

At that moment, he realized he still held her in his arms, and worse, that he wanted to keep her there. With a flinch worthy of a hot coal, he let her go.

"Perhaps I can sneak you out the kitchen door."

"Oh, I wouldn't. Servants see everything. Kitchens are the most likely places to start a scandal. I'll just climb back down the way I came."

He threw open the window. "It's four stories of brick, and a sheer drop to the garden. You'll land in a bloody heap and have more tongues wagging than hounds after a hunt."

"Window box, drainpipe; window box, drainpipe; window box, drainpipe, ledge," she replied, pointing out footholds. "Climbing this house is simple as a truant schoolboy."

He shut the window. "You're daft enough as it is, the last thing you need is to split that crown of yours and let the rest of your brains fall out."

"Did you hear that?" She crouched to rub Mimi the pug's velvety ear. "Your master cares about me."

"Humph."

Sunlight illuminated her pale locks and highlighted her full, pink lips and delicately blushed cheeks. Even her grubby fingers with their dirt-blackened nails, were elegant and long.

Damn and blast it, but she was pretty.

He didn't dare peek at the plump breasts, plumper still as she leaned over the mutt. Kiss her, his body commanded. Lopey's power, his brain countered. Swallowing, he took Snap by the shoulders and faced her toward the door.

"Follow me, and stay close."

All three dogs rose as one, and gathered about his legs. He waited for Snap to join the entourage.

"What's the plan?" she whispered.

He tried to keep his voice matter-of-fact, but the adventure quickened his pulse. "Out the front. The

219

butler hates the dogs; he'll avoid the entrance hall if he knows they're coming."

"Want to go out?" he asked the pack.

Immediately, Springer barked, Mini ravaged the door with both paws, and Rascal whined and turned circles.

"Want to go out?" he said again. "Walkies? Walkies?"

The animals leaped and barked in a full-out frenzy. Just as Mini was about the attack the jamb with her teeth, and Springer was climbing under a wildly barking Rascal, Gareth threw open the door and the dogs barreled out in a seething mass of fur.

Quickly, he followed the skittering claws down the hall to the stairs, Snap gripping the back of his coat. Just as they reached the mid-stair landing, Lady Dalrymple-Ross burst in the front entrance with the butler directly behind her.

"Lawks!" the woman shrieked as the herd of canines careened past.

"My lady…," Gareth said. "We were just…"

He looked toward Snap, but she'd vanished. Taking a step after her, Lady Dalrymple-Ross halted him in mid-stride.

"Captain Hart, surely you're not going to let that crazed pack race through London unsupervised?"

Word was, Lopey's guest enjoyed her widowhood more than her departed husband might have expected. The woman, who always dressed in the latest fashion and groomed so nary a hair floated free, flirted like a Covent Garden doxy. He chuckled.

"I'll catch up with the hounds in a trice. Care to join the pursuit?"

Stroking her fan across her cheek, she offered a smoldering look. "Perhaps they'd enjoy a game of chase in my garden? I'll hold the stick."

"Isn't that tug of war?"

"If that's what they're calling it these days."

He flashed his pearly whites. "*Touché,* my lady."

He enjoyed repartee as much as any man, but the vision of Snap leading his dogs into who knew what sort of mischief distracted his wits before he could think of a comeback.

"Your pardon, before my canines cause calamity."

As he bowed out the door, she blew him a kiss.

****

Gareth found the dogs in the garden peeing on a statue, digging up a lily, and threatening a squirrel on a tree limb fifteen feet above its harasser.

Returning to the house, he sauntered past the gargantuan bouquet of roses in the foyer and into the saloon, anticipating a brandy and more verbal volleying. But Lady Dalrymple-Ross and Lopey were leaning close in an attitude that spelled secrets. Their conversation stopped the instant they saw him. Lopey adopted a bright, broad smile that left no doubt in his mind they'd been talking about him.

"Discussing your mode of dress for tomorrow?" he asked Lady Dalrymple-Ross.

Her expression turned icy and tinged with scorn. "Unfortunately, I won't be able to attend the ceremony."

She pivoted away, crushing the possibility of further exchange—the aristocrats' well-practiced signal that one had violated the limits of their station. Gareth felt sick. Lopey must not have told her friends about their wedding. Lady Dalrymple-Ross merely staked her position: you are a commoner, and regardless of whom you marry, you'll amount to nothing more.

Lopey emitted a nervous giggle. "My darling, shall we ride later?"

"That would be pleasant." His mouth went dry as sand.

"Excellent." Lopey nodded—an unspoken dismissal.

He took the dogs for a long walk in Hyde Park. There was no point in returning to the manse or the ledger books. Concentration was impossible, even if he were tied to a chair and beaten with cattails. If he married Lopey, would she be exiled too? Her title would be gone; she'd spend the rest of her life as Mrs. Gareth Hart, wife of a former collector of gambling debts. But Clementine, Laura... Snap and the Fitzcarry pearls... If he didn't marry Lopey, they wouldn't be safe. Only money and influence could keep them beyond Baron Wadsworth's reach.

When the dogs were panting with exhaustion, he wandered back to Lopey's. His uncle had left no instructions to harass anyone for money, so the rest of the day dragged as Lopey and Lady Dalrymple-Ross unwittingly discussed the fate of a little girl, her mother, and a set of priceless pearls.

Later, he and Lopey toured Rotten Row. Her perfectly matched carriage horses held a sedate pace, and she looked splendid in her finest afternoon regalia. As they weaved among the other vehicles, she conversed with her friends. She spoke of Parliament with Lord Spencer, and of Parliament with Bunny Dugdale, and again about Parliament with the Earl of

Arundel.

For the first time in Gareth's life, he found that he didn't admire their opinions. In fact, they all made silly, uninformed statements about how the lower classes needed stronger deterrents to bad behavior, and how lucky the citizens of Peshawar were now that an Englishman governed them. The whole chinless lot of them unexpectedly grated on his nerves.

"I won't be supping with you tonight, Lopey," he said, as the horses pranced toward their stable. "We shouldn't see one another before the wedding, and I've some unpleasant business for my uncle. You won't miss me, will you?"

"It must be difficult business indeed," she replied. "You've been agitated all day."

"I haven't."

"Well, the horses say otherwise. They've tossed their heads repeatedly."

"Horses do toss their heads, my darling. It's hardly abnormal behavior."

"Humm," she said, then turned to nod at a colorful bouquet of feminine occupants in a passing barouche.

"You're not harboring second thoughts, are you?" Lopey asked.

"About my business tonight? No, no, not at all."

"Our nuptials, dear, our nuptials."

"Great heavens, no!" he nearly shouted. "I feel as if I've waited for you all my life."

Instead of pinking with pleasure, she offered an unsmiling nod. Then suddenly, a cloud clogged the sun and an oversized raindrop plunked onto her nose. She squeaked with alarm and brushed off the drop as if it were a spider.

Gritting his teeth, Gareth said, "Right then," and prayed she wouldn't interpret the rain as yet another omen.

He flipped the reins and the horses broke into a speedy, undignified canter.

Chapter 28

In the sewing room, Snap stood on a small platform as a seamstress fussed at the hem of an exquisite white cotton gown patterned with intricate embroidery.

Lizzie sprawled on a stack of fabric in the corner, tossing her knife in the air and catching it; Peggity occupied a footstool; Ellie perched on the cutting table, and Claire stood beside Ellie, studying a sheet of parchment blackened with lists containing the menu, the flowers, the names of musicians, and the chalk artist who, on the ballroom floor, had created a massive depiction of a ship on the high seas. Captain Hart was at the helm, though no one but Snap would know that.

"White soup," Claire said, reading off the paper.

"The night will be roasting," Snap replied. "You can't serve hot soup in June."

"But everyone has white soup at their come out," Peggity insisted.

The door slammed open and Mrs. Gower blew in like a load of snow off a carriage roof. "Merciful heavens," she panted. "So many stairs, it's indecent." Limping pointedly to Peggity, she waited for the Duchess of Hanesford to abandon the footstool.

"Allow me to offer my seat, Mrs. Gower," said Peggity, rolling her eyes for Snap's view alone.

"Don't you think the bodice should be lower?"

Snap asked the chaperone as the woman settled her bulk over the seat's three legs.

The urgency of luring Gareth away from Lopey could not be more dire. If she couldn't change his mind, tomorrow would begin with his wedding ceremony and end with her come out party. Tonight on the roof, was her last chance at happiness.

"The swells rode miles for a peek at my bubbies," said Mrs. Gower. "Of course, I had 'em to show—regular kettledrums they were."

The seamstress shot an alarmed look at Peggity.

"We don't want her appearing fast," her sister said.

"But I'm supposed to be a pearl, not an overdressed oyster," Snap argued.

Fanning herself, Mrs. Gower gave Peggity a severe look. "I know the bait that attracts the fish. Didn't I chaperone you into a happy marriage bed?"

"Not at first," Peggity mumbled.

The other siblings appeared to be fighting the giggles.

"Mrs. Gower knows that I have very specific notions about who I will or will not marry," said Snap. "And she agreed with me, didn't you Mrs. Gower?"

"And your list of demands weren't so far from the mark as to be unreasonable," the chaperone acknowledged, a pleased smile creasing her cheeks. "If memory serves, he's to have black hair, hazel eyes, be able to sail a shi—"

"Yes," Snap barked, drowning any further traits the woman might reveal. "All of that and more…"

A worried look crept into Ellie's face. "That sounds suspiciously like—"

"Have they brought the ice?" Snap asked, a little

too loudly.

"You're not still fixed on that Cap—"

"I'm going to serve ice in the punch. London will be in an uproar," Snap said, addressing the seamstress, "and everyone will dash over for a cup. Then we'll shock 'em by serving more and more. So much ice, the women will keep their shawls on!"

Claire's jaw dropped. "I thought Papa said he couldn't afford it."

"Mama approved the expense," said Snap, rejoicing that ice had supplanted Gareth as a topic.

Ellie and Peggity fell into a fervent argument with Mrs. Gower about the advisability of ice at a late June come out, while Snap, thoroughly pleased with herself, turned her back on her sisters just as the seamstress shifted to the rear of the gown. Executing a discreet head jerk, Snap roused Lizzie's attention. Stealthily, the lady's maid approached on tiptoe.

"Cut it an inch lower," Snap whispered, lifting her chest a fraction.

Lizzie gripped the edge of the delicate cotton bodice and sliced each side.

The seamstress peeked around the skirt.

Panicked, Snap said, "You're not at the right spot, Widcomb, I'll have to scratch my nose myself."

Lizzie faded into the corner as the dressmaker returned to the front of the gown. A sharp cry of dismay left her pin-filled lips.

"What's the trouble?" Claire asked.

"She poked herself," replied Snap, patting the seamstress's shoulder. "You poor, poor dear. Why don't you sit and recover a moment?"

Jerking the pins from her mouth, the woman

barked, "I do not need time." Her gaze darkened to storm clouds and lightning strikes. "But perhaps you require a different *modiste*."

"Oh no," Snap said, sweet and wide-eyed. "You are irreplaceable. A true master—or should I say, mistress—of your craft."

"What have you done, Nefertiti Albright?" Peggity said in her most commanding schoolmarm voice. She marched over and examined Snap with a military air.

"If I have to stand to see what all the fuss is, I promise my knees will buckle," cried Mrs. Gower.

In the next moment, the words "immodest," "ruin," and "reputation" were tossed like juggler's balls between the *modiste*, Peggity, Ellie, Mrs. Gower and occasionally, Claire. At the height of the ruckus, Lizzie slipped a small pouch of coins from Snap's reticule and surreptitiously passed it to the dressmaker.

A few deep breaths later, the seamstress cooed, "It's nothing, ladies. A slip of the scissors, is all."

As the clamor died, Snap studied herself in a full-length mirror.

He will not be able to resist me.

She turned to examine her right profile and then her left.

He will love me, and forget everyone else in the world.

****

The early evening light softened London's stone edifices, blurring the city's grimy streets and filling each hollow-eyed window with a hint of rose. In the lesser neighborhoods, mothers gathered on the front steps to gossip in the spring air, while their little ones scampered after round stones or played with rag dolls.

From the taverns, came the murmur of men who'd had just enough gin to be happy, but not enough to get them fighting. When he reached Mayfair, its streets were all but abandoned as gentlemen gathered at their clubs and ladies retired to cards and nips of ratafia.

At the back of the Davenport residence, Gareth stealthily cracked the garden gate. Its old hinges shrieked objections.

"Saint Criminy," he muttered, and, head down, quickly passed through.

Between the roses on a trellis just inside, he spied the house and got a good view of the garden. Not a soul stirred. Employing the same crouch he'd used on military missions, he made his way through a fringe of shrubs to the base of a towering oak. The tree possessed a conveniently long limb overhanging the roof. He gripped the lowest branch, pulled himself high enough to swing a leg over, and then scrambled to the next highest limb. By God, he'd spent a lot of time in trees during the war: spying, escaping, searching for food, stealing horses…

What in bloody hell are you doing? You should be readying yourself for your wedding.

With each surmounted branch, he chastised himself, yet up he climbed.

The most curious thing happened as he ascended, and at first he worried it might be a sign of ill health because his heart felt lighter. It was as if a barrel band loosened and gladness came bubbling through the slats. Two-thirds of the way up the oak, he caught himself springing like a ten-year-old from crook to sprig. When he finally climbed the mighty tree, he balanced on its overhanging bough then needlessly risked his life walking it without holding on. Elation poured from his un-sprung heart, worrying him that he'd lost his senses. Snap. Just the thought of her turned him into a pubescent lad.

Ridiculous! Sit back in the saddle and pull on the reins, man.

It unnerved him that his emotions could be jostled by a female as uncontrollable as a wild filly. He mused with hard practicality that Lopey's acceptance of his proposal was the best thing that had ever happened. He would be happy even if Society rejected him because he'd have saved his family.

And then Snap appeared. She came from around a blackened chimney like a gossamer sylph from the knotted trunk of an ancient tree.

"Hello," she said quietly.

By God, his blood shot like a geyser—the force of it pained him, and his mind went blank as paper.

"Do you admire the dress?" she said uncertainly, holding out its skirt.

He swallowed. "Let me look at you."

Facing her into the setting sun, he stepped back, giving the lump in his throat time to dissolve. Pink light warmed her pale skin and softened the white gown, lending definition to its pattern of alabaster flowers embroidered upon the snowy fabric. Throat tight, all he could think of was music—some as yet un-played melody that made him want to weep at its beauty.

"Great heavens," he said, his voice hitching, "the gown suits you."

She made to move toward him.

"No. Stay right there," he commanded.

A tendril of corn-silk hair blew across her chest,

catching in her *décolletage* and curling between her two pearly mounds. It was as if he'd never quite seen her before: the way she held her head, the intelligent light in her eyes, the delicate curve of fabric as it draped from waist to hip. By heaven, Snap was a woman—a real, honest to God woman... In a handful of hours, she had gone from a pretty girl, to...to this. With a rush of emotion, he knew he wanted her...

Snap shifted uneasily, and brushed away the errant strand of hair. "I probably shouldn't tell you this, but I'll wear the Fitzcarry pearls tomorr—"

"Shhhh," he said, continuing his study. "It's all right. I don't care about the pearls."

"But you're supposed to steal them for the baron."

When he didn't respond, Snap clasped her hands at her waist. "You're staring, Captain Hart, and it's discomfiting."

Gareth rubbed his eyes. "You're different in that dress."

"I feel elegant," she replied, her voice deeper, its music brushed with mature sensuality. "I'm looking down on other people somehow. Not in a mean way, but...something else...as if the whole world were mine to command."

Gareth chuckled. "It just may come to that."

A delighted smile tipped her plump lips. "So you approve of my gown?"

"You're ready for your come out, I'd wager..." He cleared his throat, and didn't know what else to say.

Then, through the haze of desire, rose Lopey's image. Bloody hell, he'd forgotten his fiancée, forgotten that by noon tomorrow, they'd be wed!

"I'll be going along now."

"Stay until the sun sets," said Snap, catching him as he pivoted to leave. "Truly, it's lovely from up here."

"Lopey needs me."

Wise blue eyes gazed back at him. "Not really."

True, Lopey didn't need him—he needed her.

"You won't see much of me after tonight," Snap said, the words edged with sorrow and bravery. "Maybe at a *soirée*, or in a passing barouche on Rotten Row."

If she begged or pleaded, he'd have an excuse to leave. Instead, she gathered her dress to sit.

He stopped her. "You'll ruin that frock on this sooty rooftop."

"You could put your jacket down."

"You'll see me in my shirt sleeves!"

"I know," said Snap, letting a smile play across her features.

"Outrageous chit…"

"I adore it when you call me 'outrageous chit.' It sounds like the nicest compliment."

He laughed. After removing the coat, he laid it on the slate shingles, then held her small-boned hand as she lowered herself onto it. Dressed in fawn-colored trousers, he intended to stand, but she made room for him and patted the jacket.

"Sit with me?" She tapped the fabric again.

I must return to Lopey this instant, or all will be lost. I must not waste another moment in the company of a young lady who will walk headlong into scandal…

He sat. She bowed her head, hiding a smile.

"Lizzie made the most surprising observation. She told me I know nothing about you. Not your history, and nary a jot about your family, so…I think it's time you confessed."

On the verge of saying no, he made the mistake of letting her beauty journey into his willpower and wreak havoc. But really, where was the harm? He couldn't deny her this sunset on the last night before...

"My parents came from wealth," he said. "Father inherited a fleet of merchant ships, but the manager pocketed the insurance premiums. Every farthing was lost when the fleet sank off the coast of Spain. They sold our estate to scrape together my Oxford fees and army commission. Two years later, Father died of consumption in a miserable fishing hut Uncle Wadsworth provided them at Bigbury-on-Sea. The town was so far, and so hard to get to... I had no idea of their living conditions until it... Until he was gone."

Her face crumpled in sympathy. "What a tragic tale."

"It is, rather. The war was so desolate—competing for rations, stealing blankets to keep from freezing, watching men die—yet, a cup of tea with my mother is what haunts me." He gazed at the orange sun split by a church spire as it sank beyond the park. "I was home on leave. She lived alone in that decrepit pile of rocks and thatch. From our house at Brighton, she'd saved one curtain: a gold brocade thing, heavily tasseled and trimmed. The rest of the room was nearly bare. We sat at a pine table, and she made tea. Mine, she steeped for several minutes, but her own..." He swallowed. "She poured the water through, and then put those sodden leaves back in the cupboard." His throat contracted so he pulled a cheroot from a gold case and fished a pouch with a striker, flint and tow from his pocket.

"Could you do anything for her?" Snap asked, after he'd expelled a lungful of smoke.

"The sorriest part of my story is how quickly I fell in with my uncle to keep Mother from that ungodly place. She thought working for him was a fine idea—poor thing never could see the deviltry in him. And of course, she had no idea how he made his money. But the fact is, I'd rather collect from these poor souls than let some brute in my uncle's employ do it. I captained ships for my father, and I led men in the army. I could have found a position in any office if I'd had the patience. Somehow, at the time, being stuck behind a desk seemed worse than roaming about pinching farthings from gamblers." He took a disgusted puff on the cheroot. "That was a decision I shall die regretting. And what about you?" he said, catching her profile in the apricot glow of the failing sun.

She reached for his cheroot, but he yanked it out of range. "No. It'll make you cough like the dickens."

"Don't worry. I've been smoking since I was a child."

"What?"

"Jack Nasty Face and the crew on the trawler used to get such a laugh out of little me smoking. Now I rather fancy the taste."

He shook his head and handed her the cigar. She took an expert puff, blew three smoke rings, and returned it to him.

"I had a perfectly lovely childhood, as you know, though after Uncle Sebastian died, it was lonely. Papa is always chest-deep in intellectual pursuits—Egypt and the Roman conquest mostly—and Mama helps him with his scientific studies, so my uncle was really the one who watched us. Every morning at ten, he would canter up the drive shouting, *'Ándele, ándele, vite, vite,*

vite!' which is Spanish for come and French for quickly, so my sisters and I would pile out of the house and swarm him to find out where we were off to that day. He took us swimming, galloping, hiking, climbing. Lawks, he didn't care a wit that boys go on adventures and girls sew and play the pianoforte.

"We gained the wickedest reputations. They called us 'unnatural hoydens,' which drove poor Peggity mad. She was forever telling people Uncle Sebastian didn't do this and didn't do that, but she needn't have bothered. People saw us. And Society damsels flocked to Uncle Sebastian, just as they do you. He said we were his bulwark against the horde. They'd travel to Exeter in their finery, and he'd send for us.

"We'd burst in the door; four little girls with sticky hands and dirt behind our ears. The ladies always tried to be tolerant, like it was an absolute lark to have me sit in their lap and Ellie circle them suspiciously, and Peggity lie about our good manners, and Claire... Well, Claire always tried to disappear, so they all talked to her, poor thing." She laughed, then abducted the cheroot for another drag.

"And everything changed after he died?"

Snap studied the cigar propped between her fingers. "The loss was even greater for Papa; he had to give up his studies and assume responsibility for the horse farm as well as all of Uncle Sebastian's debts. My sisters and I didn't know what to do with ourselves once we moved into the big house.

"Peggity arranged to have us taught needlepoint, dancing, and singing, but every day Ellie and I sneaked out before the instructors arrived. She took off on horseback, Claire hightailed it to a midwife for healing lessons, and I went feral as a wolf cub."

"And you haven't been reined in yet."

Chapter 29

Snap bumped his shoulder. "Would you like to hear about my days?" She didn't wait for an answer. "First I would steal the jam pot after breakfast. You're supposed to have it on bread, but it's better on your finger. I'd sneak under the kitchen table and lie on the bench. Then when the footman put his tray down, I'd snag the jam and listen to the gossip. Servants know everything—that's a fact. If they mentioned something scandalous about someone in town, I'd wait till no one was looking and escape to the barns.

"The stable boys would gather in the haymow and I'd tell them what I'd found out. Then they'd saddle my pony, and I'd ride into town. Finchy's Dry Goods was the best place to gather news, so it was my first stop. Plus, sometimes Mrs. Finchy gave me licorice. If I hid behind the pickle barrel, everyone forgot I was there. Adults say the most harrowing things when they think children aren't listening."

Gareth exhaled in an exasperated huff. "You should not—"

"Do you ever have those itchy days when you must do something adventurous?"

He cleared his throat. He wasn't about to admit to such inclinations, but Snap chatted on without waiting for his sermon.

"You have! I can see it in your eyes. Well, on itchy

days, I'd stow away on a cod boat and help Jack Nasty Face. He's a poet of the high seas—all the sailors say so—but they mean he curses a blue streak."

"I'm sure Jack taught you a few choice nuggets."

She raised her brows, and a grin of pure mischief creased her lips.

"Incorrigible," he said, unable to prevent his own grin.

Snap took the cheroot and puffed, a contemplative expression sneaking onto her face as she blew a set of smoke rings. "Life wasn't at all as it had been when Uncle Sebastian was alive." She handed the cigar back. "And then along you came and burned down the horse barn."

The cheroot dropped into his lap. Frantically, he slapped it off before it lit his pantaloons.

"Yes. And that was the stupidest thing I've ever done."

As he scrambled to retrieve the cigar before it caused a house fire, Snap said, "What did you do after your horrible uncle dragged you into disrepute?"

"Gave up."

"Gave up what?"

"Resisting the commands of Baron Wadsworth, may he rot in hell." A painful ache lodged in his chest. He took a long drag on the cheroot. "But your family's kindness helping me recuperate from my back injury, even after I burned down the barn... It changed me," he said, then returned to watching the sun set.

The lowering sun had deepened the sky to a sweep of orange, coloring the bellies of purple clouds. London seemed harmless from up here, as if there were no reason to remain under his uncle's control... Debt collecting kept him from starvation or having to fit his knees under a desk, but the job had become a nightmare.

Yet, each time he'd tried to escape, his bloody uncle upped the blackmail. The rotter pawed through church records to learn Laura had her child out of wedlock. Beautiful little Clementine would be exposed as a bastard. A sickening darkness yawned in his gut. He dropped his gaze from the horizon to find those lapis pools studying him.

"If I had the guts, I'd see that man dead." He took a final drag and stubbed out the smoke. "Yet here I am again on a mission to take your precious pearls."

"Did I have anything to do with your change of heart?"

He chuckled. "Yes you, most of all."

A delighted smile suffused her face. "How?"

He scratched his knee. "There was not one ounce of good judgement in your little body. You didn't see that I was a rogue who deserved to be booted out the door."

"Do you remember the story you told about stealing back the army's horses? What you did was heroic, not roguish at all."

"Just by chance that mission turned out well."

"But if it hadn't, your division couldn't move its cannon, so getting the horses back saved troops' lives."

He raised his hands in surrender.

With her gaze on the reddening sky, she said, "Wouldn't it be lovely to buy a merchant ship and trade in cloth and spices, and stop slave vessels? You could save those poor people and return them to Africa, but we would keep the ships and add them to our fleet.

You'd make even more money than your papa, only this time, you'd pay the insurance yourself. That would be nicer than working for your uncle, yes?"

"It's a charming dream, but—"

"My dowry could buy us that first ship, my father's an earl, and my sister married a powerful duke, so why do you want to marry Lopey?"

A million reasons skittered like rabbits into the underbrush, Clementine and Laura with them.

"That's a rather sudden change of topics." He ran a hand through his hair.

The sun had sunk low behind a black fringe of trees in Hyde Park.

Her slender fingers corseted his face, gently pulling his head around. "Please don't stare at the timber. Tell me your purpose in marrying that woman."

He took a deep breath; "I'd ruin you. I'm not a good man." He forced his gaze to remain steady.

Snap studied him a moment, then let go and picked at a primrose embroidered on her skirt. "What I haven't told you," she said slowly, "is that I've always felt as if I'd spin off this earth, banging into scandal after scandal. But when you're near…I…I love the weight of you. You bring me…understanding, and approval, and I need you so much more than she does."

A wave of sadness pressed his heart into a painful lump. "I can't. It's all too late. You're too late—and most of all, I'm too late, too old, and too corrupt to change course."

A slash of crimson rose to her lids as tears collected in the corners. He turned quickly from her to concentrate on the clouds whose bellies reflected the last vestiges of the evening's tangerine glow.

She brushed a tear from her cheek and flicked the wet from her fingers as if it were a trifle. But then another coursed down her face, quickly followed by more. He passed her his handkerchief. Now was the time to leave. He should go. Tomorrow he would marry Lopey, and all these heart tuggings and achings would end.

Suddenly, Snap balled the handkerchief in her fist, and eyes shining with tears and a desperate fierceness, she cried, "Then you won't mind giving me kissing lessons." She gripped his lapels, pursed her lips, and came in for the kill.

"Wait!" He pushed her back.

"Surely you don't want me spending my wedding night with Finnegan terrified of even kissing him?"

"You're not marrying Finnegan."

"I will. I will if you don't marry me. So, how am I supposed to kiss him? You said I was dreadful at it. Besides, it's my birthday and you're marrying Lopey in the morning, so it won't matter. It won't matter a bit."

Her eyes were bright with unhappiness and challenge, and those porcelain breasts rose and fell with each agitated breath. Frantically, his brain leaped and twisted like a beast with a leg in a jaw trap.

Think of Lopey, Lopey, Lopey, Lopey, God damn it!

Yet, his heart shattered seeing Snap's misery. His hands circled her smooth arms, and, as he drew her close, all his resistance dove out of sight. The urge drove harder. Lowering her to the jacket, he tenderly ran the tips of his fingers over the rise of her clavicle and up her neck, stopping at the ridge of her ear where downy strands of hair tangled and held him. Her tear-filled eyes widened.

"Close them," he whispered, brushing her lids down.

A tear coursed down her cheek. He kissed it away. Lips touched lips—the softness like silk ribbon. He experienced a last flickering image of Lopey before all thought drowned in a roar of desire.

****

How delicious Gareth's touch was, like bathing in warm chocolate, and the feel of his mouth against hers, fine as kid leather. Lights flashed behind her eyelids and her limbs turned buttery. This time she would not ruin their kiss; this time she knew exactly what to do because she'd looked at a dozen romantic pictures. Pinching her lips, she pressed hard against his.

To her horror, he pulled back.

"You did it wrong," he said, quirking a smile. "Relax them."

He gently tugged her bottom lip, then ran a thumb across her mouth, light as a blade of grass. A spot at the center of her upper lip tingled from his touch.

"It tickles," she whispered.

"Good."

He pulled her closer, his breath heating her, and then he kissed the corner of her mouth, moved to the other corner, deliberately avoiding the sensitive center, and then slowly, he tilted her head back and kissed her full-on. Passion filled her with such abrupt force, she turned her head away.

Panting a little, she whispered, "I feel strange…"

"Ahh, then we're doing it right."

Taking two deep breaths, she nodded. "I'm ready to try again."

He chuckled. "This time, we're going to touch

tongues."

She drew back, appalled. "Whatever for?"

"It's nice. You'll be surprised."

"If you're playing a trick, I'll push you off this roof."

He smiled and gave a slight shake of his head. "You're a funny one. But since it's your birthday and my last night of freedom..." Then he moved the tendrils of her hair back in place, leaving paths of sensation that lingered on her brow. Stroking her hair, he murmured, "Don't forget to relax."

Then he traced a line of kisses over her eyelids, her cheeks, and finally, her mouth. And that kiss was as a man would kiss the woman he loved. Snap's mind reeled with the knowledge. She was a woman to him, a woman he could wed.

Heat soared inside and met his heat, and she found herself yearning for the touch of his tongue when seconds before, she'd wanted nothing to do with it. Opening her mouth to him, she felt it—his tongue—caressing hers, so she wrapped her arms about his neck and drew him deeper.

Their tongues searched, explored, delved and sought, yet it wasn't enough. She needed to be nearer, to have more, and her need was matched by his, until they were thoroughly entwined, and she lay beneath him, her body throbbing with cravings, as if she were bursting with a thousand beams of frenzied light.

His hand slid to her breasts, confined by the pure white gown. A finger slipped beneath the fabric and touched her nipple, causing a spasm of rapture. Yet, even that was not enough. More than anything, anything, she longed to have him touch her...there.

Down there. He was hard against her thigh, so she wrapped a leg around him, pushing herself against the bulge. As a tangle of nerves amassed and gathered, she dug her heel into his back, keeping him taut against her, rubbing slowly until every fiber in her body clanged like bells.

With a rush of cold air, he jumped to his feet. "By God!" he said, breathing heavily. "Holy mother of …"

Confused, Snap struggled onto her elbows. "But weren't we getting along beautifully?"

He walked in circles, yanking on a black curl that spilled onto his forehead. When he'd calmed himself, he squatted beside her. "Look now… That was…" Scrubbing his scalp, he tried again. "I'm not sure you understand that a man—" His expression changed as something in the street caught his eye.

Snap followed his gaze. Silhouetted in the deep blue twilight was a man with a cane, which he raised in salute. Gold flashed in the light of a street lamp.

"Wadsworth." Gareth spat, grabbing Snap and dragging her behind the chimney. "You will never see me again," he said urgently. "I tell you, I am a terrible man, and too damn tainted for you. Tomorrow morning, first thing, I am marrying Lady Whitlocke."

Snap grabbed his arms. "Don't protect me from you, I won't have it!"

"Cease!" He twisted away. "Stay away from me. You must! And whatever you do, do *not* wear the Fitzcarry pearls to your party." He shook her hard. "Tell me you understand."

"I don't," said Snap, as tears rose to her eyes. "I don't understand at all. You're a hero, and there is no one else—there never will be—not for either of us, so marry me."

"My God, wipe that notion out of your silly, childish brain. It's a pipe dream, do you understand? I don't love you and I never will, and why you insist on marrying a man the rest of your family can't forgive, is beyond me. But you must not wear those pearls. My uncle will cut you or kill you."

"Then I will wear them. I'll wear them every day. I'll wear them in the park, and I'll let him cut me. I'll let him kill me!"

His hand came fast for her face, and she didn't try to block the blow. It never landed. He stopped inches from her cheek. Trembling with emotion, he took her hands and crushed them until she thought she'd scream with pain.

"Don't expect me to save you, you buffleheaded little fool."

He let go, and in a few strides and a rattle of leaves, disappeared into the oak.

****

Gareth could barely contain his rage. The bastard spied on him, made sure he was priming Snap for the theft. Well, his uncle could go to hell, and the sooner the better.

Deliberately, he headed for Hyde Park, knowing his uncle would never follow without a coach, a driver with a whip, and Beam Murphy, to protect him. He was evil as arsenic, yet terrified of dogs. The chances were good a few canines were spraying the trees at this hour.

Behind him came the tap-tapping of Wadsworth's cane. Gareth quickened his pace.

"Hart!" the baron cried.

"Bugger off," Gareth mumbled under his breath,

disgusted that he lacked the guts to yell it in Wadsworth's face.

"Hart, my man."

Gareth whirled on him. "Don't call me 'your man.' Don't."

Wadsworth fixed him with a sly smile, his black eyes glinting in the lamplight. "I see you're upset," he said. "When you're past your fit of temper, we'll speak."

It was all Gareth could do to keep from seizing his uncle's pasty neck and wringing it like a chicken's.

The baron sauntered away, swinging his cane as if he hadn't a care in the world. The point was to seem indifferent, the point was to infuriate, and the point was to make him feel utterly trapped. Gareth knew it. He knew his uncle's game, yet the old familiar despair rose like a breaker smashing him into the sand.

"Feckin' bloody devil," he said, giving a fallen branch a vicious kick.

The stick skittered sideways, bounced off a hitching post and swung around, clocking him on the shin.

You sapskull, it's bloody preposterous Snap thinks I can marry her—a chit without a ha'penny's worth of common sense. She's too damn much like spring, all smiles and fun, and—

His pace slowed. That's what she is…

He sat heavily on a park bench. "You're in love with her, you misbegotten fool," he said aloud.

The feel of her taut little body, her eagerness—it was as if she were still there, fevered and trusting in his arms. He dug his nails into his scalp and scratched so hard he expected blood.

Ever since his family's bankruptcy, he'd plotted to marry a rich widow: there had been at least a half-dozen, including Aurelia Davenport, and now Lopey. They all cared for him, coddled him, bought him fine clothes and horses, equipped him with gold cigarette cases, tickets to the theatre, and boots cut from the finest leather. In their company, servants attended to his every need. If he married Lopey, he'd never have to lift a finger again in his life. Yes, he did her accounting, but she'd be just as happy to hire someone else to do it. And once he'd escorted Lopey down the aisle at St. James, he'd bring Laura and little Clementine to his bride's home and be free of Uncle Wadsworth forever. Free.

Snap might have a hefty dowry, but she demanded a different set of skills. He'd be taking care of her instead of the other way around. Plus, the little fribble kept insisting he was a hero. Ha! And how was he supposed to live up to that reputation—a man with his list of vices... Any gentleman would have quit Wadsworth, would have escaped with Clementine and Laura, and lived in hiding even if it meant destitution. Snap was mistaken, there wasn't a snuff spoon's worth of honor in him.

He bowed his head and stared at his knees, barely outlined in the starlight. A dark tangle of emotion clogged his chest, hurting his heart, squeezing his lungs, and weighing so heavily on his soul, he was driven to move.

What he wanted to do was rid his mind of her, to exhaust every limb, to make his muscles scream and his lungs heave from exertion, so he ran. At the Serpentine, he raced along the bank to the bridge at Kensington

Gardens, and though his legs burned and each breath ripped raw into his lungs, he moved faster, and faster still, down the garden's paths until the wrought iron gates of the palace stopped him in his tracks.

It was no use. Damn it, it was no use! She glowed in his brain like a vision—a vision that offered happiness, yet insisted on sacrifice. He bent double, trying to catch his breath, knees trembling from exhaustion.

He would play courtier to Lopey, and she would marry him. With her, he'd have respectability, yet no responsibility; he'd have safety for Laura and Clementine, and they'd all be taken care of for the rest of their lives.

The plan had no flaws...

Chapter 30

Snap lay in bed, staring out the window at a crescent moon. All her dreams hung on its slender hook. As long as that moon stayed in the sky, tomorrow could not come. Tomorrow Gareth would be married and hours later, she would make her come out. All the stiff, dull, entitled bachelors of England would make their presences known. They'd have counted her dowry and decided how to spend it. They'd have examined her connections and decided how to exploit them, and they'd have learned of the freedom she enjoyed and decided how best to break her of it.

A tear leaked from the corner of her eye, followed by another and another. Her handkerchief was soaked. She wiped her eyes with the sheet.

There had been such finality in his voice. The moment he spied that horrible Wadsworth, the love she'd seen only a moment before, died. Everything died. The man she adored, seemed overcome with fear; that and a haunted, resigned, emptiness.

Her heart tumbled into a pit and just kept falling... Until it landed and bumped up against an idea.

****

Gareth stood before a full-length mirror in his room, fingers tapping his thighs as his valet, Hicks, adjusted Gareth's shirt collar.

The servant hissed when Rascal made a third

attempt to paw Gareth's leg. "Get to your corner. Go on."

Rascal gazed mournfully at his master, then went to the bedpost and lifted his leg. Hicks emitted a stifled scream.

"How dare you!" thundered Gareth at the errant canine. "You've been out this morning. There is no excuse." He strode to the bell pull and nearly yanked it off the wall.

All three dogs cowered and whined guiltily.

"Out," he said, jerking the bedroom door open. The pack scrabbled through and clattered down the stairs. "What the hell has gotten into them? And on my wedding day of all days."

"Yes sir. It's shocking, sir."

When Gareth calmed a bit, the servant approached again, painstakingly circling his master's neck with a measure of cloth in preparation for tying the knot on his cravat.

"Are you trying to choke me, man?" Gareth angrily yanked off the fabric. "I'll not go to the gallows by your hand, nor anyone else's."

"I'm terribly sorry, Captain Hart. Would you like to form the first circle, then I'll tie it at the proper constriction?"

Gareth wrapped the cloth, mussed his hair in the process, and didn't get the ends even so Hicks had to tug this way and that to set it right. Bloody blast it, why did he want to punch the man?

"And I suppose my vest still hasn't shown up?" said Gareth darkly.

The valet's fingers gave a slight kick. "Unfortunately, sir, it has not, but Cartwright is still diligently searching for it."

"Fire him. I never want to see the wretch again. That vest cost me a king's ransom, yet he 'loses' it between this house and the Cork Street tailor's."

There was a rap on the door, and though it didn't make a lick of sense, Gareth thought Snap would enter. Instead, Annie, a square-bodied maid, burst in.

"Rascal," Gareth said, jerking his head at the bedpost.

"He ain't done that since he were a pup," she replied, shaking her head. "It's this wedding business—got the lot of us nervy." After dropping a rag over the puddle, she left to fetch cleaning supplies.

Gareth glanced at the window. Snap might try climbing—a man couldn't be sure where she was concerned—but though the seconds ticked by, she didn't appear.

"What time is it?"

"Not too much longer, sir," Hicks said, soothingly. "It'll all be over shortly."

****

Fog, tangy with coal dust, stung Snap's eyes as she cantered her mare Edict south through Hyde Park—Belgrave her destination. Soon Lopey would come through the door, climb into her carriage, drive to St. James's Church, and take Gareth away forever. But not without a fight.

Riding sidesaddle and dressed in her finest habit, Snap hoped to make a stunning impression. In her mind, she rehearsed the scene: when Lopey appeared at the front door, Snap would dismount and kneel before her, and with tears streaming down her face, she would beg the woman to call off the wedding. "He loves me," she would cry, "so if you care for him at all, set him free!" Lopey would refuse at first, but soon, soon she would envision Gareth buried in Belgravia's stifled society, and understand she had to let him go.

The daydream ended abruptly when a fence reared out of the fog. With no time to stop or go around, she gave Edict her head and prayed she wouldn't fall off the cursed sidesaddle. Edict lifted smoothly into the air, but as the mare came down, she twisted oddly. Snap squeezed the saddle's leaping head and upper pommel with her thighs, managing to cling through the landing, but once all hooves hit the ground, Edict hopped and bucked, squealing in fright.

The world slowed as her grip disintegrated. A blur of foliage passed, a pine cone, grass, a jarring thump and she found herself watching the back end of an adder slither away.

Snap scrambled to her feet, but Edict was already disappearing into the fog, stirrups flapping and reins dangling. Many horses would return to the barn, but Edict loved a good romp. There was no saying where she might go, and if a scallywag caught her, a very valuable horse would be lost to the Earl of Twickenham's stables… Yet there was Gareth. And precious minutes. And London's muddle of streets that could swallow a coach-and-six, making it impossible to find Lopey before…

She pressed her hands to her chest, unable to think of what to do next.

Heart pounding, breath short with anxiety, she listened until she heard hoof beats. Blindly, she moved through the fog toward the sound until she spied Edict. With calm, unhurried steps, she got about ten feet away, when the beast lifted her head and trotted out of range.

"Damn it, stop, horse, stop!" Lud, Belgravia was so close, she could run there and not be out of breath!

It didn't take long to find Edict again; the mare was munching a patch of grass. This time, Snap relied on an age-old trick; cupping her hand, she pretended to hold a sugar lump. Interested, the horse lifted her head and waited as Snap approached. At last within reaching distance, she abandoned the ruse and made a quick grab. Edict swiveled left to escape, but the reins flapped close enough for Snap to catch them.

Minutes later she pulled Edict to a sliding stop outside Lopey's impressive mansion. Nothing stirred on the street, not even the rumble of a distant coach.

After looping the reins through a hitching post, she raced to the front door and banged its lion-head knocker until the latch moved. "Is Lady Whitlocke here?" she blurted before the startled butler could speak a word.

"No, milady, she's—"

But Snap didn't wait to hear. She flew to her horse, jumped into the saddle, and applied the whip.

****

She beat the coach to St. James's where a crowd had gathered in the street outside the church's doors. There were nobles, and beggars, and butchers with bloodied aprons; there were sweetmeats peddlers, a juggler, and at least a dozen tradesmen in leather coveralls, but women dominated the scene. Rich or poor, their skin seemed suspiciously white, their lips a tad too red, and their cheeks a jot too pink. Those who could afford a gown wore silk with matching bonnets whose feathers hung limp in the humid air. This feminine display was for Gareth's sake. Her Gareth, for whose glorious good looks women lined the streets for a sighting.

Just as Snap was about to dismount, the crowd surged toward George Street shouting greetings, and good wishes as Gareth appeared through the mist. Dressed all in black with a cloud of white cravat tucked into a vest of deepest claret and a gold watch fob at his waist, he was surely the handsomest man in England. Her heart burst with love, and pride, and… and… too much to express. She moved Edict closer so he would see her high above the scrum.

"Captain Hart!" she called, but he didn't hear.

In fact, he didn't seem to hear anybody. His eyes were locked on the road and his stride bore a military stiffness more akin to a parade of invaders than a walk to the altar.

With sudden clarity, she realized that even if she could attract his attention, he'd keep marching. A blade of pain pierced like a rapier from head to heart.

He is hers. All along, he was hers…

The torment of the rapier grew. Through a blur of tears, she watched as he mounted the stoop, and instead of acknowledging the crowd at the door, twisted the knob, and disappeared into the depths of St. James's. Her body went hollow and her limbs useless. She wanted to gallop away, and keep galloping until her agony was far behind, but she couldn't move. People talked as they drifted back to their former positions on the walkways, complaining that Captain Hart didn't wave or smile. She understood but couldn't decipher their words.

"The countess'll put on a better show," someone said. "He's a commoner and don't know what's expected."

Lopey... The thought of seeing her rival radiant and happy, stepping down from a coach drawn by six white horses, cramped Snap's stomach with such force, she doubled over, clinging to Edict's neck as tears wetted the horse's mane.

A lad raced into the park, shouting, "She's comin'!"

Like a pack of wolves, the horde streamed toward St. James's arched entrance.

Hands shaking, Snap pulled the mare's head up, and rode slowly, blindly toward home.

****

Though it was thirteen minutes before ten in the morning, candles had to be lit in the vestry as fog pressed its velvet body against the windows. Gareth fussed with his waistcoat—a dull wine-colored affair that was nothing like the embroidered green silk he'd had specially made for the ceremony.

Damn and blast it! How could Cartwright lose an entire vest? Ugh, it was unfair firing the man. I'll recall him after the ceremony.

The ceremony... Soon Father O'Leary would summon him. Aye, soon enough. Restless, he left his seat and went to the priest's desk, seeking anything of interest to keep his mind occupied. He picked up a Bible, flipped a few pages, and read, "There is no fear in love: but perfect love drives out fear, because fear expects punishment."

He slammed the book shut, dropped it on the desk and was caught midstride as the knob on a drawer hooked the fall at the front of his trousers. *Ting*—a button landed on the floor and rolled somewhere, though in which direction he hadn't a clue because the sound of it coming to rest was drowned by the rumble of a coach and six drawing to a stop.

"Mother of God." He fell to his knees and frantically searched for the button.

In the next instant, a tender *tap, tap* landed on the door. Father O'Leary leaned in.

"Your betrothed has arrived."

"For pity's sake, man," Gareth shouted, "find me a needle and thread!"

****

Snap gazed listlessly into her bedroom mirror as Malloy tugged the laces of Snap's dress. The party would begin in a half hour; she should be flashing about checking the flowers, storming the kitchen with last-minute requests, and generally making as much fuss as possible. After all, it was her night, her party, her moment of glory, yet all Snap wanted to do was cry.

"Lower your head, milady," instructed Malloy.

Absently, Snap did as the lady's maid asked, and then she saw what Malloy held: the Fitzcarry pearls.

"No!" She lifted a hand to stop the woman. "I… I thought I'd wear the aquamarines instead."

Lizzie came out of the shadows where she'd been lurking at the far side of the bed. "Them pearls is too much for a small-chested girl like milady. It's been decided she won't wear 'em for her come out."

Malloy pinned first Snap, then Lizzie, with her silvery gaze, the pupils of her eyes darkening as she sniffed a secret. "What are you two on about?"

Adopting her loftiest air, Snap replied, "I've decided against them. It's vulgar for a young lady to wear something that grandiose."

Malloy dipped her head submissively, then went to the door, opened it, and called to a passing footman. "Kindly ask Lady Davenport to come to the room, please. Tell her we need to confer about appropriate attire for the young lady."

Snap passed Lizzie a panicked glance.

With a smug glint in her tight-lipped expression, Malloy returned to adjusting Snap's ensemble. The room went silent as every ear strained to pick out amongst the cavalcade of servants rushing about preparing for the party, the pit-a-pat of a lady's dance slippers. When she heard them, Snap's heart thumped with the beat of the dowager's approach.

Her breasts arrived first, jutting past the door frame like a pair of shark fins, and then her imperious figure dominated the doorway. Dressed in a shower of amethysts and a gown of striped purple silk over a lavender underlay, she had further adorned her largest asset with ruffles that so enhanced her bosom, Snap had trouble focusing on her face.

"Chickadee, what can I help you with?"

Snap opened her mouth, but Malloy beat her to the first word. "These are a fine string of pearls, are they not?" The maid displayed them over her palm, catching their watery shimmer in the lamplight.

"Did you not notice that your mistress was about to speak?" Lady Davenport said sharply.

"Forgive me, b—"

"What is your question, Lady Nefertiti?"

Snap was not used to being intimidated, yet now her mind scrambled for a foothold. "Isn't it dangerous to wear the Fitzcarry pearls tonight?" she blurted. "Everyone is anticipating that I'll have them on."

"All the more reason to show them off. If there's anything the *ton* despises, it's disappointment. Nothing gets their tongues exercising faster. No, my dear, it would be a scandal not to sport the pearls."

She took them out of Malloy's hand as if the maid were a coat rack. "Put your head down," she commanded.

Unable to think of an excuse without naming Gareth, Snap obeyed. The pearl's cool weight circled her throat once, then twice, leaving the rest of the strand to hang clear to her waist.

"Lud, but they're magnificent," Lady Davenport murmured, and with a soft hollow click, she closed the strand's diamond and black pearl catch.

Snap stroked the necklace, her thumb and index finger caressing each perfect orb. All her life she'd longed to wear the pearls. Her sisters had on very special occasions: Ellie at the Mortimers' ball, Peggity for her come out, and Claire on her wedding day. Now it was her turn—her turn at last. Yet the honor of wearing the precious beads did nothing to raise her spirits. Tonight she felt their weight would drop her to her knees. And tonight, instead of waltzing with Gareth, she would parry with pasty-faced dandies, arrogant rogues, and woolly-headed fools who could barely climb a staircase, let alone a promontory.

"My, my, you are every inch the lady," said the dowager. "Mark my words, there won't be a nob in the ballroom who isn't at your feet."

She patted Snap's shoulder. Then, with an infinitesimal lift of her chin, signaled Malloy to follow as she floated out the door.

"What if Wadsworth sees you?" Lizzie whispered.

"I'll have to stick with you and have my knife at the ready."

Snap shook her head. "The dowager would rush you like a vulture would a carcass."

Listlessly studying herself in the mirror, Snap adjusted the strand to fall exactly center. She checked her profile, then turned to see her other side. "I look quite perfect...

"For a moment, I had my doubts, Lizzie, but now I'm confident Captain Hart will be here tonight. He wouldn't miss my come out and he'll want to protect me in case his uncle makes a try for the pearls. Plus, the adventure of sneaking in will be too tempting to resist."

Lizzie snorted. "It's his wedding night and there's two dozen guards tromping the flower beds."

"Two dozen reasons he'll come and only one minor inconvenience," Snap replied, testing a radiant smile in the mirror.

"And your papa will see him out the door with a pike in his gizzard."

"Oh pish, Papa never stabbed anyone."

Lizzie curled her lip and mumbled, "My upbringing says there's always a first time."

Chapter 31

On the receiving line, Mrs. Gower whispered helpful information to Snap, such as, "He's got twelve thousand pounds per annum," and "She's an earl's daughter, but her feet are so big she can walk on top of snow."

However, Snap's excitement banished every name and measure of income. The smiles, the colors, the perfumes, the heat of the candles, the music, and oh my goodness, the thought of Gareth seeing how beautiful she looked wearing the Fitzcarry pearls sent her heart into a tarantella of pleasure.

"Lady Whitlocke's a mad old dear," said Lady Ponsonby to the dowager. "And to think she called it off because a sparrow perched on the front seat of the coach. She said it was a warning."

The two giggled behind their fans.

"And what did my darling captain do?"

"Slunk off in a fit of the blue devils, no doubt. She swears it's only postponed, but he'll move on to the next widow, mark my words."

Lady Ponsonby's daughter wished Snap a happy birthday.

Scarcely acknowledging her greeting, Snap nudged Mrs. Gower. "Were they whispering about Captain Hart?"

"Didn't I tell you? A sparrow flew into Lady

Whitlocke's carriage this morning, so she called off the wedding. Your pick of the litter is back in the game."

Elation hit Snap with such force she shuddered.

He'll be here tonight.

"Are you catching a chill, sweeting?" her mother asked.

"No, Mama, and thank you. Thank you for the most beautiful night of my life!"

When at last she was free to enter the ballroom, she paused at the entrance to take it all in. Black marble pillars laced with garlands of pink roses ringed the room. Young ladies adorned in white and gentlemen in somber black or scarlet military gathered in clusters on the dance floor, blurring its chalk drawing of a ship on mighty seas with Captain Gareth Hart at the helm. Lining the walls were gilt benches laden with matrons resplendent in silks of emerald, apricot, sapphire, and ocher, and in the corners potted palms quivered to the thrum of the orchestra.

"Lady Nefertiti," cried a flush-cheeked buck, "may I ask to partner with you in a dance?"

"You may," Snap replied.

"I'm late," said a bright-eyed fellow with a luxurious mustache. "Can you squeeze me into a cotillion?"

Snap laughed. "I should go to the tower if I cannot."

A chorus of "Nevers," followed. One swell declared he'd catch her at the bottom, another swore he'd jump from the tower in her stead. The crowd of masculine bodies thickened, their eager, admiring eyes filling her with feminine power and the joy of certainty in seeing Gareth at the ball.

Then Finnegan shouldered through. "Your come out has inspired me, my Psyche," he exclaimed. "I think it's my best work."

From a jacket pocket, he pulled a folded piece of paper adorned with the Whitlocke family crest.

"The lady doesn't want to hear your sodding poetry, Whitlocke," Mustache objected.

"Let her be entertained," barked Blush-Cheek. "It's her birthday."

But Finnegan had a determined look on his face, so praying she could cut the verses short, Snap caught Ellie's arm as she hurried by. "Where is Papa for the minuet?"

"He seems to have disappeared, but I'll set the hounds on him," her sister replied, and dashed off.

Finnegan shook open the page and began.

"When you and I are in the throes of love,
We shall take heed of the pretty turtledove."

"Ugh! Are you in earnest, man?" one of Snap's attendees proclaimed.

But Finnegan was not to be put off.

"Raise up our ears and listen hard we will,
For doves hold secrets in their ringing trill.
Their webbed feet do tread upon the path,
And sharp their beaks do seeds a daily math—"

"Hold, my lord." said Snap, raising her hand. "Is this entire poem about pigeons?"

Annoyed, Finnegan replied, "Turtledoves. Amongst avians, they're a symbol of love."

"So if you married Lady Nefertiti, you'd be composing sonnets to birds all day?" Blush-Cheek proclaimed.

"I would add muskrats and mighty fish to my

work."

Laughter rang to the rafters, and in the mirth and ribbing that followed, the men forgot all about her. Snap sighed, and scanned the ballroom seeking Gareth—was he wearing a fake beard, or had he disguised himself as a servant?

"Just one more stanza, and I'll recite the couplet," Finnegan proclaimed above the hilarity.

He moved directly into her sightline but before his gaze could drop back to the page, she said, "Have you ever wanted to travel to the Far East?"

His pale eyes widened in surprise. "I've heard they're a bit dirty over there."

"They're nothing of the sort. Cleaner than the likes of us, from everything I've read. How about climb a mountain? Or spy on Lord Byron? Oh, never mind. See here, Lord Whitlocke," she continued, "I've got to talk to everyone tonight—the Dowager Lady Davenport says that's protocol—so the rest of your verse will have to wait." Before Finn could object, Snap turned her back on him and said to her admirers, "Who would be so kind as to flag me a glass of Champagne?"

Before a clear winner could be found amidst the jockeying for the privilege, Peggity appeared at Snap's elbow. "Ellie and I found him. It's the worst news: Papa is engaged with a scholar and he asked that you carry on without him."

"Oh no!" Snap blurted, "But it's the opening dance!"

Peggity bit her lip. "Shall I have Crewe lead you?"

That was no solution: Snap wanted to look graceful and Crewe...Crewe, the kindest gentleman in Christendom, was a boxer, not a dancer. She looked frantically around and everywhere curious glances met her gaze. They were all waiting for the dancing to begin. "I'll... I'll run and persuade him myself."

"Hurry."

As Snap hastened through the throng, a gaping pit opened in her stomach. Once Papa got talking about history, he was lost. Abruptly, she stopped rushing and a gray sadness rose inside. The feeling was all too familiar, but tonight—tonight of all nights—she hadn't thought she'd have to endure it. Papa wouldn't come. He never came...

From the crowd, Ellie's husband Hugh emerged. Quietly, he took her hand and led her to the center of the ballroom. The tinkling of the pianoforte signaled the beginning of the minuet, and then Snap moved her feet, not out of conscious awareness, but out of muscle memory.

"I'm lost," she whispered, circling close to Hugh, her eyes stinging.

"The Z formation," he murmured. "You're doing fine."

She swallowed her emotions, curtseyed, stepped elegantly right, glided in a Z across the chalk-covered floor, but scarcely felt her feet. The whole room seemed wrapped in dirty gauze. The final notes died beneath a patter of applause as Hugh led her to the sidelines.

Almost immediately, Mrs. Gower appeared. "You were the very soul of decorum," she chirruped. "So mature, so ladylike. But, my dear, you lacked sparkle. One would think you were Ophelia being dragged by the weeds."

She took Snap's arm and tugged her toward a bench partially hidden behind a palm. "Sit with me," she commanded. Safely secreted behind the foliage, Mrs. Gower threw a sly grin, then reached under her skirt and produced a silver flask. "One little sip of this is what you need to put the bloom back in your cheeks."

Numbly, Snap pressed the flask to her lips and swallowed. A blend of fire, linseed oil, and turpentine burned down her throat. She took a second gulp. About to down a third, the chaperone snatched the liquor away.

"You want bloom, not roasting coals," she said.

The liquid lounged in Snap's stomach for a minute until it got up the courage to explore. Almost immediately, it cantered to her brain and then out to her fingertips and down to her toes. She felt better. Decidedly better.

"Mrs. Gower, you're a miracle worker. Oh, and I need you to perform another miracle. Captain Hart is sure to come tonight, and you'll tell Papa and Mama he's suitable."

"I'll have to be quite the wizard for that one. Go dance, and we'll see what transpires."

Once Snap returned to the floor, it didn't take long for a sea of men to flood her banks. As she flashed past a gilt-edged mirror, led by a thick-lipped buck in cream breeches and a maroon waistcoat, she caught a glimpse of herself. The Fitzcarry pearls glimmered about her neck like a strand of dew-soaked petals; her cheeks were pink, and her blue eyes twinkled.

"Lud," she exclaimed, as they took the first steps of the maggot, "I truly am the prettiest girl here."

The young man laughed—a terrible braying that started deep in his throat and ended in his sinuses. He appraised her with unbridled approval. "And I want the prettiest girl," he said. "No horse-faced cow for me."

In that split second all the dash drained from him.

"How perfect," replied Snap, extricating her hand, "Because most of the time, I'm a cow-faced horse."

With that, she moved on to William, Earl of Craven. He hailed from a long pedigree of rakes and rogues. Though the dancing had just begun, his fine features were already puffy and rouged from alcohol. The rake and rogue part interested her, but his character seemed hollow, as if swallowed whole by debauchery.

Craven passed her to Viscount Bottomrigg. Squat, full-bellied, and bespectacled, his only asset was his title. Scanning the rest of the gentlemen in the dance, she concluded Gareth was the only suitable mate.

Bottomrigg raised his arm for the twirl as high as his scant length allowed. She ducked low, but caught her hair on his sleeve button. Bottomrigg jerked his arm, Snap let out a pained shriek, and the viscount spewed apologies while not helping at all to extricate her. The line of dancers faltered. A few off-key notes sounded from the orchestra before the Master of Ceremonies whipped the melody back into shape, but not before every occupant in the ballroom focused on her struggle.

Papa, Finnegan, the braying toff, and now this?

Snap was on the verge of ripping the tress from its roots when a pair of deft fingers took control of the tangle. Was it Gareth?

"Captain Hart?" she whispered, but got no reply.

"Come with me," a masculine voice said, low, deep, reassuring, but unfamiliar.

Catching a glimpse, her heart quickened. Julian van Eck! Cleverly, he'd dressed as a soldier in red coat and gold braid.

They might think he's one of our brave men at arms. Gareth probably lent him the coat.

With a light touch on the small of her back, he urged her toward the arched exit to the back of the house. As they walked, he passed a lacy handkerchief. She waved it off.

"It's all right, I'm not crying."

"Pretend to. It will make them more sympathetic."

She accepted the bit of cloth and daubed the corner of her eyes.

They were passing Lady Pemneux when the grand dame of Almack's caught Snap's hand and gave it a pat.

"Viscount Bottomrigg is as welcome as a rat to a larder. You will not see him next Season, my dear. I'll make sure of it."

Before Snap could reply, van Eck urged her away.

"Would you like to go somewhere private to recover yourself? The ladies' retiring room, perhaps? Or would you risk a pleasant surprise?"

"Is he here?"

Van Eck smiled. "Hush," he replied, holding a finger to his lips.

"Lead the way," she whispered.

Heart thumping like a gypsy drum, she passed guests chatting in the hall and prayed her eyes wouldn't betray her excitement, prayed she wouldn't be linked to the artist as she quickened her pace to keep a discreet distance between them.

Turning a corner into an unoccupied section of the passage, van Eck came to her father's study. The portrait artist opened the door, then closed it quickly behind them. Not a jot of light illuminated the black interior.

"There's someone here to see you," he said *sotto voce*.

Chapter 32

"Captain Hart?" Snap whispered.

A clandestine meeting in the dark—how thrilling!

But no one answered. Van Eck said nothing, just stood at the door behind her. She could hear him breathe, quick, unsettled breaths that raised a niggling doubt in her mind.

"If you intend to scare me, Captain Hart, you've failed miserably," she announced.

A sound, like a dog panting, came from the inky darkness. Then a flint struck, a lit tow flickered uncertainly, and the skeletal bones of Baron Wadsworth's face glowed in the wavering light. In one outstretched hand glinted the muzzle of a pistol.

"If you open your mouth to scream," the baron said, "this gun will fire before the first squeak."

His body convulsed, eyes flashing with unearthly joy. He lit a gas lamp, illuminating a room bursting with furniture stored there for the ball. Between them was a tight path of stacked chairs, divans, and side tables.

"My nephew said you're an easy doxy to lure."

"No, he didn't." Her hand involuntarily covered her heart.

Wadsworth grinned. "What I tell him to do, he does."

"He never said I'd come."

A chuckle hissed between Wadsworth's yellow teeth. "How else would I know a likely room for our rendezvous? You blithering bit o' muslin, your lover gave you up without so much as a rub to the chin."

She cut a burning stare at the hideous man. "Captain Hart has never been in this house. He wouldn't know this room from any oth—"

Suddenly she was yanked backwards. Choking, she slammed against van Eck. For a moment, she hung, strangled by the Fitzcarry pearls before the ancient strand broke and she hit the floor, beads clattering wildly about her.

"Idiot!" Wadsworth screamed.

Panicked, the artist hurled the broken necklace at the baron, who dropped the pistol to catch it. Snap lunged for the weapon, closing her hand over its metallic casing just as Wadsworth bent for it. Boom! Fire, smoke, the acrid taste of sulfur in her mouth, stinging her eyes, pain shot down her elbow converging with pain ringing in her head as the gun's recoil knocked her backwards.

Van Eck's dance slippers skidded on the floor, kicking pearls that shot past her and under the furniture, the beads banging and bumping into chair legs, and rolling under the divans.

"Baron?" he said.

But Wadsworth lay still on the ground.

The painter turned and ran, opening the door to distant voices down the hall, then slamming it shut. The sound of his footsteps disappeared down the corridor.

Movement drew Snap's attention. Not five feet away, the baron twitched, and then writhed, moaning and grunting. With increasing rapidity, his arms flailed, his legs pumped, and he gulped and gurgled as blood spat from his mouth. Both legs kicked straight, stiff as battering rams, cracking the legs of a delicate table that crashed onto his prone body.

Overcome with horror, Snap shot to her feet and screamed. She screamed so loudly the whole room seemed to shake with her terror. An explosion of glass and shards *plinked* against her face, in her hair, against the folds of her dress, and her next wail of horror crammed the back of her throat. A stack of chairs careened toward her, leaning, crazily teetering, and then Gareth appeared. He turned her from the sight of Wadsworth's tortured writhing and held her against his chest.

"Hide, love," he whispered. "When they're not looking, blend with the crowd." He pressed her down then, under the protective covering of a divan. "Deeper," he urged.

So she flattened and slid farther.

"What's this!" a male voice cried, bursting through the door.

A muddle of frightened exclamations followed as the room quickly filled.

"I've killed him," Gareth announced.

A woman shrieked. Men shouted. The roar was deafening.

Snap's father joined the ruckus. "What's happened?" he cried. "What in bloody hell are you doing in my home, Hart?"

Too frightened to make herself known, Snap dragged herself further under the furniture and inched toward the door until she got close enough to appear as if she'd just come in.

As she eased to her feet between the wall and behind a cluster of tailcoats, her father shouted, "Seize the bloody murderer!"

Before Snap could shout her father down, someone grabbed her arm and yanked her from the room. Ellie, wild-eyed, herded her through the growing throng and pushed her up the servants' stairs.

"No, Ellie," cried Snap. "I have to go back. Papa is having Captain Hart arrested!"

"By God, Snap, he murdered his uncle."

Collapsing on the stairs, she looked helplessly at her sister, then covered her face. "It was me." Her body shook, and tears burst from her eyes followed by a wail, thin and high as a fox's scream.

"Stop talking nonsense." Abruptly, Ellie hauled her back to her feet. "We have to get you away from that room." Shoving her hard, she compelled Snap up the rest of the flight and down the hall to Snap's bedchamber.

No sooner had they settled on the bed then Lizzie burst in. "Did he take it?" she blurted.

Unable to speak, Snap nodded miserably.

"Who? Who took what?" Ellie gave her a shake.

"Blister it," Lizzie exclaimed. "He nipped the pearls!"

"The Fitzcarry pearls! Snap, where are they? Who stole them?"

"The baron, the baron," sobbed Snap. "They're all over the floor."

Ellie stood abruptly and ran for the door. A fraction away from hurtling out, she stopped. "Get down there and summon my mother and sisters," she directed Lizzie. "Then crawl on your hands and knees, but collect every one of those pearls."

Lizzie tore from the bedroom, and pounded down the hall.

Rejoining Snap on the bed, Ellie put an arm around her shoulders. "Don't cry, little one. We'll make everything right."

But her words of comfort only thrust a sword deep into Snap's heart. She crumpled on the eiderdown, clutching her middle, the anguish tearing her apart. Claire, Peggity, and Mama came in.

"My darling," her mother cooed, moving damp tendrils from Snap's tear-soaked face. "The main thing is you're safe. Lizzie said he got the pearls, but I'm unconcerned, poppet. They're nothing to me compared to your life."

The sweetness in her mother's voice drove Snap to greater paroxysms of despair. Claire gently pressed a handkerchief into Snap's hand as a fresh gale stained the coverlet.

"But why did you go to Papa's study?" Peggity asked.

Pressing the hanky hard to her eyes, Snap said in a strangled voice, "I thought Gareth was there."

"Gareth who?" her mother coaxed.

"You don't mean Captain Gareth Hart?" Peggity exclaimed.

"We've been meeting secretly, and...and I love him."

The room went deadly quiet.

"Oh, Snap, no," breathed Claire.

"You can't be in earnest." Ellie leaped off the bed. "He is our absolute enemy!"

"I should hit you," added Peggity whapping the

mattress. "You've been naughty before, but this is going too far. Captain Hart, the man who burned down our horse barn? The man who collects debts for Baron Wadsworth?"

Ellie barked, "What made you do it? How could you?"

Rather than answer, Snap tightened into a fetal position and covered her ears. Eyes pinched shut, she felt her mother pry her hands lose and pull her into a sitting position.

"Look at me, Snap. This is very serious." Her usually soothing voice was strained with emotion. "Why would you form an alliance with such an individual when we specifically told you not to?"

"The devil himself would be more suitable," Peggity said, disgust dripping from every syllable.

"Don't you say a word against him. He's a noble, wonderful man, and I've loved him ever since I was a child, and at this moment he's sacrificing his life for me, so not a word—" She glared at her family. "Not a word against him."

Again, a stunned silence.

"Did… did he kill Baron Wadsworth to save you?" asked Claire.

Violently wiping tears from her eyes, Snap shook her head. "No, I fired the gun. Don't you see, I murdered Wadsworth, and now Captain Hart is taking the blame!"

She threw her legs over the side of the bed and started to rise when Ellie nabbed her by the back of her gown.

"Where are you headed?"

"I have to stop Papa."

"You can't go down there!" shrieked Peggity. "Confess to a murder in front of every member of the *ton*? My God, Snap, we've all had our share of scandal, but this… this…"

"Your papa wouldn't listen anyway; he's too upset," their mother said. "Let's let a little time pass."

Snap struggled out of Ellie's grip, but Claire quickly took her hand while Peggity sprinted across the room and blocked the door.

"Sweeting, tell us what happened," said her mother, trying to ease her back onto the pillows. "You must have been frightened to death."

"Oh Mama, he twisted and thrashed like a cut snake. I'll never rid myself of the image—he'll haunt me. He'll drive me mad, I'll be in Bedlam and you'll visit me through the bars!" In a gale of woe, she buried her face in her mother's lap.

"Poor darling," Lady Albright murmured, "and the straw is so dirty there."

Snap sat up. "You're funning me, Mama, but you've never killed a man as I have. Watching someone die… It's the most terrible, horrible thing in the world."

"But you…you did it to protect Mama's pearls," Claire said, touching Snap's back. "Surely that acquits you of ill intent."

She whirled to face her sister. "I didn't do it intentionally! He had me at pistol point and his accomplice yanked the pearls from my throat. I fell backwards, and the baron must have lost control of his gun because there it was on the floor right in front of me. I grabbed it, and… and there was a bang. A hideous bang. A dreadful, hideous bang.

"Then smoke everywhere, and the baron…the

baron lay on the ground—blood pouring—squirming, crashing into the furniture… Oh God! I wish he'd shot me instead." She dropped facedown into her mother's lap again.

"And Captain Hart," said Peggity, "where was he?"

"Outside. He crashed through the window."

Silence.

Softly at first, and then gaining volume, Ellie said, "I know what love is, Snap dear, and it makes us blind sometimes. Blind to someone's faults."

"I love his faults." She choked.

"Blind to evidence of knavery of the worst kind. Captain Hart knew Wadsworth's plans. He had to have known or he couldn't have come through the one window to the room where the baron was robbing you."

"Shut your gob, Ellie!" Snap tried to bolt from the bed, but her mother and sisters formed a blockade. Scrambling to her feet on the bed, teetering on the soft mattress, she yelled, "He wouldn't do that!"

"They'll see the pearls—then they'll know I was there. They'll know I killed Baron Wadsworth, not Gareth… Not Gareth!"

She leaped over the bedstead and raced for the door. As she reached for the latch, the panel swung violently toward her, revealing Lizzie who glowed with triumph.

"I got every last one of 'em," she said, displaying an apron full of pearls. "And not a swell in the room took notice!"

Chapter 33

For a fleeting second, light from the guard's lamp flashed into the corners of the cell before the officer slammed the metal door, and with boots echoing down the corridor, left Gareth in total darkness.

As he stood riveted to the spot, a terrible cold seeped into his body—cold generated as much by the damp cell as by dread. How many years working for his uncle had he feared this end, locked away in Newgate like the poor debtors he'd trailed, demanding payment to Wadsworth, money before rent, food, or surgeons for their children. Society, at last, had brought him to account.

He remained still until his eyes adjusted to the blackness and he could make out, high on the exterior wall, a barred window through which shone a single star. "I'm grateful to you," he told the star.

Dimly, he perceived a thin bed along one wall, and tucked in the corner, a table upon which rested a pitcher and cup. In the other corner squatted a chamber pot that, based on the stench, hadn't been emptied.

He took a step toward the bed, got caught in his leg irons and found himself face-to-face with the filthy stone floor. His palms stung from breaking the fall, and it horrified him that he might become diseased, might die in this wretched cell even before the trial. Lurching swiftly to his feet, Gareth fumbled for his handkerchief and realized he was shaking badly.

"Calm yourself, man," he said, sinking onto the straw mattress. "Everything will be better in the morning."

This terrible room, this pitiful bed, he knew to be reserved for those with position and money. What commoners endured in the Stone Hold, he couldn't bear to think. But the keepers at Newgate were happy to take bribes. By the light of morning, he'd have his shackles off, and with a few shillings, a lamp, clean sheets, good food, and as much liquor as his gut allowed.

I'll be all right.

Whereas Snap, if she were taken—chained in this dreadful place—her smile, that lit a room like a vase of flowers, would disappear forever. Thank God, he'd gotten there in time. Thank God, her father hated him so much he believed him capable of murder.

They call me hanging Johnnie, he hummed.

Hang, boys, hang.

They say I hang for money,

Hooray, Hooray!

But saying so is funny;

Hang, boys, hang.

The ditty did nothing to raise his spirits. In the morning, he'd improve his lot… And he had saved her—burned her family's barn, but redeemed himself.

****

Scattered glasses of half-drunk champagne cowered under benches along the rim of the smeared chalk on the dance floor, brown-tipped rose petals and evergreen needles cross-hatched the marble stairs at the entrance, and most of the hundreds of beeswax candles had been snuffed—scarcely burned. Her come out party broke up when the Bow Street Runners arrived and hauled Gareth away. The guests followed the officers, eager to see Gareth in chains.

In her bare feet, Snap padded through the wreckage, avoiding the sympathetic glances of servants busily clearing the debris.

It wasn't enough to see the ballroom, Snap wanted the knife to stab deeper—penance for failing to confess her crime—so she went to the dining room to witness the untouched place settings, the mounds of food now destined for alms houses or pig troughs. Among the untouched splendor at the supper table, sat her parents deep in conversation. Papa raked his fingers through his hair, while Mama leaned close, patting his hand.

Under the arched entrance to the room, Snap hesitated. "Papa?"

He straightened. "My darling," he said, his voice gruff with emotion, "we'll have another party for you next year. No scoundrel is going to ruin my daughter's chances for a happy life, by Jove."

Snap shook her head, and her mother's eyes flashed a warning.

"Papa, I need to tell you something about Baron Wadsworth." Her chest tightened so hard she could scarcely speak. "I killed him. It was me, not Gareth—not Captain Hart." The ocean of tears that had pooled since the gun went off, now spilled. She sank to her knees at her father's feet and took his hands. "You mustn't prosecute him, Papa."

He removed his glasses and vigorously rubbed the lenses against the lapel of his jacket. "What are you saying?"

"Because I am in love with him." She rested her

cheek on her father's knee, "He's the man I want to marry."

"What is she talking about?" he asked his wife.

Mama tried to raise her off the floor. "Oh Snap, you choose the most inappropriate times."

Her father's legs twitched. "That man has foxed her, Sofia."

Taking Snap's arms, he lifted her into a chair, pushed his glasses into place, and scowled. "Did he tell you to say this?"

"No, no. You mustn't think that." She tried to wipe the tears from her eyes, but the flood kept coming.

Her mother snatched a handkerchief from her husband's jacket and pressed it into Snap's hand. "You're distraught, my darling. Why don't you talk to your father in the morning?"

"Men like Captain Hart manipulate women," he said. "They make a study of it, and use their charms to profit from the naiveté and vulnerability of the weaker sex. You come from a very wealthy family, Snap, and I fear he's preyed upon your emotions."

"But he hasn't. If anything, I've preyed upon him."

He took the handkerchief from Snap's hand and held it to her nose. Dutifully, she blew.

"Now my sweet girl, tell me truthfully, did Captain Hart ever…touch you?"

She caught her mother's eye, but the look was not returned. Instead, Lady Albright studied the floor.

"No…"

"Don't protect him, he'll hang whether he did or not."

"Papa!" Snap said, wringing her hands, "I… I… We did touch, but only because I wanted him to. I practically forced him."

Her father scraped back his chair and stood so abruptly he slammed his hip into the dining table, rattling an army of uncleared plates and silverware. Agitated, he patted his jacket for his handkerchief, and not finding it, snatched a napkin and scrubbed his glasses. "Did he… Did he defile you?"

"Oh, Papa, no. Truly, no—he would never."

"But he kissed you?"

She didn't know what to say. If she told the truth, her father would explode, but if she lied, he'd know, and the same thing would happen. "You don't understand him at all—"

"Oh, but I do. I understand a great deal about men like Gareth Hart. Furthermore, I know the harm a man of his nature can cause a young woman."

A terrible light burned in his eyes, and for the first time in her life, Snap was genuinely afraid. Papa was going to do something awful to Gareth, and with absolute certainty, she knew she couldn't stop him.

"Go to bed," he commanded, and then paced so stiffly to the arched doorway he seemed made of wood. With his back to them, he added, "Sofia, please order your daughter a hot milk posset and see that she goes to her room."

As her father disappeared, the last of Snap's emotional strength collapsed. Heedless of the Spode place setting, she put her arms on the dining table, buried her face, and wept as piece by piece, her heart tore into bits.

Her mother stroked her hair and kissed the top of her head. "Poor sweeting," she said, "what a terrible, terrible muddle."

Chapter 34

The next morning, Gareth stood in the dock at his inquest in the Public Office, chained at the ankles before Harrow Dent, a Bow Street magistrate. A huge man, Dent's face was a mass of carbuncles, interrupted by lips thick as slugs, and a heavy, unforgiving brow. He eyed Gareth from beneath a powdered wig while lines of disapproval creased his jowls.

To Gareth's right and left, sat the spectators, a sad lot of merchants, laborers, and journalists who studied him with the hunger of jackals eager for scraps. And standing before him, grave as a guillotine, was Lord Albright.

Though Gareth could not see the face of the man who wanted him swinging from the gallows, he could feel his lordship's searing determination, his will to put his daughter's lover in hell, and, what was worse, the man was an earl... The weight of that fact harbored in Gareth's gut like an anchor. Defendants in an English court, especially murder defendants, were outgunned as it was, but against a wrathful earl and an unmerciful judge... Licking dry lips, Gareth gripped the rail that separated him from the rest of the court and waited for the unhappy drama to begin.

"This man has been a plague upon my family," Lord Albright announced, his voice choked with suppressed emotion. "Several years ago, he burned down our horse barn in an attempt to collect a gambling debt accrued by my deceased brother, which I, by law, did not owe. Furthermore, as he recovered in the confines of my home from a back injury incurred during the destruction of the barn, my wife's most prized possession, the Fitzcarry pearls, were discovered looped about his neck. Now, the filching lecher has disgraced our home and plunged my family into scandal by choosing it for his most heinous act to date: the cold-blooded murder of his uncle, Baron Wadsworth."

The jury chattered, the magistrate's wig swayed like hounds' ears, the pencils of the press scratched furiously, and the onlookers tilted forward, straining to catch every syllable.

A lump formed in Gareth's throat, tight as a hangman's noose. He'd been in scrapes before—clinging to a tree as enemy soldiers marched below, caught by a jealous husband beneath his wife's skirts, and pursued by bees into a raging river, yet none was as dangerous as this. Was he truly willing to die to keep Snap from scandal? The girl was bound to get herself into some sort of public trouble sooner or later, why should he sacrifice himself?

Luck had brought a boar that ripped through the woods, scattering the soldiers; quick thinking gave the wife an opportunity to block her husband as Gareth leaped out the window, and chance had delivered him from the bees and rapids to a smooth surfaced lake... But the law was a clock ticking toward Society's demands for justice—and Society was notoriously impatient... and prison bars, notoriously unyielding.

"Captain Hart, how do you answer this charge?" boomed Dent.

"Which one?" asked Gareth, hoping roguish charm would put the jury on his side. "The horse thieving, the barn burning, or the killing of my uncle?"

Lord Albright turned. Eyes glowering through wire-rimmed spectacles, his lips were pulled into a grim line so tightly, he looked as if he'd never smile again.

Gad, was that ever a mistake.

Still, he'd played the saucy devil so long, he wasn't sure what else to do. "I wouldn't say I'm guilty, your honor," he said, and swallowed.

Jurors sat back, the magistrate snorted, and the earl's grave demeanor fired with spots of angry scarlet.

"Did you not confess to the murder at the scene of the crime?" the magistrate demanded.

"That would be accurate," Gareth announced, "but in the heat of the moment, a man is likely to say all sorts of things."

"Are you saying, Captain, that you did not murder your uncle?" a juror asked.

"Bounder!" Snap's father barked with the force of an exploding cannon. "You were found standing over the body, and the first sentence out of your mouth was a confession."

"You are understandably upset, my lord," Gareth began, then stopped. He'd rehearsed what he would say last night, but in the light of day… Should he tell them the truth to save his neck? Would it matter if he did, given Lord Albright's mood? And above all else, what would happen to Snap?

****

The bedroom was dark, all the curtains drawn against a shining summer sky. Snap lay in her sheath, a tangled mass of sheets curling vine-like over her body.

Her pale hair clumped in streaks against a damp forehead, and pages of balled and torn newsprint littered the floor.

She stared blankly at the ceiling. Over and over again thoughts sped through her overwrought mind. What should she do? How much time did an innocent man have? The papers were filled with ridiculous accounts of Baron Wadsworth's death. One said Gareth slashed his uncle with a knife and left him to bleed; another claimed he led a brigade of masked bandits into the house to carry out the crime.

Once the populace made up its mind, he was guilty, the evidence wouldn't matter a wit. Each minute the untruths compounded, the man she loved moved closer to death. Yet here she lay paralyzed by fear of prison, ruin, her father's wrath or all three.

Snap rolled onto her side and let an arm dangle over the edge of the bed. She swung it a little, but was reminded of a swaying body at the end of a rope. Moving the limb tight to her chest, she groaned.

A bold knock sounded on the door. It was Lizzie's knock—she never scratched deferentially even though Malloy had tried a dozen times to teach her.

Snap did not say "Come in." What she wanted was absolute quiet until she could work out what to do, but Lizzie didn't wait for permission. She pushed open the door and mutely stood about a foot away. Silence was the worst sort of disruption. Snap could practically hear Lizzie's thoughts. Though she didn't know what they were exactly, she was positive they were accusatory.

"What do you want?"

"So you've decided to lie in the dark, eh?"

Snap flipped onto her back. "Go away."

"There's a fine solution. And if I leave, what then?"

"Who's to say! That's the problem, Lizzie. I've wracked my brain, and I still can't find an answer."

The lady's maid shoved Snap's legs over and sat on the bed.

"If I were you," said the maid, tucking her ankles crosswise beneath her, "I'd let the man do a good turn and sacrifice himself."

Snap jerked upright. "Are you dicked in the nob?"

"Men love that sort of thing—dashing in front of coaches to save babies and leaping into lakes after a woman's hat—"

"Pish! Taking the blame for something as terrible as murder can't be compared to baby and hat rescuing."

Lizzie shrugged. "The captain's already got the reputation of a boar on a nut farm. And though it's a miracle to me, your reputation's still a prime piece he thinks is worth preserving. Now here's his chance to do the noble and get buried a hero, so what's the good in spoiling his plans?"

"I won't hear another word out of you," Snap said, swinging her feet off the bed and stalking away. "You are an odious creature, Lizzie Widcomb."

Yanking back the window curtains, Snap studied the garden gate. "If I did confess… Do you think they'd hang me?"

Lizzie cleared her throat. "They won't. England don't prosecute the gentry—it's your papa who prosecutes—and chances aren't high he'll want his daughter swinging… at least in public."

"But if I say a word, I'll die a spinster."

"You see, one more reason to keep mum."

"Yet, if I don't…"

Her hands drifted under a mullion, and she gave it a slight upward tug. The window didn't move; she gave it another, harder tug, but it remained steadfastly closed. Nearly running, she went to the next window. It too refused to open, and the same thing happened at the corner window.

"He nailed my windows shut. Papa had them all nailed shut."

Lizzie grimaced sympathetically. "And I hate to be the bearer of bad tidings, but Malloy's stationed at the top of the stairs. She's darning a pile of her ratty ol' stockings, so I don't expect she'll move soon. His lordship alerted us that you ain't to visit the captain, let alone go to his inquest."

Snap bit her lip. "So it's no use…"

"There's even a guard planted outside." Lizzie nabbed a pillow and fluffed it. "I'll tidy up the bed so you feel more comfortable."

Snap sank into a chair and watched miserably as Lizzie fluffed the second pillow, then dismounted from the bed and began carefully smoothing the linens.

"If I wrote a letter to the magistrate, would you deliver it in secret?"

"Oh sure, and he'd be happy to halt the proceedings for a note carried by a lady's maid. Besides, whatever you tell 'em's going to be in the court record."

"You're being awfully cavalier about this, Lizzie Widcomb. A man's life is at stake, and all you can do is make the stupid bed." She scrambled to her feet, tore the coverlet back, snatched a pillow, and hurled it across the room.

"That'll make a world of difference," said Lizzie, resting a fist on her hip.

With a defiant stamp, Snap grabbed a second pillow, beat the bed mercilessly with it, then hurled her cudgel full force across the room. It bonked a bottle of Milk of Roses lotion, which rolled threateningly close to the edge of the dressing table.

"Why aren't you helping me? Why are you being dreadful in my hour of need?" Borne upon a wave of despair, Snap hurled herself onto the bed and wept into the coverlet.

Silence.

"You know I ain't meaning to be mean." Lizzie touched her shoulder. "You never been like this, is all. If I got a clue how to save you and that Hart fellow, I'd tell you to get on it quick. Truly I would." All the fierceness had drained from Lizzie's eyes; her sharp pinpoints of hazel gone soft with worry.

"I'm sorry. You're the only one I can take my anger out on," Snap said, lips trembling with quickening tears. She took Lizzie's hand, and together they gazed out the window.

"I wonder what a mature person would do?"

Lizzie shrugged. "Stay put, I suspect."

Shadows of trees jutted across the lawn shading a single black starling who poked its beak repeatedly into the grass. Despite its efforts, the bird appeared luckless. No matter how many times it pecked or how far it searched, the creature's beak remained empty.

Chapter 35

Sending up a silent prayer, Gareth tried to think of a way to cool Lord Albright's anger. "I don't deny that my uncle is dead," he told the court. "That I tracked him to your home to do the deed is false."

"Poppycock!" roared Lord Albright, shoving his glasses abruptly into place.

Before the unhappy father could disgorge another word, the magistrate interrupted. "You will explain yourself, Captain, I presume."

"I will indeed, sir." Gareth studied Lord Albright a moment, and deciding a confident pose would certainly work better than cockiness, he adopted the posture of a great orator, one foot extended, both hands gripping his lapels. "On the night of your daughter's come out party, I learned that my uncle planned an attack on your household."

A rumble of talk among the spectators followed this announcement.

"Baron Wadsworth's purpose was to steal the Fitzcarry pearls, a necklace, as you mentioned earlier, that is your wife's prized possession. Sna—Lady Nefertiti certainly would don it for the event. Knowing of my uncle's plans, I followed him to the Mayfair abode of the Earl of Davenport and his wife, your daughter Lady Ellie, whereupon I secreted myself in a bush in the garden. The particular shrub, I conjecture, was woodbine."

The magistrate rolled his eyes and thumped the bench. Aiming an impatient glance at Gareth, he said, "You may squawk like a parrot, Captain Hart, but you are still a murderer until an acquittal in the court of England. By this I mean, tell your story in plain language."

Thrown, Gareth sensed the blood draining from his face. Had it come to the confession so soon? The truth and Snap be damned, or the lie? The truth... or the lie? "From behind the honeysuckle," he began slowly, "I kept a close watch on Lady S—Nefertiti through the windows. Then I spied her being escorted from the ballroom by an inveterate gambler, who is in debt to my uncle for fully five-thousand-thirty-eight pounds due next week. Sir," Gareth said, addressing Dent, "dire straits can drive even a good man to reckless deeds."

The lawman nodded, but Lord Albright swiveled to land a diamond-hard glare at Gareth.

"In the middle of the dance," Gareth said tentatively, "he...approached her." Sweat prickled his armpits and stung at the hairline of his forehead. "He abandoned her in the ballroom, but I couldn't see if he'd poached the pearls."

With the lie spoken, a glaze of unreality narrowed Gareth's vision. Everything seemed distant and banked in fog. The courtroom chatter sounded as if it echoed from one mountain to the next.

Mopping his brow, he continued. "Minutes later, a light flared in the study, and I saw the man I mentioned—"

"His name, please?" commanded the magistrate.

"A painter...of portraits...Julian van Eck."

"Alert the runners to find van Eck," said Dent to a shabby court clerk in boots too big for his feet.

The clerk conveyed the burden of this request with every shambling, buckle-clinking footfall as he made his way out the door.

"Continue, Captain Hart," said Dent.

"Returning to the study, Mr. van Eck consorted with my uncle, who ordered him to get back to the ballroom. He demanded the painter take Sn—Lady Nefertiti by force, if necessary, and bring her to the study. My uncle swore to personally cut her face again and again until she took the pearls from her throat and gave them willingly."

A mumble of horror circled through the spectators and jurors, then stopped with a puzzled look from the magistrate. Only Lord Albright's features failed to change.

"One question," growled his lordship. "Why should you care for my daughter's safety? You've been Baron Wadsworth's henchman for years. It was you, was it not, who set fire to my property? It was you, was it not, who was caught in possession of the necklace even as my daughter Claire tended to your injury?"

Swallowing hard, Gareth replied, "I'll not deny it. But it's critical for you to know, Lord Albright, that that event changed the course of my life." He tightened his grip on the railing and with every ounce of his soul tried to pierce the man's armor. "Your family reminded me of happier days in the bosom of my own. And don't you remember how your daughter doted on me as a child?" A well of sorrow filled his heart. "You must believe that I would never harm her. For her, and for your family, I swear I would lay down my life."

The court erupted. Pencils flew, mouths gaped, and the magistrate's lower slug protruded as his brows clenched in a perplexed V. But Gareth's focus remained on Lord Albright. The man stared at him as seconds ticked by. For a fleeting moment, his lordship's expression lightened, and it appeared the aristocrat saw the possibility that Gareth might be telling the truth. But then Gareth smiled. It was an inviting smile, a "please believe in me" smile. Too late he realized it could be interpreted as an ingratiating grin.

Snap's father straightened, his face taut—the bleak line of his mouth pressed hard against his teeth. "My son-in-law hired at least two dozen guards to patrol the property because we knew Baron Wadsworth coveted my wife's pearls. You could not have gone from a view of the ballroom to the window of the study without being caught. Captain Hart, it is obvious you secreted yourself in the study early in the day, and then shot the baron to gain sole possession of the necklace."

To his dismay, Gareth's teeth chattered as he registered the logic of his lordship's argument. With clenched fists, he took a deep breath to steady his nerves. "You forget, my lord, that I broke through the window from the outside."

A juror sporting a single yellow tooth and a bald pate leaned forward. "So you heard all that talk about yanking the pearls through a closed window? That don't signify."

In a storm of panic, his brain went blank. Caught, well and truly caught! And yet his lips formed words though his mind scarcely understood them. "The baron is not known for his even temper," he said, surprised by the calmness of his voice. "Call a witness from the rookeries, and they'll all say his shouts could be heard in Scotland."

"If this case goes to trial," growled Dent, "we'll have plenty of time to hear from the residents of St. Giles."

"Who's to say you didn't break the window to make it appear you came from outside?" demanded Snap's father. "Sir," his lordship continued, addressing the magistrate, "the perpetrator went to great lengths to hide the theft of my horses. He planted carcasses from the knackers in each stall so it would appear the animals had been lost in the fire. There's no doubt he would have planned this murder as carefully."

Dent coughed and averted his gaze. "Have we any witnesses who were present in the study after the gun went off? We need someone who can attest to the position of the glass."

A feminine voice came from the spectator rows. "I was there, your honor."

Gareth swung around to find Lopey gazing back at him, an unreadable expression in her gray eyes. His pulse quickened. What was she up to? She hadn't been at the ball. Finnegan went alone.

****

The starling strutted under the skirt of an alder buckthorn and then emerged triumphantly with a fat grub clutched in its yellow beak. First devouring its prize, the bird then took wing.

Snap jolted as if stung. She let go of Lizzie's hand, "I'd like tea... and cakes, and toast, and a rasher of bacon, and Sally Lun buns, and butter, and jam, and... and, I'd better have chocolate and coffee too."

"And maybe you'd like a side dish of sautéed

elephant?" Lizzie grumbled, eyeing Snap as if she'd gone daft.

"Don't ask anyone for help carrying it up," she said, ignoring the maid's remark. "Bring it all on one tray, and make sure I have the proper utensils for each dish: butter knife, dinner knife, fork, napkin—"

"What've you got up your sleeve, and how much trouble am I going to be in once you've done it?"

Snap swallowed. "I'm hungry, that's all."

"That ain't it. You got that look in your eyes." Lizzie shook her index finger and stepped slowly backward toward the door. "Too hungry is my guess."

"But you'll bring me the tray all the same?"

"If it'll get you out of bed…"

Hands wringing, heart pounding, fear rising, Snap tried to appear the soul of calm. "Tell them I'm ravenous," she said. Then, unable to help herself, added, "So hurry, please hurry."

****

Urgently signaling to Lopey by mouthing the word no and infinitesimally shaking his head, Gareth tried to avert disaster.

"I am Lady Penelope Whitlocke, the third Earl of Whitlocke's widow," she announced. "And I believe I can shed some light—"

"Mr. Dent," Gareth interrupted, "may I have a private word with the court concerning Lady Whitlocke's testimony?" The magistrate reared back in his chair, and Gareth could feel the denial coming. "It is of the utmost urgency."

Lopey rose and started squeezing past the knees of the other spectators in her row.

"Please, sir," he begged.

In a race to address the magistrate first, Lopey gained the center aisle, but fortunately caught her reticule on a man's coat button and had to stop to disentangle it.

To avoid the guard, Gareth vaulted over the dock's rail, his chains racketing over the metal rod and clanking like a plow horse as he shuffled to the bench.

Just as the guard clamped onto his arm, Gareth whispered to Dent, "She didn't attend the party, and I don't want to sully the reputation of a lady of her standing."

The wig rocked forward, emitting a rank, unwashed odor, and the magistrate whispered back, "So you're doing the beast-with-two-backs with her; that's the right of it, eh?"

What Gareth wanted to do was sock those slugs back into his carbuncled face, instead he nodded.

"Lady Whitlocke," the magistrate said, as Lopey hurried forward. "We're going to meet in my office. It's a more suitable surrounding for a woman."

Her mouth opened to protest, then shut.

"Am I to hear what the witness has to say?" Lord Albright demanded.

"Of course, my lord," Dent answered. "Just want to give Lady Whitlocke a bit of privacy before I summon you."

As they filed into a small room behind the court, Lopey hissed in Gareth's ear, "Finnegan saw her leave the dance and he saw the pearls on the floor."

Gareth's breath stopped.

Cool as a Gunter's ice, she settled on a wooden chair in the bare-bones office while the magistrate took his seat behind the desk. Anxiously wondering what she meant to do, Gareth remained standing.

"Good sir," she said, "It is immensely kind of you to agree to this meeting. I can't tell you how deeply I appreciate your protection."

The wig swayed as Dent's features formed into a mass of delight. "Whatever I can do to be of service is my soul's pleasure, my lady."

"I knew you would be amenable. On the way here, the trees were nodding, which means you are a positive force in nature, good sir."

Chuckling, the magistrate replied, "Truly, my lady, the trees and I have no particular understanding."

"But we are all connected to the natural world—as much here to do its bidding as it would do ours—and clearly you hold mighty sway over both fauna—" She gestured toward Gareth, "—and flora." She tipped her fingers toward a filthy, viewless window.

"You do me too much honor." The slugs leaked a spot of pleased spittle.

Her brows went up as if she'd just thought of something. "Were you in earnest just now when you said you would help me?"

"Of course! Of course! What would you like? The court is at your feet."

She held a thumb and a forefinger about an inch apart. "This much time to speak with Captain Hart. Alone."

The lawman's forehead wrinkled, and the slugs puffed in doubt, then his expression lightened. "Ha! Very cunning, my lady, but I suppose you've outplayed me." He hoisted his bulk from the chair and maneuvered around the desk. As he passed, however, he shot Gareth a look meant to crush any hope of escape.

Gareth smiled in return. Once the door closed, he whispered, "What are you about, Lopey?"

She didn't look at him. "The window was open this morning, and in my garden was the prettiest goldfinch pecking about the lawn. Then, quite suddenly, a red squirrel chased it away. Whatever that finch had, the squirrel wanted, do you see?"

"Not at all," Gareth answered dryly, though his heart sank.

"Nature, my darling, takes what it wants without sympathy or doubt. I know you do not love me, and it's reasonable that you desire a young, beautiful bit like Lady Nefertiti. Even I admit you'd make a lovely pairing. Her adventurous spirit is so much like your own, yet... You make me happy." She shrugged her shoulders, glanced at him, then focused on the desk. "I can save you, or I can tell the court that Snap, as you call her, left her come out unescorted with an infamous rogue. That she followed this disreputable fellow to the room where Baron Wadsworth was murdered. And, I may also add, she was there when the gunshot was heard."

"That's blackmail, Lopey," Gareth said, trying to keep his voice gentle. "And that's not like you."

Her large gray eyes took him in, guileless as a toddler's. "But you're used to blackmail, Gareth. You've been under your uncle's thumb for years. I promise my blackmail will be much more pleasant."

Chapter 36

When Lizzie arrived with the tray, Snap grabbed the butter knife and went to the window. A screw had been inserted from the bottom of the frame into the sill. Because it was a temporary measure, the fastener hadn't been flattened to the wood—an excellent advantage.

She fit the tip of the butter knife into the screw's groove and twisted. Her hands trembled so badly, the knife kept slipping. Stripping off a bit of fat from the bacon, she applied it to the wood around the screw and tried again. Only after tremendous effort could she get the fastener to turn even a fraction.

Lizzie watched impassively.

Whirling around, Snap demanded, "Are you going to help?"

"A screwdriver would have been handier."

"Just get the bleedin' window open, and make haste!"

The maid's brows shot to her hairline, but she said nothing as she took the butter knife, dropped it back on the tray, and picked up the dinner knife. Instead of applying the utensil tip-down, Lizzie inserted it in the screw's groove sideways as if she were about to slice the fastener in two. With minimal effort, the maid maneuvered the screw a full half turn.

Snap stuffed her knuckles in her mouth to keep

from shouting in relief. "It's coming," she whispered.

With a few more turns, Lizzie pulled the screw from its hole and dropped it in her apron pocket.

"Tell me to eat my eggs," Snap whispered. "Say it loudly."

Lizzie tiptoed to the door. "If ya think I'm going to be toting eggs and the like up here the rest of your days—" Under cover of Lizzie's voice, Snap jerked the window open. "You can sleep sound knowing it ain't going to happen," Lizzie continued.

From the clothes press, Snap fished out a plain sand-colored frock decorated with a pattern of dainty blue flowers.

"That's the ugliest costume on the lot. Don't you want to wear the blue with that fine looking bonnet while you do whatever it is you're going to do, which I don't want to know nothing about?"

"Not to climb in," Snap replied.

Lizzie closed her eyes. "I told you not to tell me."

The maid slipped the dress over Snap's head.

"Tie up the laces, and hurry before I lose my courage."

When the last tie at the back of the plain little gown had been secured, Snap pulled its skirt between her legs and secured the hem by tucking it in the waistline of her petticoat.

"Oh, sweet la," said Lizzie so softly she could scarcely be heard. "I wish you wouldn't." Then loudly, "Ain't that bacon a nice compliment to them eggs?"

Voice quavering, Snap whispered, "Everyone's said I need to stop being a child. Adults take responsibility..."

Lizzie grunted, and her eyes went misty. "Take a

nice nip o' the chocolate," she barked at the door. "That'll make you feel more yourself."

"This is our last adventure," said Snap through a throat so tight she could barely get the words out. With that, she kissed Lizzie on the cheek, climbed over the sill, took a hard grip on the drainpipe, and shimmied into the shrubbery.

****

Before Gareth could utter a word in protest to Lopey's blackmail plan, a respectful knock sounded on the office door and the magistrate popped his head in. "Finished, my lady?"

Lopey didn't look at Gareth. She rose, took Dent's beefy mitt in her white gloved hand and said, "I am, and thank you from the bottom of my heart. You've made a great concession for my comfort today."

Beaming, the bedazzled man humbly lowered his head and mumbled, " 'Twas nothing."

"Oh, but it was," she cooed. "And I hope that for your kindness, you'll consider attending my soiree Thursday next?"

Dent practically swooned. Gareth barely kept himself from rolling his eyes. Lopey didn't hold soirees on Thursdays; hers were staged only on weekends. Gad, he could choke on her falsehoods.

"This is a great honor," the magistrate said, scraping a ridiculously low bow.

She was about to tell the poor devil another Banbury tale when heavy, jangly footsteps approached. A moment later the clerk entered appearing exhausted, harried, and resentful.

"Sir, I got something private to tell you."

The clerk and magistrate stepped into the hall

where the lesser man whispered in the court's ear.

"Puzzling," Dent said when the clerk finished his message.

"I'm thinking the same, sir, but that's the long and short of it."

"Very well then."

The clerk clumped away.

"Had that anything to do with my case?" Gareth asked when Dent returned.

Rubbing a lump on his carbuncled chin, the magistrate said, "We may postpone the rest of the inquest until tomorrow."

"But you mustn't!" cried Lopey. "I have something deeply important to say today, before this poor man spends another night in jail."

Gareth took a deep breath. "You are beyond solicitous, Lady Whitlocke," he said, casting her a meaningful look, "but a night's contemplation might benefit us all."

But Lopey would have none of it. She broke from his side, took Dent's arm, and guided him toward the door. "You would indulge me one more favor, good sir, I'm sure of it," she sang. "I can see in the width of your forehead, that you are a man who seeks justice no matter the hour."

"It's not the hour, my lady, it's—"

"Then you'll let me speak? Oh, you delight me, sir. Truly you do."

Helplessly, Dent allowed her to ease him from his office.

****

Before traffic began to slow at the approach to Covent Garden, Snap peeked out the window of the hack to examine the pedestrian situation. A gentleman in a top hat entered the premises of a gin shop; two flower girls cornered a mother and child, pressuring them to buy bouquets; and a porter stomped toward the Garden with a burden on his back so enormous he'd have to turn completely to see what was behind him. In other words, conditions were perfect.

Though the carriage horses held a brisk trot, Snap swung the door wide, maneuvered onto the step, quietly closed the door, and leapt into the street. She experienced a tinge of guilt at not paying the fare, but carrying coins in one's pocket while climbing was not possible.

At the formidable entrance to the Bow Street Magistrates Court building, Snap smoothed her dress, but mussed her hair—not much, just enough—then, with a heavy gait, in she marched.

The vestibule was large, bare, and echo-y, with grim stone walls and a few plain chandeliers that weakly penetrated the gloom. At an undersized wooden desk sat a red-faced guard sweating in a buckled coat and top hat adorned with a matching buckle. Across the desk lay a wooden club. She would swear there were bits of hair and blood on it.

"Your name, miss?" said the man.

"Lizzie... Elizabeth Widcomb," replied Snap, trying to sound as much like Lizzie as possible.

"Your business?" he asked, already bored and refilling his quill.

"I'm here to testify at Cap'n Hart's trial."

"Inquest," the guard said, grinding the word as if he were smoothing rock.

"Beg pardon. Inquest. Right then."

With a jerk of his chin, the guard indicated an opening in the wall to the left. "Up the stairs. Take a right, another right, and it's the first courtroom."

Overwhelmed with nerves, Snap stood meekly in front of the guard, watching him scratch Lizzie's name in a ledger as if he were signing the maid's death warrant. When he finished, she moved off, the fearsome thunder of her footfalls reverberating against the rock walls.

A thin, antiseptic hall led to the courtroom, which was accessed, not with stately double doors as she'd expected, but a somber single door only slightly wider than the norm. Her plan had been to burst in by flinging back double doors and announcing to the court that she murdered the baron, but the lack of dramatic potential this door offered gave her pause.

Strangely, it sounded as if everyone inside were talking at once. She had pictured the accused and the prosecutor debating like fighting dogs. This noise was not at all expected.

Cautiously pushing open the door, Snap witnessed a mass of chaos. Men with pencils tucked behind their ears stood in groups conversing at full volume; female spectators pointedly kept to themselves, and one juror lay snoring, fully stretched out in the seats as his fellows clustered in a secretive circle. As for the dock and bench, neither Gareth nor the magistrate appeared to occupy them.

She took a few tentative steps inside for a better view, when her gaze locked with her father's. She drew a breath of alarm as his gaze widened first with surprise, then fury. Quickly, he hid his expression by finding a speck on his glasses and wiping it off. Ever so casually, he rose and walked toward her appearing for all the world, to be heading out for a smoke or a cup of tea.

Snap froze.

About ten feet away, he flashed a stiff-jawed, squint-eyed look that demanded she leave the courtroom. Once as a child, she bit Peggity as they fought over a doll. It was Peggity's doll, but she wouldn't share it. As a result, Papa gave Snap the only real spanking she'd ever had (Gareth's didn't count because it was terribly exciting). And at this moment, Papa had the exact same pre-spanking expression on his face.

She hurried into the hallway, bolted down the stairs, and sustained a rapid pace until she reached the Covent Garden market and dove into the crowd.

Chapter 37

Lopey and Gareth filed into the courtroom, followed by Dent.

Lord Albright rushed the bench. "Is there new information I should be privy to?"

The stiff locks of the magistrate's wig swung round as he shifted focus from Lopey's well-endowed rump to his lordship. "It's been determined that Lady Penelope Whitlocke shall testify."

"But she didn't attend the party!" Lord Albright exclaimed.

"I've been made aware of that, yet, it's been explained she has information important to the case."

Reluctantly, the earl extended a suspicious nod to Lopey and retreated to his seat.

"My lady," said Dent, "the floor is yours."

Gareth, who had returned to the dock, sat on its hard narrow bench and tried to breathe.

Bloody hell, what kind of mess is Lopey about to cause? Damn her blackmailing hide.

"Ladies and gentlemen, perhaps you are unaware that yesterday the clouds over London amassed in a most foreboding manner." Lopey scanned the jury and newsmen. "And yet, there was no rain—an ill omen, as keen observers of nature will tell you. I therefore, knew something awful was about to happen and chose not to attend Lady Nefertiti's come out ball. However, my son, heedless of my warning, did go."

The journalists shot sidelong glances at one another, and Gareth saw one poke his neighbor and whisper, "Cloud is spelled C-L-O-U-D."

Gareth prayed the press would count her testimony as the ravings of a lunatic.

Lopey continued oblivious to the journalists' snickers. "I came today in my son's stead to keep his good name out of the press. Alas, my intentions were thwarted, but I will impart to the court all that he told me."

"But don't we need your son's name for the legal record?" asked a very small juror in an ill-fitting suit.

The magistrate beamed indulgently at Lopey, then glowered at the occupants of the courtroom. "If Lady Whitlocke has chosen to honor us with her august presence, then I hold that the least we can do is respect her wish to keep her son's name out of the gossip sheets."

Crimson rose to the forehead of the outspoken juror, and the press shifted uncomfortably in their seats. Lord Albright rubbed his glasses with a handkerchief that he abruptly stuffed back in his pocket. Clutching the bench until his fingernails penetrated the wood, Gareth fought a war with his temper.

"My son," Lopey continued, "was speaking with Lady Nefertiti when the man Captain Hart mentioned earlier, Julian van Eck, approached. The pair danced until Mr. van Eck quite suddenly abandoned her." She nervously fingered a row of lace at her bodice. "Curious to see what the man was up to, my son followed. Though he kept his distance, he observed the notorious painter enter the study. Moments later, there was a scream and the sound of breaking glass. That's when my brave boy burst through the door in time to see the villainous Mr. van Eck standing over the body of Baron Wadsworth, the smoking pistol gripped in his guilty hand."

A babble of shock and amazement swept through the courtroom, every pencil scraped in a frenzy, as Gareth swung between relief she'd left Snap out of her tale and dread that her lie would plunge him permanently into the clutches of another blackmailer. His stomach cinched into a knot. Even Dent seemed perturbed, tucking an index finger under his wig and giving his scalp a scratch. Only Lopey appeared unfazed. She stood regally on the raised floor of the court, not deigning to look down on the expectant faces of the audience.

"Julian van Eck," she continued, "is rumored to paint society women in the nude, though they have personally sworn to me that they neither granted him permission to do so nor disrobed."

During the ensuing uproar, Gareth lowered his face into his hands.

Hell and damnation, van Eck's a blackguard of the first order, but even he doesn't deserve Lopey's lies.

Rising over the cacophony came the voice of Lord Albright. "My dear Lady Whitlocke, if Mr. van Eck pulled the trigger, why was the window broken?"

"Captain Hart came through it, of course. Everyone said the shot came first."

"Why'd he do that?" a sharp-nosed journalist asked.

The magistrate drew back his chins. "Questioning of witnesses is the prerogative of the court, sir!"

Cowed, the reporter sullenly studied his notes, but his question lingered. The jury looked to the magistrate and everyone waited for him to ask it.

Lopey's fingers returned to the lace at her bodice. "Captain Hart..." she said slowly, not daring to look at Lord Albright, "must have heard the scream and jumped through the window to save his uncle," she finished with a vivid smile.

Heads in the jury pool bobbed in agreement, and Dent straightened in his chair, an imperious, "there, you see," look on his lumpen features. "You there," he called, waving at the exhausted clerk. "Didn't I order you to send the runners after Julian van Eck? Tell the runners, to fetch him at once and bring him to Bow Street."

"Before you go," said Snap's father, raising an index finger to halt the clerk, "I have an additional question."

The courtroom went silent. Tension mounted as his lordship paced the floor, looking at no one and appearing as if he were pondering every angle of the thing.

"You've made an excellent case, Lady Whitlocke, and I don't doubt the word of your son... However, something troubles me... If van Eck shot Baron Wadsworth, why did Captain Hart confess to the murder?"

Lopey nearly pulled the lace from her dress. Her gaze danced this way and that as she desperately sought a logical answer.

Too disgusted to watch, Gareth shook his head and stared at the floor.

This is what came of lying. His lies, and her lies.

And then Lopey giggled. "Well, I'm not sure. Why did you confess, Captain Hart?"

****

"You're an out-and-out sham, and a coward, and a fraud, Snap Albright." She sat on a basket of cabbages in the Covent Garden vegetable market. "There is no excuse for your behavior. None." She gave her thigh a hard punch, but it wasn't enough. "White livered, hen-hearted, vapored cowa—"

"Are you a' right, dearie?" A woman with a face as dark and fissured as dried mud gazed at Snap, her red-rimmed eyes filled with concern.

"Am I ruining your cabbages?" Snap asked, starting to get up.

"Not at all. You roost on them as long as you want." A kindly smile creased her furrowed cheeks. "Troubled in your mind, eh?"

It suddenly struck Snap that this woman had probably never tasted beef, enjoyed an ice at Gunter's or even ridden in a hack. Her sack-cloth apron was tattered and stained, and the fringe of loose threads that hemmed her frock barely covered the tops of boots so worn her blackened toes peeped through. The aristocracy, Lady Davenport had explained, was supposed to set an example for the poor and give them behavior to aspire to, yet someone with nothing could afford to be kind.

"I'm sorry," Snap said, standing. "I do think your cabbages have suffered, but I haven't a ha'penny to pay for the damage."

The woman chuckled. "Don't you fret, miss. They'll sell all the same."

"Thank you. Thank you so very much." She

dropped a curtsey and, fighting a legion of conflicting emotions, pushed through the throng back to Bow Street.

Her pace slowed as she approached number four, the Magistrates' Court. Having once been the writer Henry Fielding's residence, it was not large, nor were its walls difficult to scale; the brick provided footholds, a sizeable lintel extended below deep window sills, and to cool the courtroom the window was cracked wide enough to get a handhold and lift it open. The trouble was getting above the first floor. A boost would be required. Also, Bow Street appeared to host a battalion of prostitutes, thieves, and worst of all, bored urchins. How was one to discreetly scale a wall with an audience in attendance?

Scanning the crowd, Snap whipped around at the feel of a tap on her shoulder. "Lizzie!" she exclaimed. "Lawks, you scared me."

"Only the guilty is startled by a nudge," the lady's maid replied. "What're you planning?"

Ignoring her, Snap said, "Isn't that my new bonnet?"

"You run off without anything on your head, which ain't fitting for me, let alone an earl's daughter." She removed the hat and handed it over.

Beneath her chin Snap tied the pink ribbon of the pale blue bonnet with its high conical crown trimmed in rosettes. Then she smoothed its blue ostrich plume, curling it slightly with her finger so it wrapped around the crown. "This is the bonnet Captain Hart gave me," she said.

"You mean the one you bullied out of 'em. Anyway, I knew it would dress up that plain gown you're wearing."

And it did, Snap noted. The blue and pink reflected perfectly the flower pattern on the dress's sand-colored background. "Perhaps, he'll remember the milliner's shop when he sees me. It may be his last glimpse of me." Then with a sigh, she took Lizzie's hand and led her to the corner of the building below the courthouse window. "It's a stout, well-secured pipe," she said, pointing at the drain. All we need is a distraction."

****

Gareth's eyes were open, yet he perceived nothing, not his lap, or the floor, or the spectators waiting for his answer. What he did see were the years he'd spend with Lopey. No doubt, if he attempted something not to her liking, she'd threaten him with revealing Snap's secret. He'd live his life the same way he did with his uncle: forever in fear. He wouldn't even have the dignity of hanging to save someone he loved... loved?

I love her.

A flood of light buoyed his thoughts. He wasn't sacrificing his life to protect Snap's reputation; he wanted her free; he wanted her to go on adventures, to climb mountains, and dance the waltz, and above all, he wanted her to be happy. Thinking of her made him want to laugh with joy; remembering a noose would keep them apart, made him sick with sorrow.

Gareth lifted his head and gazed about him at Dent, Lopey, the jurors, the press, and the audience. Their curiosity pierced him like a thousand darts; what would he say about that misbegotten cad, Julian van Eck? Nothing. He couldn't let an innocent man hang. But was there anything, anything he could say that would give him a life with Snap?

Slowly, he rose off the bench and approached the dock's thin railing. The chains binding his ankles clanked with each step. He took a breath, swept his gaze across Lopey's anxious features, and the spectator's ravenous expressions, and the magistrate's suspicious eyes.

"I confessed," he said, "because—"

A sharp *tap, tap* on the window interrupted his speech. The whole court turned as one toward the noise. Pressed against the glass, was a woman, her gown flattened by the pane. He couldn't see her face, but he had no doubt who she was.

Lord Albright apparently had no doubt either. He rushed to the window and carefully raised it, keeping a firm hand on the folds of the dress. "Widcomb!" he said in shock, "what in blazes are you doing here?"

"She climbed at my request," came a response from the back of the courtroom.

Though the speaker was mostly masked by the crowd, Gareth saw the delicately curved crown of the bonnet he'd given Snap, its blue ostrich plume a brilliant spot of color in the dull court. "Oh please, no," he groaned, sinking into his seat.

Her father helped Lizzie through the window and at the same time, called over his shoulder, "Snap, go home!"

But Snap pushed her way through the crowd, her lovely face fixed and determined. "Sir," she said, curtseying before the magistrate. "A word with you is all I seek."

Startled, the man's brows ascended so high they disappeared beneath his wig.

She didn't wait for permission. In full voice, so that

everyone could hear, she said, "I caused the death of Baron Wadsworth."

****

That evening, while everyone else was at dinner, Snap lay in bed staring at the ceiling. Occasionally, she wiped her face as tears leaked from her lids and burned itchy trails down her cheeks.

Lizzie had not been given the chance even to say goodbye. She was dismissed with no references and just enough money to pay for a coach ride home to her grandparents. Malloy, that wretch, relayed every detail of how Lizzie wept as the servant's door slammed behind her—all her possessions tied together in an old apron.

Another tear streaked down Snap's cheek and she rolled on her side, the pain too bitter to bear. Not only had she ruined Lizzie, her confession had been for nothing. The magistrate didn't believe her. "My, my, my" he had said. "That's quite the revelation, milady."

Then his focus shifted to Gareth and a malevolent glint sharpened his glare. "You've got them young and old defending you. Quite the way with the weaker sex, Captain Hart. Your name is apt."

Snap was laughed out of the courtroom, her reputation shredded, Lizzie was gone, and Gareth was still in chains. Tomorrow morning the papers would be full of headlines blaring her name and describing Gareth's hold on women. Especially his ability to manipulate them.

All he had wanted to do is spare her ignominy and shame, yet now he would go to the gallows for nothing. It had been awful on the roof when he ordered her to stay away, but now was so much worse. At last she knew he loved her, yet he would die for it.

Unhappiness sank to the bone, and a fresh gale of weeping curled her into a ball of misery.

A gentle knock sounded on the door and the next moment, her mother softly entered. "Sweeting?" She went to Snap's side and placed a small tray on the bedside table. "Eat something, my darling. It will make you feel better."

The sympathy in her mother's voice caused a wave of pain that split Snap's heart in two. Overcome, she convulsed in sobbing woe.

"I would, but I can't."

"No, I suppose not." Lady Albright moved a dish or two on the tray. "Here's a fresh hanky." She pressed a napkin into Snap's moist fingers.

"Thank you." Snap held the cloth to her eyes so hard it hurt.

"Poor, poor sweeting." A comforting hand rubbed her back and brushed soaked strands from her face.

Another, heavier knock sounded, and her father came in. "I'm sorry you're so downcast, Snap," he said quietly from across the room, "but I want to speak with you about your conduct today."

"John, perhaps you should wait for your daughter to recover herself a bit," her mother said gently.

"And I would, Sofia, but Lady Davenport just advised me that Snap might be better off out of London tomorrow when the papers hit."

"Oh," replied her mother.

Snap uncurled herself, sat up, and gave her father a hard look. "That means you would like me to leave tonight?"

Tugging his earlobe, her father avoided her gaze.

"Before I go, I would like to show you something I tried to introduce at the courthouse today—before you ushered me out amidst the laughter of the press." She yanked open the drawer of the bedside table and dumped handful upon handful of pearls onto the coverlet.

Anger spiking her every word, she said, "I would have been strangled by Wadsworth's henchman if the strand hadn't broken."

"Are you talking about Mr. van Eck?" her father said, picking up the necklace's black pearl latch.

"The baron dropped his pistol to get the pearls. I grabbed it and it fired—" Her throat closed, allowing nothing but an anguished sob. "It fired, Papa," she cried, tears streaming down her face. "I didn't mean it to, but it did."

Her mother's arms wrapped around her, and Snap buried her wet face in the comforting shoulder. When her gasps subsided, through the folds of fabric she heard her father shuffling about the room.

"Fuff…" he said. "Well…" His glasses clattered on the floor. They scraped the parquet as he retrieved them. "I couldn't have known."

"But you could have." Snap jerked away from her mother. "I tried to tell you last night, but you wouldn't listen. You never listen, Papa. You've ignored me all my life, and now, now, suddenly you want to deny me the man I love?"

"Don't deny you've often been unreasonably provoking. It's natural I assumed your infatuation with Hart was just another way to upset me."

She scrambled from the bed and stood holding the footboard, clinging to it for fear she'd do something unspeakable. "Why do you care who I marry?"

So shocked he backed into her vanity chair, her father said, "I haven't ignored you."

"You didn't even dance with me at my come out! Why do you think I went to the study alone with a man I hardly knew? Because you broke my heart, Papa! You broke my heart, and I was confused, and so upset I just wanted to leave. That's all I wanted to do, and Julian van Eck led me away." She collapsed to her knees and sobbed, covering her face with her hands.

He knelt beside her and tentatively patted her shoulder. "Sofia, what do I do?"

"Sit there, John," her mother said sadly. "Just talk to her, and listen…"

Chapter 38

In the morning before the second day of the inquest began, Mrs. Gower came to the jail with a message. Complaining of a thousand aches and pains caused by her walk up the stairs, it took her at least a half hour before she mentioned the reason for her visit: Snap, she told him, had been sent from London sometime after midnight, otherwise she would have come this morning.

Gareth tried to be glad for Snap's safety, but his ribs seemed to close around his lungs, making it hard to breathe.

Clucking in sympathy, Mrs. Gower said, "Oh, she'll miss you something terrible, Captain. The girl begged for my help, don't ya know, and seeing how her heart was set on you, and as how I liked the look of you—I've a fondness for the ne'er do wells—I did my best to make the hitch."

He nodded, his lungs too crushed to thank her for her efforts.

"That's all right, lad. Here, I brung you something to keep you up–to–date." She squeezed a thick bundle of newspapers through the bars of his cell.

Again, he nodded.

"I'll be off then, poor soul." She took a few steps and turned about. "Would you like a nip of sherry? It's ever so therapeutic."

He dipped his head, and she bestowed a motherly

317

smile. "I hide my flask where it isn't decent, so you'll have to avert your eyes."

He turned away, but closed his eyes to avoid looking at his dismal cell.

"Here it is," she said brightly, handing him a silver flask. "Drink it all, dearie. It'll fortify you."

After downing the contents, he gave the flask back. "Thank you."

"That's all right, happy to do it," she said, as she wobbled away.

Gareth sat numbly on the narrow board serving as his bed and went through the newspapers. Each carried an article outlining lurid details of his prowess with the ladies: they claimed he had populated the Lake District with bastards, wore out the whores in Seven Dials, and seduced every rich widow from Scotland to Wales.

Additionally, he was accused of having faces slashed and fingers broken for gambling debts amounting to no more than a few shillings. Every bloody crime his uncle committed. And, most damning of all, a reporter from the *Tattler* claimed Gareth rigged fights, races, and card games in order to line his pockets.

In other words, in the court of public opinion, he should already be dangling at the end of a noose.

****

Women, sneaking curious and seductive glances at Gareth from behind their fans, occupied the majority of seats in the courtroom, forcing the reporters to line up in the aisles and lean against the walls. Their combined bodies heated the air to that of a fetid swamp. The noise, the temperature, the stench, and the pack of ravenous eyes made Gareth dizzy. He rubbed his unshaved jaw as he sat in the dock with his chained ankles tucked under the narrow bench.

Julian van Eck, wide-eyed with fear, beads of sweat shining on his bald head, sat beside him. The painter glanced furtively at the spectators, and connecting with a pretty damsel, held her gaze until she smiled. The interchange seemed to give him confidence because he leaned back against the dock's railing, a pleased tilt to his full lips.

Hell and the devil, Gareth wanted to batter those lips into a bloody mass. It may not be fair to blame the artist—Gareth knew how his uncle could twist the kindest soul into carrying out heinous acts—but he still wanted to corner van Eck someplace dark where his fists could do some damage.

The room buzzed with talk until the magistrate entered. Dent lumbered toward the bench, and then, struggling to lift his considerable frame, hoisted himself onto the dais.

"If it pleases the court, I would like to say something before we begin," Lord Albright declared.

Dent nodded, his wig sliding slightly forward. Gareth prepared for the worst.

"I am withdrawing my prosecution of Captain Hart."

The silent courtroom exploded into a cacophony of unruly questions from the press, squawks of concern from the jurors, and delicate gasps from the ladies. Gareth felt as if he'd been hit by a wave, or a horse, or a falling tree. He wondered if he'd fainted and dreamed Lord Albright's declaration.

"So you will now be pursuing a case against Mr. van Eck?" asked the magistrate, quieting the crowd with his menacing baritone.

"I will not, sir," replied Lord Albright, nervously licking dry lips. "In fact, I am dropping the case altogether."

A wily expression narrowed the magistrate's mouth. "On what grounds, my lord?"

"I was presented with evidence last night that has convinced me both men are innocent…of the murder."

"I see." Tenting his fingers, Dent pointedly asked, "What evidence?"

Tensing, Gareth waited for the man to utter an impossible lie the court would see through instantly.

Lord Albright removed his glasses and fixed the bewigged man with a haughty, contemptuous glare. "That is a family matter that I do not intend to discuss."

The words rang through the courtroom, loaded with the entitlement of the aristocracy. There wasn't a British citizen in the assembly who didn't know that meant no disclosure—Dent included.

The magistrate tapped his fingers on the bench, considering. "Thank you, Lord Albright. Please let it be noted, ladies and gentlemen, his lordship's case is no longer active."

Fog whirled in Gareth's mind. Could he possibly be free?

"Captain Hart." Dent's voice sliced through the fog. Training a malevolent gaze on him, the magistrate said, "Have you any relatives?"

"A sister and her daughter."

"Ahh, well then, they have an interest in your uncle's estate. Therefore, I am going to keep this case open on their behalf."

This elicited shocked babble from the spectators

until Dent banged a beefy fist on the bench.

"But sir, they've been virtual prisoners at my uncle's Exeter residence," Gareth blurted.

"Therefore, they have been in the baron's care, and will appreciate seeing his murderer hang."

"In his care, sir?" Gareth rose to his feet. "My sister and niece got their living from my pocket."

"Sit down, Captain, or risk being returned to your—"

"He would have starved them, destroyed them, ruined my sister and kept her daughter in misery had I not intervened!"

"I demand that you—"

"Miss that spawn of the devil?" he continued furiously. "My sister and niece will dance a jig when they hear he's gone."

"Enough! Enough!" bellowed Dent. "I will not suffer such insolence. Another word, Captain Hart, and I'll have you bound and gagged."

Gareth threw himself onto the bench, his gaze darting wildly over the sea of reporters as they scratched zealously at their notes.

"This proceeding is now in session," announced the magistrate. "You may step out of the court area, Lord Albright."

Snap's father turned toward the spectators, a dazed look in his eyes. He moved slowly, taking small steps, as if he'd forgotten how to walk.

Without waiting for his lordship to fully depart, Dent straightened, and barked, "First witness."

A wretched woman in ragged clothes, with shoes tied to her feet by string, mounted the rostrum.

"Your name?" demanded the magistrate.

Cringing, and keeping her face averted from Gareth, she said in a small voice, "Suky Hauser."

"Do you know the accused?"

"The Cap'n, I know 'em," Suky replied, "but the other one I ain't seen."

"And how did you make Captain Hart's acquaintance?"

"He collects for Ol' Spaz, I mean the baron. Gambling chits and the like."

"One day, according to your written testimony, Baron Wadsworth beat you and your child with his whip, yet the captain did nothing to stop him, is that correct?"

Suky winced as if Dent had just administered a blow himself. "I ain't lying," she said defensively.

"And when the baron left, did Captain Hart assist you in any way?"

She let out a shuddering breath and appeared unable to speak.

Gareth sat forward on the bench. Poor Mrs. Hauser. More than anyone, he knew how many shillings, or even pounds, it took to lure poor Suky from St. Giles.

"Did he help you?" snapped the magistrate.

Shrinking like a whipped dog, Suky crossed herself and barely above a whisper said, "He threatened me. Said if I didn't find the gel's knife, I'd get it worse."

"Knife?" asked a juror.

But before Suky could explain, an officious little man with old fashioned rosettes on his black knee breeches, made his way through the onlookers and stepped onto the raised court area.

"Sir," he announced with a cursory bow, "Pardon the interruption, but as coroner, my testimony has direct

322

bearing on any further statements here."

A rumble of curiosity cantered through the audience.

Taken aback by the disruption, Dent took a moment to collect himself, yet it was a moment too long. The little man turned and addressed the crowd.

"As coroner, it is typically my privilege to speak first at inquests. However, I was waylaid by the corpse of Baron Wadsworth. That is to say, that determining the cause of death took considerably more time than expected. The reason, you may ask? There are no bullet holes in the body."

"What?" roared Dent, as the courtroom burst into a thunder of shouts and mayhem.

"I repeat, the baron was not mortally wounded by pistol shot. He suffered a hemorrhage in the brain, and died of blood loss."

Chapter 39

A month after the inquest, Gareth sat on the terrace at Budleigh Abbey, the fifty-thousand-acre estate granted to his uncle by King Charles III. It was only two miles from the Albright stronghold. Only two miles from Snap. He'd gone to Exeter every day since he'd arrived, hoping for a glimpse of her.

On the lawn, his niece Clementine chased Rascal, who frisked away just as the little girl tried to nab his stick.

Gareth stirred in his chair. It was painful to see her at play. Her joy reminded him of Snap. More painful still, the weather glowed with sunshine, reminding him of his days with her in London. He rose to go inside, but then heard the laughter of his sister Laura. She was being entertained by Squire Roddy Hancock, a prosperous man with a horse farm and a fleet of fishing vessels. The squire adored Clementine, and the little girl worshiped him. An engagement was eminent.

I'll buy them something wonderful. Something big and expensive.

He took a deep breath and stepped toward the French doors.

"Cap'n, Cap'n, look!" squealed Clementine, holding the stick high as Rascal leaped to seize it.

He mustered a wave and a nod, checked to see if the governess had her eye on his niece, and then passed into the house.

"My lord, a gentleman has come to see you." His butler Kettleridge, presented a card.

"Who?" Gareth asked, thinking he'd put the man off since he was feeling too old and dull to be good company.

"Lord Albright."

Gareth's heart banged in his chest. The man was here to confront him about being in Devon. Should he tell him that total separation from his daughter was worse than hell? Should he demand that he let him see her? Tell him he'd steal her off to Gretna Green if he didn't grant them permission? Or...or should he slink away and allow a better man to marry her?

"I've put him in the Sunset Saloon."

"How appropriate."

"You know what I'd do if I was you?" said Lizzie, as she sauntered across the drawing room with her knife thrust into the ribbons of her apron and a feather duster in hand.

Kettleridge whipped around, landing a frightful glare on the girl, which Lizzie ignored. Gareth had tried to warn him it was no use teaching the maid her place. The lesson wouldn't stick.

"What would you do, Lizzie?" Gareth asked.

"I'd ignore that old fellow—send him a who's who message. Didn't he just about ruin your life? Ain't he a stick for driving you off from Snap, I mean Lady Nefertiti?"

Taking a deep breath, Gareth replied, "Lizzie, you have an uncanny knack for making odious statements that drive one to do just the opposite."

"I'm thinking 'odious' means 'perfectly

reasonable.' " She turned her back on him to give a porcelain clock a few useless flicks with the duster.

****

Standing in a shaft of late afternoon sunlight, Lord Albright studied a Goya sketch on the wall. Gareth cleared his throat as he came in the door.

"It was kind of you to see me," Lord Albright said.

Woodenly, Gareth offered a hand, and they shook. "It is my pleasure, of course."

"I don't imagine it is, really."

Gareth looked away. "Won't you have a seat, my lord?"

"Should I address you as Baron Wadsworth now?" he asked, slipping into a wingback chair.

"Ugh, I suppose it's right and proper," Gareth said, biting his lip, "but I'd rather you call me Hart."

"Understood."

Lord Albright folded and unfolded his hands in his lap. It struck Gareth that the man seemed ill-at-ease, even nervous. After giving his glasses a vigorous scrub on his lapel, his lordship said, "I came to ask you a question."

"What would that be?"

The man swallowed. "Why did you try to take the blame for my daughter?"

Gareth rubbed his forehead. "Sn—Lady Nefertiti has a spirit that made my heart…she made my heart unfurl. It was the oddest sensation. Every time I looked at her, I could burst with joy. And that's never happened before… Others must feel the same way about her. She's so charming and mischievous…I couldn't bear to see a spirit like that ruined by a public scandal. It's inconceivable—like locking a butterfly in a dungeon."

With a curt nod, Lord Albright pressed on. "Then why were you on the property that night?"

"Ahh... Well, Lady Whitlocke and I were to be married that morning, but my fiancée called it off for reasons too complicated to explain. We were going to postpone, but then I realized Mistress Fate had saved me from a disastrous blunder."

The moment had come. The fight would begin.

"I went to Mayfair to sneak in and see Snap in her gown with the pearls shimmering around her throat and a hundred men gathered at her feet. You would have had my head cracked on sight, but I had to know if her marriage proposal still stood."

"Her proposal?" Outrage flared in Lord Albright's eyes, but then he seemed to reconsider. "Yes, yes, of course. She would, wouldn't she?"

"But even more importantly, my lord, I had to protect her because Wadsworth was fully prepared to maim, kill, or burn to have those pearls. I know you took precautions, but...I circled the house and spied a guard who owed my uncle fifteen pounds on a gambling debt. That's all the leverage it took for the baron to get into the house."

Lord Albright fidgeted with his glasses. "I believe you."

"So with twenty pounds to the same man, I gained access to the garden and a clear view through the window. Then S—Lady Nefertiti left the dance floor with Julian van Eck. She trusted him because she once saw us together.

"When she screamed, I bashed in the window. I tell you, I would have torn down the walls to get to her."

The earl took a deep breath and his face looked stiff and unnatural. "It was my fault she left with that bounder, not yours... I'd invited an expert on the Roman occupation of England. You see, I suspect there's an ancient ruin running through the garden and out to Hyde Park, but I needed to speak with him about it, so—"

"Wait," said Gareth, briskly going to the bell pull and giving it a yank. "Go on, Lord Albright. Forgive the interruption."

"So...so I missed our minuet. We'd even rehearsed. It was unforgivable, but it's difficult to divorce oneself from one's passions, isn't it? At least it is for me, and—"

Kettleridge entered. "Tea or brandy, my lord?"

"No, no. There's a red lacquer box on my desk. Bring it to me." Gareth returned his attention to his guest. "Did you want refreshment?"

The earl shook his head.

"You were saying?"

"Not much more... Except... Except, all the light seems to have gone out of my little Snap, and frankly, I'm worried. She's so sad. She won't eat, she doesn't climb drain spouts, or ignore what we tell her, or even gossip with the servants. In fact, this morning...this morning, the dowager Lady Davenport was teaching her to embroider." His lordship paused, his voice too choked to continue. I fear...I've done irreparable damage... So, I wondered if maybe you would—"

The door swung open and Kettleridge entered with the lacquer box on a silver tray.

Gareth took the box and opened it under Lord Albright's nose.

"By God, where did you get them?"

"In your son-in-law's garden at Mayfair. I was looking for pebbles to toss at your daughter's window, and I picked these up instead."

"May I?"

At Gareth's nod, he removed three gold coins and rested them in his palm. "That is the face of Aureus Tiberius," the earl explained, his voice soft with reverence. "Heavens, this is Emperor Constantius II! Exquisite. Just exquisite. And this one—Oh, devil take it, I'm doing it again!" He dropped the coins back in the box as if they'd been dunked in poison. "I've come to discuss the happiness of my child, and instantly I'm distracted by bloody Roman currency." Though it obviously took all his will, he closed the box and pushed it toward Gareth. "Take them out of my sight."

The coins jingled in their velvet-lined casket. Gareth bit his lip. An idea occurred to him. On the verge of saying something, he balked and walked away instead. Halfway across the saloon, he halted, then slowly turned and said, "I have a proposition for you..."

****

Julian van Eck curled his finger, and Snap walked toward him, though she sensed danger, disaster, she couldn't stop herself. And then he tore the pearls from her neck in front of everyone, and the people at the ball gathered, watching the beads clatter and spin, while they jeered and laughed. And the pearls *pinged* on the marble floor, *ping, ping, ping.*

The ballroom and the taunting faces vanished as Snap eased out of her dream, yet the *pinging* continued. And then came the sound of a bird, but not like any real bird, more like a… a very poor imitation of a bird.

Without bothering to put on her slippers, she flew to the window and searched the moonlit lawn until movement caught her attention. Two stories below, a man waved. In his other hand, he held the reins of two white horses.

Gareth? Her heart leapt to a gallop. After yanking open the window, she leaned out. "Is that you?"

"None other," came the reply.

"But why are you here?" With all her heart, she prayed for the right answer.

"Climb down and I'll show you."

Now her breath came quick and fast, but Snap had learned her lesson: behaving recklessly only sank one into a pit of despair and ruin. "I don't climb anymore," she called. "Silly children do that sort of thing. I've matured greatly since you saw me last."

"But it's made you sad."

"I'll get past it."

The night went silent. Snap held her breath, listening for a cough or a boot moving in the grass. She wished the tree frogs and night insects would cease their chatter so she could hear him. Was he thinking of leaving? Would she never see him again?

"I've been sad too," he said at last. "Hollow, really… So, climb down, love. I promise you won't regret it."

He said "love"!

Snap gasped, and was about to dance a jig, when she remembered how mature she'd become. "I'll walk down the stairs."

"Climb, my love. Only an adventurer will travel with me to the jungles of Africa, the mountains of

China, the bazaars of India, and across the wide-open seas."

A surge of mad, wild, uncontrollable joy, tore through her every vein. Gareth. Her Gareth! "Wait," she cried, "let me change my clothes."

She dashed from the window and threw open the clothes chest. Tearing through its contents, she remembered she'd given all her adventuring clothes to the maids. There was nothing here but silks and satins and lacey gewgaws.

She bolted back to the window. "I'll just put on my slippers."

Gareth laughed, a rich throaty sound, warm as coffee and sweet as honey.

"Oh pish," she cried, sticking her leg out the window. "It's easier to climb barefoot."

A word about the author...

In addition to writing historical novels, Elf Ahearn tutors students and slavishly tends to every whim and fancy of her cats, Puck and Jilly.

Prior to the arrival of these demanding felines, she spent thirteen years as a reporter for the *Litchfield County Times*, an award-winning newspaper, edited an award-winning corporate newsletter, and composed back cover copy for Penguin Random House.

She is happily married to a knight in shining armor who is also fond of cats. They live in New York.

****

www.elfahearn.com

****

If you enjoyed this story, leaving a review at your favorite book retailer or reader website would be much appreciated. Thank you!

Thank you for purchasing
this publication of The Wild Rose Press, Inc.

For questions or more information
contact us at
info@thewildrosepress.com.

The Wild Rose Press, Inc.
www.thewildrosepress.com